A Ring in a Case

Northwestern

University

Press

A Ring in a Case

YUZ ALESHKOVSKY

Translated by Jane Ann Miller

Hydra Books

Northwestern University Press

Evanston, Illinois 60208-4210

ISBN 0-8101-1138-1

IN THE HOSPITAL

They stood, as if at a shop window,
Almost blocking the sidewalk.
The stretcher was pushed into the van.
The orderly hopped in up front.

And the ambulance, passing by
Pavement and doorways and idlers,
The bustle of night on the street,
Dived headlights first into the dark.

Passersby, streets and faces
Flashed by in the headlights' glare.
A paramedic swayed back and forth
With her vial of smelling salts.

It was raining, and at the front desk
A drainpipe gurgled drearily.
In the meantime, line by line,
They scribbled the admissions form.

They gave him a bed near the doorway.
All the wards were full.
The air reeked of iodine vapors
And a draft blew in from the street.

The window-square framed part of the garden,
A little scrap of sky. The newcomer
Studied the ward and the floors
And the hospital gowns.

And suddenly, from all the questions
Of the nurse who sat shaking her head,
He realized that he wasn't likely
To get out of this fix alive.

Then he cast a grateful glance
Out the window, where the wall
Was lit up from the town side
As if by a housefire's spark.

There in the glow the gates gleamed red
And in the town's reflected light
A maple's gnarled branch
Made a farewell bow to the sick man.

"Oh, Lord, how perfect
Are Thy works," the sick man thought.
"The beds and the people and walls,
The death-night and the night-city.

I've taken a sedative dose,
And cry as I tug at my kerchief.
O God, tears of agitation
Keep me from seeing You.

It's sweet in the dim light
Just barely falling on the bed
To recognize my life and my lot
As your priceless gift.

Dying in a hospital bed,
I feel the warmth of Your hands
You hold me like a hand-wrought thing
And hide me like a ring in a case."

BORIS PASTERNAK
Translated by Jane Ann Miller

CONTENTS

On the eve of Russian Orthodox Christmas, just as the USSR is entering the final stages of collapse, Helium Revolverovich Serious, native son of the Russian Revolution, lies freezing to death on a snowcovered Moscow street, the sounds of Mozart's *Eine kleine Nachtmusik* ringing in his ears. So begins Yuz Aleshkovsky's account—part satire, part philosophy, part hallucination—of one decisive night in the life of a "paladin of the intellect," a professional atheist who has made a career of fighting against what he claims does not exist.

Two things immediately strike the Western reader as odd: that atheism could be a career at all, and that it could be not only a career but a calling. The first can be explained in part by the Kafkaesque nature of Soviet bureaucracy, but the second has its beginnings in the psychology of nineteenth-century Russian radicals. The western atheist thought that God simply didn't exist; the Russian atheist like Ivan Karamazov thought that He *shouldn't*. As Andrei Sinyavsky points out in his book *Soviet Civilization,* the western atheist simply negates God, while the Russian one resists Him: hence the adoption of the Greek term theomachy, *bogoborchestvo* in Russian, which can be translated as god-battling—or god-wrestling, like some Yakov going hand-to-hand with the angel. Or better yet, like some rebellious

Lucifer locked in titanic combat with the divine Autocrat. (Lunarcharsky went so far as to give Milton and his Satan revolutionary credentials, bourgeois rebels though they might be.) And this, says Sinyavsky, accounts in part for the Bolsheviks' "extravagant acts against sacred objects. . . . as when they lined them up against a wall and shot at them, as if . . . the icons were living beings."

For all that it happened years before Helium's birth, one of those extravagant acts is central to the novel. The place in which Helium's demons first appear is the "Moscow," an enormous, heated, open-air swimming pool, its eerie clouds of vapor spreading wide over the embankment. But more is at work here than Aleshkovsky's instinct for the absurd, or the pool's obvious resemblance to some reeking, steaming maw of hell. This was where Christ the Savior had once stood, an immense cathedral seventy years in the building, erected to commemorate the Russian victory over Napoleon. Both its size and its cost were staggering—a lavish monument to empires both earthly and divine. Not the first church to be razed by the Soviets nor the last, it was certainly the biggest, and its dismantling and spectacular detonation left a hole in the Moscow skyline which Stalin planned to fill with an even grander project, a Palace of the Soviets taller than the Empire State Building. A new foundation pit was dug, but the year was 1931, and the project soon stalled: whether Stalin became simply too distracted with his purges to follow through, or whether indeed, as Moscow folklore had it, the pit simply swallowed up every pile driven into it, every slab laid—who can say. But what materials were left were needed for the war effort, and afterwards the site stood abandoned and overgrown, the haunt of drunks and derelicts. So in 1960 Nikita Khrushchev ordered the installation of an outdoor swimming pool—not quite a palace, but still, the world's largest something. Again, rumors spread—this time of demons who infested the depths of the pool, grabbing at swimmers' legs and dragging the unwary to a watery grave. (By the fall of 1994, several years after Helium's last fictional encounter with it, the pool itself was no more; workers had begun dismantling it to make way for a new Church of Christ the Savior, to be rebuilt from the original architectural drawings and old photographs of the finished church.)

Cynical careerist Helium is hardly a Faust or a Prometheus, for all the grand rhetoric his profession has coopted. In developing Helium and his demon-ridden consciousness Aleshkovsky takes his cue from Dostoevsky; from the crass familiarity of Ivan Karamazov's shabby Mephistopheles to Helium's own incessant calculations of "enlightened self-interest." Like Dostoevsky, Aleshkovsky is preoccupied with the presence of evil in human society, and with the human need for theodicies, those rational vindications of a God who would allow such evil to exist. But clearly the chief inspiration here is *Besy*, a title for years translated as *The Possessed*, but more accurately and literally as simply *The Demons*. A petty demon incarnate, nihilist Peter Verkhovensky escapes after wreaking havoc on a provincial town, while corrupt Stavrogin and mad Kirillov are exorcised from the body politic when they commit suicide; Helium's demons, who bear a grotesque collective resemblance to certain figures on the contemporary, post-Soviet scene, make their grand exit in an outrageously farcical take on the epigraph Dostoevsky chose for *The Possessed*, the verses from St. Luke in which Jesus casts the unclean spirits out of the body of a man possessed and into a herd of Gadarene swine, who promptly rush down a steep shoreside cliff to drown.

But *Ring* is a virtual catalog of demons and devils in Russian literature—all of which would be familiar to the Russian reader. Helium boasts to Veta that his favorite poem is Lermontov's romantic *Demon*, who, saturnine and cosmically bored, of course ends by killing the only thing he has ever loved, the Georgian Princess Tamara. (Helium's friend's lame joke about the Aragvi—Georgia's chief river, for which a popular Georgian restaurant in Soviet Moscow was named—also plays on lines from Lermontov.) As Helium wanders through Moscow in the blizzard, he mumbles garbled lines from Pushkin's *Demons* ("The clouds scurry, the clouds whirl") and *Winter Evening* ("drink, good friend of my luckless youth"), both set amid howling, malign storms. Even the comic, folky little demons of Pushkin's *Tale of the Priest and His Servant Balda* make a brief appearance. The plasma-like instability of Helium's little goons is reminiscent of the nearly formless dust-devil of Fyodor Sologub's *Petty Demon*. A struggling Helium takes issue with Mikhail Bulgakov's "unpardonably romantic" treatment of the Devil and his minions when, in the novel *The Master and Margarita*, they descend on Moscow as the conjurer Woland and his entourage, to raise a little hell but also to dispense a little justice. And these are just the *direct* references.

Not only Helium but the text itself is aswarm with manifestations of the Archfiend and his ilk. They appear not just in curses, but in common adjectives, idiomatic expressions, including Latin cognates (*d'iavol, demon*) as well as the Slavic words (*chort, bes*), as well as the collective designation of Helium's tormentors, *nechist'*, "the unclean," which can mean either evil spirits or everyday vermin or, as Aleshkovsky has made the case here, both. Moreover, many of the verbs and adjectives formed from those nouns denote not so much a likeness to the devil, or evil intent (as in the English devilish, diabolical, satanic), but a state of madness, fury. The common, colloquial verb *besit'sia*, for example, means to be enraged, infuriated; *beshenstvo*, a noun derived from it, means rage—and also rabies. Aleshkovsky relies on all those associations, evil-rage-madness-disease, and the very frequency of such words in the text forces them out of cliché, out of their secularized, purely emotional context and back into their original framework. That, plus references to the various afflictions of Party leaders—Suslov's tuberculosis, Chernenko's emphysema and Andropov's kidneys—leave the impression that both Helium and the world around him are suffering from a nasty case of demonic possession.

The most direct counterpoint to the demon motif, the melody which eventually replaces it, is Boris Pasternak's poem, which flickers in and out of Helium's memory as he stumbles through both Moscow and his own uncomfortable history. Just as Helium cannot remember the words of Dostoevsky's epigraph, let alone understand them, until the very end, he cannot remember his true self until the poem is whole. If ever there was a case of poetic image being "bodied forth"—here it is, as the poem restores itself, the Mozart resolves itself, and the restoration of memory coincides with the revelation of the real, material ring. (The poem itself is traditional in form, with regular rhyme and meter. The English version sacrifices both of those to preserve the key words and sequence of line and image that organize Aleshkovsky's text.)

Aleshkovsky has a songwriter's ear, and like his protagonist, he hears a certain music in events, music by turns angelic, by turns obscene. *Ring* is full of the rhythms and melodies of Russian culture, high and low, refined and raunchy. There are direct musical comparisons, like the persistent Mozart motif, or snatches of folk or popular songs ("Let there always be mama," "didn't I groom," "banana-lemon-Singapore") that accompany events in the novel. But as often as not, reality will simply compose itself into a refrain ("against the streetlight's iron base") and leave readers wondering just where they've heard it before. Russian poetry as well as song becomes part of the text, as Pasternak presides over passages related to Veta—the image of the candle burning on the table in the midst of a blizzard, the storm over all the earth. Pushkin, too, is a constant presence: it's not that Aleshkovsky consciously quotes Pushkin or Pasternak at every turn, but that Pushkin's "free element," for example (from *To the Sea*), is part of Russian consciousness in the same way that "a rose by any other name" is part of English. If a line starts with "farewell," then "free element" can't be far behind.

But Aleshkovsky's prose does not run on literary allusion alone. Like Gogol's prose, like Tsvetaeva's poetry, it is driven by metaphor and by sound and word association. There are passages reminiscent of Russian Orthodox liturgy, theological discourse; there is the ominous rhetoric and bombast of Soviet officialdom, Stalinist watchwords like "socialism in one country taken individually"; the buzzwords of the intelligentsia; the latest word on the street—none of it neatly confined to its own "cultural space," but spilling over into its neighbor's.

Sometimes that means an extended metaphor that runs through the entire novel. The verb *naplevat'*, for example, means simply and literally to spit. But the expression *mne napletvat'* (roughly, "I could spit on that") doesn't signify contempt, as a literal English translation might. Instead, it means sheer, emphatic indifference—Rhett Butler's famous "frankly, my dear . . ." in Russian. (The attitude even acquired its own name in the stagnant Brezhnev years, as newspapers fulminated against the *naplevism* of the young.) And that is how the phrase is most often translated: "I don't give a damn, I couldn't care less"— unless, of course, you're translating Aleshkovsky, who has his characters hawking up loogies to launch at the face of heaven and falling into metaphorical buckets of their own warm spit.

Helium's own ridiculous patronymic, Revolverovich, is another case in point. The word "revol'ver" does exist in Russian, and calls up images of the pistol-packing, leather-jacketed Cheka of Old Bolshevik myth. But, it is also a play on words, a parody of the truncated names of early Sovietspeak—*revol*iutsia plus *ver*a (faith). And Khrushchev's association with pigs in the text has as much to do with his name (*khriushka* is a colloquial word for a pig, an "oinker") as it does with his fleshy pink jowls. Even Veta's poet himself doesn't escape Aleshkovsky's grotesque reality. The word *pasternak* means parsnip.

The restoration of Helium's memory is dependent not only on the restoration of his memory of events, or of a poem in its entirety, but is contingent on his understanding of the links, the relationships, the roots of true words and true meanings. Central here is the Russian root *rod-*, which is the basis of *rodina* (motherland), *narod* (nation, people), *rozhdenie* (birth), *Rozhdestvo* (Christmas, Nativity) and the ubiquitous adjective *rodnoi*, which can mean native, kindred, related, familiar, and dear all rolled into one. So when Helium's voice in the wilderness finally finds the right word, it finds God too.

The challenge of translating a novel that works by wordplay is obvious. Russian and English morphology are different; word associations are different, and the translator can produce only a partial impression of how Aleshkovsky, in full voice, sounds. I would like to thank the author for his faith and patience, and Lev and Nina Loseff for their constant help and encouragement in translating this work. Any inaccuracies or outright mistakes are mine alone.

Jane Ann Miller

1

OUR HERO'S MOTHER was a physicist, an expert on super-low temperatures. And so she named her son Helium in honor of the remarkable element, master of matter's lowest freezing point.

She was a quiet woman, immersed for entire days—and sometimes nights—in the world of her super-low, strictly top-secret temperatures, and after the little one was weaned she took almost no part in the business of raising, feeding or spoiling him. All these cares lay on the shoulders of one of his grandmas, a townswoman. In the summertime they shipped Helium off to the country grandma.

But our narrative will leave aside many of the poetic details of our hero's childhood, boyhood, and youth. We will merely say that he grew up not in what one would call a prosperous family, but in one which had, in the first few days following the October catastrophe, jumped ahead of the game and established itself in one of the nomenclature's little niches in the material-base-primary-phase-Party-apparatus safehouse.

It was in these niches that the very biggest parasites and their light-fingered flunkies were based. They had swarmed in during the malevolent, suicidal whirlwind that had swept away the very order of life—an order that was hard, but quite acceptable, i.e., naturally tragic and (this is the main thing) perfectly suited to sinful human society, something that was soon discovered by people easily carried away by revolution but nonetheless basically normal.

So it was in this very niche that Helium lolled around from the day he was born. True, this circumstance didn't turn him into a twit, nor did it impart to his nature any of the revolting plebeian snobbery so characteristic of practically all representatives of that lowbrow ruling caste of bald bedbugs, whiskered cockroaches, dung beetles, house fleas, pubic lice, maggots and numerous other parasites on the System.

On the contrary, he was sociable, pensively curious, and could clean a bully's clock, although he always impressed certain schoolteachers and people older than himself as a young man somehow dissatisfied and listless for his age.

It seemed that he, like them, was a virtuoso at putting the desire to puke at the nauseating spirit of the age right out of his mind and psyche but, like them, lived in anguish and fear that the stifled puking spasm might suddenly repeat itself at, say, a Komsomol meeting and then . . . well it was better not to think about that.

If he was troubled by any sort of inner discomfort, brought on by so-called multiple complexes, it was only because of his family's pet name for him, Heelie, because of his odd patronymic Revolverovich and a surname obviously derived from an old Party gangster alias—Serious. Therefore when making people's acquaintance he would inform them darkly, "My name is Hal."

He clearly preferred Mozart to the light classics of Soviet composers. He could listen to a recording of *Eine kleine Nachtmusik* over and over, all day long. One time his parents brought him a dozen copies at once, since Helium wore them out so quickly.

When he started up his favorite serenade, rather than listening closely to the sound of the parts or savoring, with a fine-tuned internal ear, their musical detail, he would seem to be gazing quizzical and spellbound into a structure that hinted to him of something. In those moments his face became the face of a man frustrated and tormented by the impatient reminder of something once known, something very familiar, very close, almost kindred, which had suddenly disappeared in the thickets of memory and which was now slyly and mockingly inviting him to play a game of hide-and-seek . . . .

2 AND THERE IT WAS, his favorite music—or rather, the leitmotif from one of the parts of Mozart's serenade— ringing in Helium's brain on Christmas night, as he lay freezing in a snowbank on a street in central Moscow.

Helium was freezing, but because of the little musical excerpt from *Eine kleine Nachtmusik* that kept ringing in his brain as persistently as if the needle had landed in some little pit on a damaged record, it didn't even enter his mind to crawl out onto the pavement, fall on his knees before some car—they were rare, but still occasionally passing at that time of night—or at least to try to use a pay phone to call either an ambulance or the cops.

If in those moments he did have any sort of desperate wish, it was not for salvation but for the key—one instant before death or no—to the true meaning of his favorite composition. The meaning which had been intentionally communicated to him by Mozart's genius or else had been organized in some unforeseen fashion, seemingly all by itself. Regrettably, it's extremely rare, but this happens, not just with sounds but with words that acquire (not without the loving permission of a truly great-hearted artist and creator)—a moment of freedom to develop freely on their own . . . .

Helium was freezing, but the fragment of *Eine kleine Nachtmusik* kept stabbing, sharper and sharper, into his brain, and he couldn't understand anymore whether he, having mustered his last remnants of bodily and spiritual strength, was the one grasping at the essence of the musical meaning that so clearly hinted at something, or whether the music itself was demanding of him some final resolution, acknowledgment . . . .

The freezing man would drift off now and again, and then it would seem to him that his Lifetime—within which he could clearly, but quite fearlessly, discern a mood of pre-departure packing for a trip to the unknown—had started taking a disordered inventory of the past. Here it was stirring up things he'd completely forgotten, putting insignificant things, trifles like his pining over the candy wrapper filched by a neighbor kid, into the dark recesses of some invisible satchel, but then taking something that once seemed so very valuable and tossing it the hell away . . .

3 IN CHILDHOOD Helium had loved reading as well as music. Ever since his school days, he had adored the magical interaction of parts within the all-powerful figures of formal logic, which imparted to the world of phenomena accessible to him the features of harmonious communion with a Higher Order. And what watched over this universal order was a conjugal pair forged over centuries' time—Cause and Effect.

This legendary couple he unconsciously linked with the images of his parents, although in his family everything was reversed: that is, the Cause which gave birth to all of life's certainties was in fact his papa, Revolver Fomich.

In general, nothing caused his psyche such nagging frustration as did the back-and-forth associated with all manner of certainties.

People noticed that even in the first months of life, for all that his mind and experience lacked any criteria for comparison, some very strange (for this age) "bookkeeping" instincts were manifesting themselves in the infant being. For example, wrinkling up his little face in excruciating doubt and obviously weighing something in his little mind, he would spend a long time choosing which breast he preferred for this feeding—left or right. After taking, say, the left, he still wouldn't start greedily smacking away, squirming and red-faced from hunger though he might be, but instead would seem to be having doubts: was I wrong? have I gotten the short end of the stick? have I taken myself for a ride? what exactly was it that guided my choice?

And that's how it was. Cream-of-wheat or buckwheat? . . . Movies or theater or concert? . . . The Crimea or the country? . . . Valya or Lida? Streetcar, bus, or metro?

It cannot be said that finding himself in a situation requiring choice always frustrated him (a situation in which each of us finds ourselves several times a day without, by the way, even noticing it), not just in an airplane, in the dentist's chair, in prison or in front of a Stalin-era ballot box, that is, in places where the fantasies and caprices of our free will are extraordinarily limited and where of course there's no getting away from anything foisted on you by circumstances, a run-amok regime, or the whim of chance.

More often than not, Helium would turn any choice into a game. And then his psyche would fall slave to calculation. However, it wasn't the final result that was the goal—this he unconsciously shoved into the background—but instead the prolonging and the savoring of the calculation. Calculation of this sort seemed to divide his choice into several absolutely unexpected, independent problems that would make him simply lose heart.

This at times left Helium with neither strength nor desire to keep on living, but simultaneously imparted to his reason a very brief illusion of all-powerful dominion—within the bounds of that moment—over chance. In such moments his ever uncertain reason imagined itself the captain of a wrecked and sinking ship—but captain all the same. Or else Stalin, after losing out to Hitler at the debut of their revolting, mutually-dirty little game and cravenly hiding in the john during the initial days of the Second World War. Scared shitless—but Stalin all the same.

Very often, after relishing all the doubts, mental maneuvers, unexpected whims of the soul, and all the psychological nuances of gaming combinations, he felt himself utterly drained, and immediately—to the great amazement of those near and dear to him—turned traitor to all his calculations.

He would retreat, slip away from his chosen position like a candy-ass staff officer trying to escape enemy encirclement—that is, he would get himself captured right off by yet another choice and then bitterly regret that he hadn't stood fast to the end, that he'd acted this way and not that. Then for months he would grope for the root of his latest bookkeeping muddle.

But he also knew how to free himself easily enough from the heavy mental yoke—by out-and-out refusing to make a choice or by assigning it to, say, a piece of chocolate and a gumdrop—Tanya and Manya. Then when the gumdrop seemed to pop into his mouth all by itself—it was Tanya who suddenly appeared on his sofa.

True, at such moments Helium gave people—and perhaps candy too—the impression of a child, boy, man who was a bit dissatisfied, a bit annoyed by whatever had happened, who morosely harbored suspicions that someone-or-other was plotting and scheming out there . . . .

Finally, after two years of intense work by his "internal investigative organs" and of family discussions on the topic of KGB versus theoretical physics, both of them together versus foreign trade, diplomat versus physician-dietician for the Soviet figure-skating team, Helium surprised his teachers and his parents alike by settling on history.

He chose the study of history, of its laws and its philosophy, with the goal of gradually immersing himself in the narrow field of the role of chance occurrence in the multilayered Napoleon torte–like structure of historical events. He was also attracted by the analysis of quantitative characteristics of everything random that, one way or another, creates if not the shape, then the quality of whatever has occurred, and which has deservedly—or sometimes even undeservedly—attained the historical status of an unforgettable event.

4 BUT UNFORTUNATELY, as it turned out, in his very first year at the Lenin Pedagogical Institute Helium Revolv-erovich Serious found himself—not, we should emphasize, of his own volition—a "very promising career" in the war on God, on theology, on the whole Heavenly Host, clergymen of all confessions, rank-and-file believers and, naturally, on Religion As Such.

This unhappy occurrence took place on the day he was accepted into the institute. That evening Helium and his father, one of the chief wheeler-dealers in the Party's Central Committee food combine for the upper-level nomenclature, had an Important Discussion. They were in a private dining room at the Prague. After saying the usual "in memoriam" for the wife and mother taken from them in untimely fashion, they drank to this important milepost in Helium's life.

We shall return without fail to this Important Discussion, inasmuch as this is where, apparently, the whole thing started. In any case, Helium, battered and freezing in his snowbank, kept returning to it as if to some arcane, fateful first cause, the beginning of all the ugly troubles of his existence.

Quite a few years had rolled by since this tavern discussion. Everything happened just the way Revolver Fomich—with Helium's tacit agreement—had planned. The resolution of the curious but seemingly minor question—is there a God or isn't there?—Helium had more or less delegated to his father, who was considered the hereditary family expert on "the mystical origins of dead matter, proteins and the business of life in its oozy primeval bouillon."

In his graduate work at the institute Helium had specialized in a variety of questions of so-called Scientific Atheism. He felt no particular liking for or even interest in any of this drivel.

His thesis and later his dissertation were ghostwritten by a defrocked priest, driven both from church circles and from his post for a multitude of sins unbecoming to a man of the cloth, and also for the sale of a unique sixteenth-century icon to a Swedish diplomat. In the same fashion, and with the same ease, Helium might just as well have delegated his wedding night with a fictive bride to some other man.

The dissertation written by the seedy hustler had quite a romantic title, in the view of Revolver Fomich and the history Ph.D-to-be.

STORMING THE HEAVENS: THE FUNDAMENTAL METHODOLOGI-CAL PRINCIPAL IN THE ATHEISTIC TRAINING OF THE SOVIET CREATIVE-ARTS INTELLIGENTSIA, CONSIDERED IN THE LIGHT OF RECENT PARTY AND GOVERNMENT RESOLUTIONS, AND BASED ON EXAMPLES OF ANTI-RELIGIOUS PROCESSING OF MALE MEMBERS OF THE MOSCOW WRITERS' ORGANIZATION.

Helium had been gabbing with writers, poets, and critics for about three years or so (either in the drinking establishments of the Central House of Writers or sometimes in the writers' own kitchens or at arts centers) about all those things that the Moscow intelligentsia (which considers itself innately spiritual) tends to gab about.

His dissertation defense went brilliantly. They drank to it in that very same room at the Prague. True, when the dissertation was being reviewed by the Supreme Academic Commission someone deemed it necessary to remove the expression "EXAMPLES . . . OF MALE MEMBERS" from the title and put the period after "GOVERNMENT RESOLUTIONS."

For about five years Helium toiled in some arcane little section of the USSR Council of Ministers Committee on Religious Affairs. At the same time, he began establishing himself as the major theoretician of Scientific Atheism inside the lecture-circuit nomenclature of the "KNOWLEDGE SOCIETY."

Naturally he would drop in at the House of Writers fairly often, since he'd finessed a Writers' Union membership by way of the criticism section; he was also getting to be rich and, as they say, distinguished.

PAPA REVOLVER had once introduced his indiscriminately lecherous son, who in the end had gotten himself mixed up in triple-column bedroom bookkeeping, to the daughter of one of the Central Committee section chiefs. The young people often went to Moscow theaters to see dress rehearsals of plays subject to imminent and irrevocable ban.

They would spend hours in restricted museum storerooms where Vetochka would rapturously educate Helium as to the perfect charm of paintings and sculptures by those native Russian geniuses who were fierce foes of Socialist Realism. They would sit in box seats at performances by virtuosos and the world's finest orchestras.

As if sensing that Vetochka's intellectual tastes were somehow off-key, as if guessing her soul's reverence for the very Heavens he was storming and for all the dogmatic myths of the Holy Scriptures he himself had had a hand in refuting, Helium had never uttered a peep about the nature of his provocatively proud profession, nor of course did he ever display his bold scholarly profile in conversation with the girl.

For Helium was in love. Chiefly, this was exceedingly clear and absolutely obvious—so obvious, that it never occurred to him to weigh in his mind, did he love her or didn't he; to sit down and mull it over, to give thesis or anithesis either one the litmus test of high-minded doubt.

And, it seemed, his love was not unrequited. And in comparison to what he was now feeling for the first time in his life, Scientific Atheism, God, the devil, the hosts of Light and the hordes of darkness, the Bible, the Committee, the Church, the global titans of theomachy all looked rather inessential and strangely substanceless.

The young people were more and more drawn to one another. Helium decided to declare his love to Vetochka in the "Moscow," that is, the swimming pool. The watery ambiance, he thought, would lend their bodies an illusion of weightlessness (a property mistaken by idealists of all stripes, including any number of cosmonauts, for much-vaunted spirituality).

At the hour reserved for the ablutions of family members of the high-level Party and government nomenclature, the young people descended into the chlorinated vapors of the gloomy foundation pit.

Sensing intuitively the passions of Vetochka's soul and the

delusions of her intellect, Helium chose the indirect approach and, floating on his back, told her that he was a Voltairean, in the purely Pushkinian sense, but that his favorite poem was Lermontov's "The Demon." In the interests of greater guile and to lend the decisive moment all the attributes of complete mutual understanding, he added that here in the pool those amazing lines of the Bible's initial verse always came to mind, in the translation of a certain remarkable poet-and-drunk: "and the spirit of God moved upon the waters . . . "

Then, as if to urbanely downplay any superflous pathos and also to advertise his knowledge of Lermontov (for Helium, this particular genius was among the elementally Luciferean theomachists) he quoted a joke by one of his boob friends in the operetta department of the Ministry of Culture: "In the streams of the Aragvi, he ordered some tsatsivi . . . "

Vetochka laughed and told him that her favorite poem in the literature of all times and peoples was Pasternak's "In the Hospital."

Helium wasn't familiar with the literary masterpiece. The very name of this poet who, word had it, had died with a smile on his face for "priestianity," usually roused him to quite understandable fury. But here in the foundation-pit waters, he rather nicely imitated the exceedingly artless manners and esoteric breathiness of the high priests of our kitchen-intellectual culture, touched his foot to his beloved's shoulder, and drawled, "So reci-i-ite it to me, I'm li-i-i-stening, . . . ple-e-uz . . . "

Later, especially in moments when alcohol had sharpened his senses or in the absolutely blunt despair of a hangover, he not so much remembered as felt—with every single nerve-ending—everything that then took place in the "Moscow" pool.

Moreover he remembered it in a light so piercing that it pitilessly revived in that space of remembrance a full complement of minor details, right down to the shallow slapping of the water, the chlorine which guaranteed the continued health and well-being of the swimming masses—its importunate reek reminded him of that strange whiffiness under the blanket after his first wet dream, and the turmoil in body and soul that kept him awake until morning came—right down to the Kazbek butt someone had prankishly flicked into the water . . . right down to the note hung on the door of his changing-room: "ironclad promise of intimate compensation for the finder of my designer bra" . . . and the roiling, roiling, roiling of the hateful vermin . . . it all came back to him in such piercing light that reality, each time obsequiously yielding place to recollection, seemed the latter's rather pitiful, artificial shade . . .

When Vetochka concluded her barely audible recitation of the "Judas-poet's ultra-religious doggerel" with the wondrous lines "You hold me like a hand-wrought thing / And hide me like a ring in a case," Helium was about to dissemble, to say something cryptic and neutral in kitchen-intellectual lingo, or else just get by with a weighty silence.

But suddenly realizing in horror that not the tiniest bubble of his own will remained to him, that it had all left him and was burbling out around him the way air burbles out into water after bursting through a ripped air-mattress—all of a sudden he began flailing his arms in fury, slapping the water with his feet, then hoarsely, boorishly, mockingly, he cried—or more strictly speaking howled—like a man possessed: "R-i-i-i-ng in a c-a-a-a-se my a-a-a-s . . . g-i-i-i-ft my a-a-a-a-ssss . . . what frigging hand-job? . . . and who the hell's g-i-i-i-ving it to us any-wa-a-a-y?"

What happened next was something which should, by all laws of nature, never happen in a surface-water environment laden with evaporation and the fiendish chlorine vapors that flatten the ripples of sound and, with sadistic pedantry, refuse to allow their childish game of "echo."

Suddenly, there in the foundation pit, an acoustic marvel took place. The boorish, jeering howl suddenly took on such concert-stage volume and artistic purity that Helium's very eyes popped out of his head in horror and dismay.

It was as if he'd been struck by paralysis. In some utterly strange fashion, he didn't sink, but neither was he able to "butterfly" over to Vetochka, to avert something irreparable, to urbanely say that God, apparently, did not exist (though it was possible that He did) . . . but that in any case Helium himself didn't believe in his existence but did consider that out of sheer respect for the laws of language that the word "God" should be capitalized, even in the newspaper . . . it would be just crazy for us, Vetochka, crazy, crazy, to quarrel over such obscurantism on Pasternak's part . . . and as far as his metaphors go, well, they're really great . . . if you want I'll run out and buy a carnation from the street-vendors . . . we'll lay it on the steps of his old apartment building . . . it's right close by, not far from this pool, on Volkhonka . . .

But Vetochka, utterly stunned by the thrice-repeated echo of Helium's boorish howl, had already begun swimming away . . . swimming away, away forever, swimming toward the steel handrails of the pool ladder.

She swam then and many years later, in wretched Helium's memory, with unusual, unnatural speed. In the movement of her body he could sense precisely the sort of horror with which we try to escape some hideous monster pursuing us through our dreams.

Meanwhile he himself, comprehending nothing, stared at the strange, dirty-green little forms—not quite objects, not quite beings—hopping-skipping-jumping over the agitated water: inside each one of them, just like inside laxative grapes filled with castor oil, jiggled some sort of heavy, disgusting, greenish gel.

This was his first encounter with what he immediately dubbed, in his own mind, his demons, imps, devils, and other assorted lowlife goons.

HELIUM COULDN'T REMEMBER climbing out of the pool, or anyone helping him dry off, or getting dressed, or coming out on the embankment which bore the name of the famous anarchist, or making his way to the restaurant at the House of Writers.

It was absolutely clear to him just who in that establishment was forcing drink after drink down his nondrinker's throat. He had no doubt but that he was in the personal custody of a horde of hazy grayish-green gremlin-waiters who were hopping up and down the marvelous carved banisters, who were splashing in taiga-oak Zhora Markov's and Party-skunk Verchenko's soup, burrowing into Kiev bard Longiomo Andriushko Voznesensky's cutlets; sitting on the sterling silver rim of Bob Rozhdestvensky's bowl, their paws dangling, froglike, in his black caviar; pissing foamy-yellow in Lenin-rhapsodist Voskresenkaya's mineral water. For Helium there was a certain mockingly derisive savor to this devil-crew's consorting with bearers of scriptural, so to speak, surnames, all these Ascensions and Assumptions and Nativities . . . . The demon brood picked at the crust of a layered pie on Tolyana Safronov's plate: one imp was lobbing floury cakecrumbs at snitch Lesyuk's hyenalike chops. . . .

If it hadn't been for the natural fear of looking like a crackpot and ending up in the bin, then—given everything that had just happened—Helium might have tried, foaming at the mouth, to prove to his pals and drinking buddies that demons *do* exist in that "objective reality accessible to our senses"—in the favorite words of a certain goateed Someone bearing both an inner and outer resemblance to that well-known functionary, chief administrator of the underworld.

It was they, Helium might have maintained, who broke off our betrothal, who poured filth on the union of two hearts. They have unlimited psychotechnological means at their disposal. They mysteriously plugged in to my consciousness. The demons put that rash howl about the damn ring-in-the-case right in my mouth. Give me a blank piece of paper and I'll form—more like deform—them right down to the last little smirk, the last horn and hoof, all those spectral little demon-figures swarming in the pool like sprats at spawning time. O-o-oh, yes. They appear extremely rarely, but they do exist. *He* doesn't, but they do. They do! And herein lies atheism's problem of problems and its theory of relativity. That was an ingenious maneuver—distracting Scientific Atheism with a war on something that doesn't exist at all, so it would leave them in peace or, if worst came to worst, pawn them off on the psychiatrists and pharmacologists. . . .

He was drinking himself blind by then. He was trying to stifle a feeling in his soul which (this was extremely clear) would never leave him and which (purely because the mind is not used to putting words to anything anecdotal, tragicomic, or irreversibly awful in our lives) he wouldn't have been able to define, even for himself, as the feeling that his love and happiness were dead, now and forever.

He tried hanging himself with his belt in the Central House of Writers toilet, but didn't quite manage it. Although he did get the belt out of his trouser loops . . . . But he tied one end to a pipe and when, with the help of those nastily smirking imps, he stuck his head through the leather noose . . . both feet slid from the wooden seat right to the bottom of the toilet bowl.

The laughter of the smutty little goons was just as rasping, slaplike, noisy, and obviously prankish as at the pool. It was bad enough that he'd torn the belt off the pipe—he'd also plopped into a pile of turds covered with the crumpled pages from a book of Felka Chuyev's poetry. And it was obviously that simply ingenious and crafty dissenter Zhenka Yevtushenko who, as a sign of comfortable protest against the introduction of the Brezhnev tank doctrine into Prague, had refused to flush it into the nationwide plumbing system.

In this state Helium returned to the dining room. For a while he suspiciously and severely scrutinized the faces of the wining-and-dining critics, writers and poets, the Party's faithful helpers, as if trying to search out the coquettishly and profitably dissenting Yevtoo, in order to settle the score once and for all.

But then the incredibly stupid and half-blind bard of the irrepressible friendship of world youth rushed over to give him a slavering kiss, and then a Literary Institute student (a boy from the Urals, a future Central Committee agit-prop instructor) obligingly wiped the shit away with a brand-new issue of *Young Communist*.

Finally a female acquaintance from the World Literature Institute, aging but still quite active in all manner of venues, abandoned her drinking companions and lustily led Helium out of the dining room, accompanied by the nasty mummer's laughter of a certain hideous critic and snitch. Whenever he'd had a snootful, this critic always tried to convince Helium that "one ought to believe not in God but in Man, that is Russian Man, that is in the general human sense."

Overcoming her squeamishness with a little forced humor, the philological lady slipped off Helium's shoes and trousers in a little courtyard next to a high-rise. Somehow she also managed to provide him a certain extraordinarily acute satisfaction. Then she took his half-naked, half-dead body home in a taxi. He sobbed the whole night through on the imported silicone bosom of this resourceful specialist in erotic motifs in Greek and Roman literature.

There was something symptomatic and diabolically absurd in this nocturnal wake for his lost love. No doubt, he thought, this was all contrived by that same gaggle of demons. Neither chance nor some archenemy could have devised a more refined outrage—spending the night after the shit-dumping of a lifetime with an aging nymphomaniac who, according to gossip, in her days as a loyal Komsomol girl had slept with our paralyzed myth Ostrovsky. The scabrous anecdotal Writers'-House version of that affair was entitled "How Madame de Stahl Was Tempered."

After seeing the lady out, Helium suffered all day long, from both despair at being doomed to an obtuse, loveless existence—

and his utter failure to part with it. But he made no more attempts either to hang or poison himself.

7 NOWHERE DID HE ever again encounter his former love.
He could no more telephone her than he could telephone a dead woman, or—rather—than could a dead
man call out to a living woman passing by his gravemound.

He became a quiet, respectable drunk. From time to time,
moreover in the most offical manner, he performed his functions in the beds of ladies of the exotic-hotel-room sort. He was
considered an eccentric luminary of Scientific Atheism. He and
another philosopher practically owned one department of the
Academy of Social Sciences, Central Committee Branch.

He often served as a highly-paid consultant on films based
on works by Gogol and Dostoevsky in which evil spirits played
some part, or else characters of dramatically profound and sincere faith were featured.

He often traveled abroad with various delegations. Over
there he had a good rep—that of an eminent religious scholar,
author of monographs and articles. So he could allow himself
the luxury of not bringing to bear the most refined, devastating
arguments of Scientific Atheism (the tattered rags of which reveal an unseemly, nakedly plebeian mind and spirit which
arouses in those people who are either naturally aristocratic
or else simply intelligent a feeling of embarassment at the
speaker's public self-humiliation).

It was enough for him, at some academic discussion of, say,
the Shroud of Turin, to shrug his shoulders and smile a plu-
ralistically correct smile, and the poison of terminal doubt in the

authenticity of the crucified Savior's raiment would seep into the brains of those who still wavered . . .

But why talk about the waverers? Thanks to such well-practiced niceties of public demeanor, this eminent (but ignorant, by virtue of the primordial stupidity of atheism) religious scholar looked to be an extremely tactful figure—even in the eyes of highly-educated foreign Jesuits and our own native underground- and kitchen-cultivated theologians.

And why not? His entire mien seemed to appeal for mercy and magnanimity toward the One who, after the successful storming of Heaven, had been personally cast down into the dust of objective reality. . . .

And this, in the eyes of liberal believers, appeared to be an obvious symptom of neo-official recognition of the existence of God, who was now to be found in undoubtedly temporary captivity, prisoner of the diabolical power of the Prince of Darkness, with something like the special status of a Napoleon or a Fieldmarshal Paulus.

In a word, from the outside, everything seemed just okey-dokey for our hero.

Pasternak's fateful last lines about the handwrought thing and the ring in the case, which he'd mocked so lustily in the pool, had literally never entered his conscious mind, as if they hadn't been lines of verse at all, but instead fatal, random bullets piercing his soul on the fly and leaving it bleeding and alone, while they disappeared scot free into the emptiness of the world's immensity.

And his friends and colleagues attributed the strange fact that Helium's athletically boyish good looks had, with unusual rapidity, become those of a person who, though still impressive-looking, had grown old before his time, to either the stress of unending grief over the deaths of his parents or else to exceedingly reckless overexhaustion in the wilderness of solitary bachelorhood.

And naturally no one knew that what had taken up residence within him and now would never ever leave his being, was a melancholy horror at the instantaneous death of his love, the old horror which had engulfed him in the chlorinated hell of the swimming pool.

He got himself plastered so respectably at his infinitely sad private wakes that it never occurred to anyone to suspect him of morose drinking binges and daily drunks.

Moreover, he soon became convinced that he never stank of liquor, strange as that might seem, given the violent excesses usually perpetrated by chemical substances on the hungover organism of the drinker.

Of course Helium couldn't help seeing a connection between this phenomenon and with the influence of the unholy vermin who, ever since that ill-fated moment in the pool, had watched slavishly over his thrice-damned life and totally useless career.

In public Helium bore the vermin's presence with stoic decorum. True, it seemed to certain ladies of the hotel-room sort that during the sex act their partner would sometimes begin rolling his eyes in baleful and menacing fashion, like a dog bothered by some pesky fly buzzing right in front of its nose at the very climax of intimacy with a juicy bone.

But these ladies were never able to analyze their impressions more closely, by dint of their irresistible impulse toward higher things, an impulse which never triumphs over daily life and its petty annoyances with more remarkable power than in chance sexual encounters of the hotel-room sort.

Whenever Helium got plastered in complete solitude, he

would either sadistically and vengefully torment the hateful little devils, imps, and demons (who were slightly larger in size) with a reproduction of some icon, or else peer at them with the squeamish curiosity of a child peering at spiders and wood lice.

There were fully materialized single-goons and crowds of goonlets in various configurations. Moreover all these anti-creatures were so fidgety and so taunting in their fidgetiness that fixing any of their external features either in fleeting observation or in long-term memory was utterly impossible.

Sometimes they seemed to be nothing but playful globs of thickened air, assuming various shapes and changing color, but with the dirty-green tones always the dominants in their capriciously faithless coloring.

Sometimes it was the other way round, and you could look at all these little goonlets as strange holes in folded space—a variety of holes in paper snipped out by the darting scissors of a fluey child marking time in his illness and his life simultaneously. But when the multiply folded planes are unfolded, the uneven, random cutout becomes—thanks to that magical moment when it acquires symmetry—a number of finished configurations of the holes shaping the emptiness. And, for whatever reason, they rivet the attention not only of small children but of solitary childlike natures. This happens, perhaps, because shaped emptiness draws the gaze of such natures away from the menacing content of our absurd reality.

It goes without saying that Helium had classified the whole revoltingly persistent vermin cast (extras and all) and had, in accordance with their various smutty inclinations and the functions they performed, assigned them appropriate titles and sometimes casual nicknames as well.

And although he couldn't deny that the goonlets' attitude

toward him was gracious and at times almost too deferential, although without their obvious involvement he would have enjoyed neither foreign nor domestic success, no deals, no profitable connections, affairs, acquisitions et cetera et cetera—Helium, with provocative ingratitude, ridiculed and taunted every devil and demon that came to hand.

8

FOR EXAMPLE, just recently, Helium had been trying to hail a taxicab outside the House of Writers on an inclement holiday eve, when catching one of these urban-insult vehicles is virtually impossible. If a person does manage to snag one he's usually so stunned by his unprecedented luck that he in all sincerity consigns this rare occurrence to the sphere of the miraculous rather than to any flicker of humanity in the thrice-damned permafrost of the Soviet service sector.

So there Helium was, trying to catch a cab. Many of the "horseless" writers with their sweet literary groupies or their lawful wedded life's companions had already given up, and were straggling off, pedestrianly squelching through the slushy snow.

Helium could just catch the echo of their literary squabbles and nervous perplexity over the cheerless perspectives for creative-arts workers in the not-so-distant future.

One of them was fretting over the disintegration of the imperial friendship of peoples, which had resulted in the collapse of the "time-honored institution of subsidized translation, since that nightingale of generals' shorts, Prokhanov, has decreed that henceforth anyone translating from Ukrainian, Chechen and Tatar should be considered a hired Russophobe! . . . " "Well that vile Koziol, to the very end of his days, translated those traitorous Chechnya and all the other wog-gook-ragheads he could find . . . " "The marketplace, gentlemen, will soon sort out just who's who. . . . " "So, gentlemen and Leninologists, we've had enough of you collectively kissing the Party's stinking ass and swarming like nomenclatured crabs all over Socialist Realism's frigid groin . . . " "Frigging Bullsheviks! Brrrr. . . ." "Don't worry about it, Bob, Nabokov was a cut above you in genius and style but even he held his nose and did his share of grunt work in some trade school for girls before getting rich on his pornita-Lolita . . . " "Well and Joyce's consciousness tended to stream in the direction of foreign currency too . . . " "It wouldn't hurt you bastards to keep in mind that back in '17 Nabokov lost about a hundred times more than the whole lot of us ever made . . . ."

Moscow is dreary in the November slush, and the despair enfolding the outraged souls and chilled bodies of writers suddenly cut off from their sovereign bankrupt's largesse was driving the temperature of their sorry common lot straight down to some infernal zero.

And here was Helium, after the criticism section's usual idiotic discussion of parapsychology, after a marvelous dinner in the unbearably loathsome company of writer-patriots, former Brezhnev doormen and lackeys with excellent appetites, humbly standing on Insurrection Square, in an enormous human line so plastered with wet snow that it by now resembled some enormous, homeless, derelict monster.

There he stood, uninvolved in discussions of the future of the Writers' Union, of the provincial greed and pathological belligerence of the new first secretary, summoned from Tashkent to be lord and ruler of the palsied Writers' Union and thereby raking in the privileges and tossing them into his shoulder bag (with both hands) just like the mythical junior heroine-of-labor Mamlakat Mamlayev at her cotton-harvesting marathon; from discussions of the gathering social darkness and the estrangement of the people from absolutes and ideals. It was those atheist Yid Freemasons and all that other financial-monopoly Zionism distracting the Russian people from all that was sacred, suggested the hideous critic.

The little green cablights of hope and comfort flew past, occasionally spraying the now nearly faceless parts of the monster consisting of critics, writers, and poets of either sex with the slush and chill of unadulterated Soviet indifference, the most mocking and inhuman in the world.

The critic was cut off in mid-word by a certain stupendously intellectual lady, who declared that members of the Writers' Union were duty-bound and obliged to channel all their unused creative energy not into unsafe sex in a time of plague, but instead into the greatest project in the history of all times and people, i.e., toward the resurrection of the dead and our literal re-union with our forefathers who have kicked off before us. Someone optimistically objected that, given Yeltsin's decree on the liberalization of prices, this grandiose project would soon be accomplished by natural means. And, really, why cook up schemes to disturb the natural and heavenly order just so that our ancestors can quit their empyrean repose to report back to this barracks, this brothel, this filthy, frigging mess where they'd have no food, no home, no decent constitution, no rule-of-law, and no opportunity to apply their talents. We should show our ancestors a little mercy. It would be shameful to bare, even for an instant, the stinking sores of our debased post-Soviet civilization. Why rub their noses in something they were so kind as to help create? Although, mused someone, I wouldn't mind smacking both Belinsky and Chernyshevsky around a little. . . . No? I'd take those little goatees and splat! . . . . face-down, right in our puke. . . . goatees and all. . . . yessir! Excuse me, but we're still wondering how we're going to get over one cosmic and anthropological catastrophe and you, madame, are already possessed with the notion of another rebellion, this time against the natural and God-given order of things, not the Tsarist one. You know what you can do with your satanic "versus" . . . ?

"That guy is absolutely right," thought Helium, since the lady's call to curtail sexual activity had markedly lowered the general temperature not only of the writers' immediate physical environment but also of their already hardly congenial existence.

To distract himself from all the squabbling, Helium turned his interest to a curious version of what, in the tipsy interpreter's view, was practically the main subtext of the inspiration—or rather the image—behind Nabokov's marvelous *Lolita*. His interpretation came down to this: this great aesthete, the master of his own opulent inner world, suddenly, magically, got sick of it all: sick of penury, of his penchant—suppressed by upbringing and a sense of right and wrong—for enchanting little nymphets, sick of drudge-work in a girl's school atmosphere, of the longstanding, sadistic aloofness of worldwide Fame, and other domestic inconveniences. But the main thing he'd gotten sick of was Dostoevsky's genius—all those tortured, repenting and ruminating protagonists, those sensual despoilers and destroyers of schoolchildren. . . . It was absolutely delightful how Nabokov had managed to kill two birds with one stone. It was great that he'd gotten both rich and rightfully famous and then skipped out with his wife to a Swiss hotel, as far as possible from the miasmas of a young ladies' finishing school—and, in the sweet asphyxia of inspiration, amused himself to his heart's content composing a novel about what he had stoically, bravely, and truly decently renounced his whole life long. He renounced it and allowed himself only the most refined, purely symbolic, indetectable, secret indulgence in his primordially shameful passion. And all this took place amid his pursuit of ungodly (excusez-moi) beautiful butterflies, his loves and his victims, later to be pitilessly splayed and pinned onto little scientific beds in various shades of velvet. And then Nabokov could really thumb his nose at hateful Dostoevsky! Here, says he, here, Fyodor Mikailovich, here's the way to sin in novel form and then instructively chastise the villain, and the way to sinlessly save beauty without expecting it to save the world, here's how you bring the Sleeping Beauty of Russian belles lettres back to life while aristocratically disdaining to resort to ideological sermons or appeals to native down-and-out dopes. Gentlemen, this is an artist and naturalist—not some Tolstoevsky moralist—impressing upon us that setting our perplexing criminal tendencies loose is not only permissible but also quite useful—as long as it's in art, not life . . . And what have we been doing the last seventy-five years, nearly all of us pissant poets—with the exception of maybe a dozen names— what have we been doing? Furiously screwing ourselves and everyone else along the way, shitting personally on all that's holy, and who's it swinging the stinking censer over the casket of our poor, violated belles lettres? . . . all the rotten Svidrigailovs and rancid Stavrogins and Petie Verkhovenskys, reincarnated in that petty little demon Limonov. . . . And here we are whining for alms from our bloated powers-that-be and discoursing on God Almighty . . . What kind of God lets the police run scared while the taxis run amok. . . ?

Then all of a sudden a free cabbie pulled up and stopped—more like bucked up and reared—at the head of that enormous, assembled monster and in crippled Russian, with palsied accents, bawled out the driver's window, "Whereyoufuckin-suitsgoin??"

All at the same time, the writers, critics and other literati and their girlfriends and wives obsequiously (which is understandable in such weather, but makes even a dim-bulb streetlight feel a little embarrassed for man and his sovereign nature) called out their chosen destinations. Of course not a single one of them, near or far, was to the mug's taste.

But one little demon got Helium by the tongue and, almost against his own will, he said, "Klin. The Schnittke House and Museum, Pakhmatova Wing," and at that very moment, out of the blue, he was suddenly seized with a hatred for the former's refined modernism and the latter's stinking Komsomol music.

The pug cabbie, who happened to be a native of Klin (though of course nobody except the imp knew this), flung the door open wide. The monstrous line stood stunned and amazed at the unpredictable behavior of the proprietors of our willful means of transportation.

The imp flitted straight into the heavenly warmth of the cab. With crass familiarity it cocked the pug's military cap down low over his shifty brow. Helium tumbled in right behind the brazen little goon.

The taxi roared off in the direction of the Leningrad highway without even thinking to take any of the writers who lived in the literary dorm by the Airport metro stop, which was right on its way. They, in the meantime, found solidarity in their agreement that the Klin House and Museum could not possibly belong to either the great Schnittke or that hack sidewoman of stagnation, as well as in their burning hatred (which did warm them up a bit in such weather) for the lucky religious scholar.*

The religious scholar, in his turn, was warming up his chilled innards with hypercynical spite: "So what do you lowlifes expect after years of Storming the Heavens with your spitballs? How about a juicy gob of wet snow down your backs, gentlemen and atheists? *This* is how you deny the Deity, like I did, ready for anything, be it dirty tricks or a lucky twist of inanimate nature—in other words, with a grateful merci, you can all go to hell, allons au taxi! "

Meanwhile the pug cabbie was behaving the way that not only lone citizens but million-strong crowds do when under the irresistible influence of unholy spirits.

He was speeding, without the slightest clue why, in the direction opposite the former province of Tver—though his shift had long since ended, though he never connected his place of birth and their destination, and his taxi-barn was located at the other end of town. It wasn't just that he was too intimidated by his strange passenger to exchange some stupid chitchat—he couldn't even bring himself to take a peep at his well-groomed, lordly profile.

Meanwhile the little goonlet demon, who looked like a whirling, green-plasma top, hopped from the steering wheel to the gearshift and popped out onto the windshield where it squiggled back and forth along with the wiper blade, dissolv-

*The Tchaikovsky House and Museum is located in Klin, about an hour from Moscow.—TRANS.

ing, then reforming into a plasma-puddle and looking clearly overjoyed at pleasing its ward.

But Helium, instead of mentally thanking the little imp for its menial services, up and—in the most natural of fashions, just to spite it—made the sign of the cross over all the expanse outside the windows. And laughed like a madman, laughed and laughed.

It struck him as funny, and fun, that the imp was flustered, that the twerp writers were left grousing in the wet snow, that ahead of him lay homely warmth, a shot of Cuban rum and the oblivion of dead-drunk sleep, and that the pug-ugly taximan was just a pitiful toy in the hands of this rank-and-file vermin.

"Stop!" ordered Helium suddenly. "I think I'll just stop in for a bang at a certain lovely lady's." He handed the lewdly sniggering cabbie a five-ruble note (from which that dickbrain Voznesensky—probably out of naive, avant-garde but no less fawning stupidity—had tried to persuade old gomer Brezhnev to remove Lenin's face); the green-plasma goon dissolved all over the bill. The cabbie, reaching into his pocket, again like the millions of people fallen under the spell of demons and failing to realize how fateful were their own acts in October of 1917, was about to cause irreparable damage to his own eventual mood and the social equilibrium as well.

He gave Helium change for a hundred rubles and with fawning eagerness refused to accept a tip, then tore off in such haste that his "Volga" first spun like a top on the slimy asphalt, then skidded right up onto the grassy snow-covered median and zoomed out of sight.

After which the ungrateful Helium again frustrated the demon with the words, "Begone, bane of existence. Begone, before

I use the sign of the cross on you again, you squiggy little freak."

We should note that not one single goon out of all that unholy flock ever bore any grudge toward Helium. Their lack of rancor was amazing, although they couldn't abide rude gestures and would meekly slink away like dejected pets whenever Helium began taunting and tormenting them.

On the contrary, what *didn't* they do for him, veritably spitting on their own pride. Once he was almost murdered at what was then a clandestine gathering of nationalist-fascists, where he'd been taken by the same hideous critic who, denying God, affirmed his faith in Preferably Russian Man.

Helium had sat there, drinking, chewing, brushing the demons off the rim of his glass, listening to the revolting crap spouted by these freakish offshoots of the Russian family tree, grieving that the better part of his great nation had unfortunately been totally destroyed by an infernal, decades-long experiment. And in its place this little crew was spreading its stink. And they called themselves patriots, the scum-suckers. . . .

Religion in general, and the very words God, Jesus, the Virgin, et cetera, always made Helium a bit queasy, but even he was horrified by the talk among this sullen, brainless bunch about how Christianity was really just a Yid-Freemason scheme cooked up to spiritually enslave the Aryan nations. One person suggested that, for a start, Russian children be recruited into pagan arts-and-crafts clubs where patriotically-minded educators would teach them to carve wooden images of the ancient gods tossed into the Dnieper river by that tenth-century agent of international Zionism, Prince Vladimir. Helium drank, and listened to this stunningly dim-witted rhetoric lacking any hint of form or artistry, which reduced all the nation's historical woes, without exception, to the politico-economic whoring of the lost tribe of the Khazars as well as the ongoing global conspiracy of Yid-Freemasonry's financial oligarchies.

By the time they asked him to say his piece, he could hardly move his tongue, and he bleated out something-or-other, but suddenly, involuntarily, at the look of their ugly faces, their crudeness, their logic which insulted the hapless soul of a nation and grossly cheapened the meaning of Russia's hellish trials, everything in him felt suddenly outraged—his intellect, his taste, and his sense of tragic Russian history. He himself had hardly a clue to the reasons for the trials which had befallen Russia (and not only Russia) in this century, but he could sense some kind of devilish warp in this crowd's reduction of all cause-and-effect to the devious machinations of Zion.

Helium felt so nauseated that it was as if he'd stuck his finger down his throat and turned himself inside out right then and there. But he didn't palaver, didn't try to change the minds of these wood-lice hatching out under the floorboards of their once great, ruined and crumbling house, but puked this right in their faces: "I myself don't believe in any god," he said, "but I do still believe that our nation's fate is nothing if not instructive. But you, you don't believe in God, or in Russia, or in her language or her culture or her history, or in hope, or in fate—you, gentlemen, don't believe in anything. You don't even believe in the Devil. And as for the future—well, what can I say. Seems the only thing you rock-solid believe in is the Yid-Freemasons, and that's unbelievably mindless idiocy. Here's twenty-five rubles for the drinks and the eats. Merci, gentlemen. . . ."

They let him leave the building, but caught up with him

outside and coldcocked him with something. When the pain woke him up, he realized that these lackeys of the latest pseudo-majestic, pseudonational idea were hammering the crap out of him. They were working him over and working themselves up more and more as they went along. It was a dark night and an out-of-the-way side street. Helium was already calmly saying his farewells to life when he saw three men running toward the fracas. At the group's head sped the demon flock, looking just like a bluish-green cloud of plasma from an American science-fiction movie. The newcomers, his saviors, lunged at the attackers and and went about professionally kicking butt. Later, Helium learned that a vigilante group had organized to protect the neighborhood from local punks and muggers. . . .

He couldn't count the number of extraordinary incidents in which either some solitary lowlife goonlet—or else the whole hideous mass—acted the hero.

Helium let himself go, stopped even trying to write anything, didn't bother traveling the profitable lecture circuit, blew off his career, was in no rush to go abroad, never plotted, and refused to snitch—with a look that suggested he'd long since been recruited by Andropov himself and was just waiting in deep cover for his big moment. With the same look he stayed clear of the Party—and still everything went like clockwork. His savings account grew and grew, women fell into his lap, languidly beguiled by his unfeigned indifference; his superiors assumed that Helium Revolverovich's career was being handled at the highest government levels and that his professional stasis was merely temporary camouflage for another significant post.

After successfully turning several deals on junkets abroad, he didn't want for foreign currency. Thanks to his connections, made exclusively by "all those frogskins," he never had to pass regular customs but could savor his cognac in the VIP departure lounge instead.

9 ONCE, IN AMSTERDAM, Helium struck up an intimate acquaintance with a woman scholar, an esoteric-religions specialist. A couple of months later it was discovered that the charming heavenstormer had AIDS. The unfortunate nymphomanic, who had been at a scholarly conference representing the forces of atheism in a young African government's war on tribal idols, gave a sworn statement to Interpol (which had long been dogging the sexual trail of this highly-cultured femme fatale).

In her statement her partners' names or else their distinguishing features came to the surface easily enough. And so it was that first the mole on Helium's privy member, then the little scar under his left nipple, and finally his name surfaced. He was slightly cheered by the prospect of a complex illness and an inevitable, not-too-distant outcome. It was, after all, not the worst way of escaping the relative shabbiness of his existence.

In a restricted, highly classified medical facility the horrified technicians took a blood sample for testing. In the office of the Deputy Minister of Health (he and Helium had been pals for a long time) Helium was about to relate the piquant details of his dramatic infection, but at that very moment, to his own great surprise and, as always, clearly not of his own volition, he denied that there was any truth to the wild, slanderous tales of his, as it turned out, quite observant sexual partner. "Sheer bull, my friend," he said to the Deputy Minister. "Utter nonsense. There was nothing between me and the lady except a conversation over a glass of champagne, when we discussed the sadistic and vandalistic details of the Dnieper River idol-tossing incident provoked by Prince (and presumably Zionist) Vladimir. What, do you think I haven't got my own pretested Rubensesque honies there in Holland?"

Both Helium's first and second blood tests came out negative. So the demons had protected him after all, those few nights in the hotel, from daily disgrace and a lingering death. And it was they who'd egged him on to flat-out deny everything in his chat with the Deputy Minister. True, the DM had suspiciously wondered out loud just how this woman with whom Helium was not intimate had managed to spot the mole on Helium's, as he put it, "performing snake." Helium responded weightily and severely: "Western covert operations, and also lyrical-intelligence leaks across the border."

He was on the verge of somehow expressing his appreciation to the little goonlet who had, by the way, been flitting worriedly and meaningfully around the hotel bedsheets, right in front of Helium's nose, while Helium was trying his best while in the throes of passion to prove himself a worthy representative of our mighty Empire. But his insurmountable hatred of the vermin that had murdered his love and happiness prevented him from ever uttering, even mentally, a word of personal gratitude to the goonlet who had somehow kept him from contracting AIDS and who knows what the hell else. "By that," the DM had remarked, "I mean the resplendent bacterial bouquet from the ardent woman scholar's phenomenal venereal collection." That bouquet had already been entered into the gold reserves of modern venereology under the name "TRIPTYCH-AIDS." . . .

10

IN A WORD, our hero, watched over by his unholy vermin, might well have coasted right on into hoary old age and death itself, never wanting for a thing. It was only occasionally, when hungover, that he felt any inner pain at the recollection of that awful moment where love had died right before his eyes. The life he led in his enormous apartment or at the dacha left him by his parents was an unbelievably monotonous one.

But finally, an ultimately insurmountable disgust wore down the patience of Time Itself.

That is, Time puked, and puked in full public view—from the utter worthlessness and stagnant ineptitude of those heaven storming strategists who had for half a century brazenly considered themselves Its (Time's, that is) Mind, Honor, and chiefly Conscience.

Time did its own mental reckoning, and finally stood up for its shit-covered Mind, its trampled Honor and its injured Conscience—and suddenly took note of the most sensitive and weak-willed of top-level leaders now in the Kremlin.

The chosen one naively took nauseated Time's visceral spasm for his own historical-spiritual-political initiative.

"Well, more power to him, as they say," thought Helium, "because in submitting to Time, this not-particularly-bright fellow's had to start powdering over all those toxic red splotches of reality, and start that slam-bang repair called Perestroika."

Of course, it couldn't help but gall Helium that Time's chosen but hardly remarkable politician was gallivanting all over the West in the VIP chariot of a victor. Back here, understand, there are mountains of uncounted skulls, here before your eyes the horrifying graves of the past are being dug up, and the sorry wreckage of Russian civilization is being laid bare; here, either still missing-and-unaccounted-for, or still languishing in jails are those who fearlessly pressed on to the embrasures of our dim-witted piggish regime, and over there he's dashing around triumphantly, taking it all as his due, all the laurels due someone who has singlehandedly delivered humankind from the barbarous spread of Communism, and has saved his own people from the commies' suicidal bungling. "Just try and figure out," thought Helium to himself at times, "if this is just some tasteless prank on the part of Mama-Historia or some vindictive, ugly irony at the expense of the ignominiously despatched dead and the emotionally gutted living. . . . "

At these very same moments he was also gripped by a feeling of infinitely melancholy impotence, which aggravated his already painfully ambivalent frame of mind.

Religion had not merely flown out of the church crannies where it had nestled submissively in balmy belief in the One who did not exist and never had; it was flapping shamelessly out onto the pages of Party newspapers and magazines.

Triumphant, incensed, it again occupied and dirtied all the strongholds and nesting places of Scientific Atheism—that is, the minds, hearts and souls of squadrons and squadrons of unprepared and utterly dismayed heavenstormers.

Religion started clucking and crowing all over the place as lustily as as if Helium never had wrung its neck, hacked off its wings, plucked it clean to the last little pinfeather and singed the carcass just like Papa Revolver had long ago singed his primary-phase pheasants when a shipment of the rare birds had once been sent by the Madagascar People's Liberation Front to grace the November banquet tables of Politburo members. . . .

Religion's sad victory—that's what Helium called recent events—horrified him greatly. He tried to rise above the spiritual disturbances of a society once again overcast by monks' hoods, cardinals' skullcaps, white-on-black wimples, turbans, bare skulls, and Hasidic hats.

He tried to find a common language with the masses by striking a scabrous Voltairean note in a talk at the House of Composers.

However, not only was he abruptly put in his place by both Left and Right, he was foully slandered in the Moscow papers by the whole scared-shitless, dazed-and-confused lot of them.

In their version, he and his fellow godless-intellectuals busy spitballing the heavens were the ones to blame for the spiritual bankruptcy of the cretinous leadership and indeed for the tragic catastrophe of the nation—he, not the criminal party of the heavenstormers or the Lenino-Stalinist architecture (viable only for red bedbugs and other domestic parasites) of our communal gulag barracks.

If you hadn't aimed your spit in that direction, said they, and taught us to do it too, then maybe He Who does, by all rights and lights, objectively exist and observe but is somehow not accessible to our senses—unlike shortages, rampant crime, the rapid shedding of red skin by old Party reptiles and the rampant whoring of the young, newly-hatched vipers of commerce and politics—maybe He wouldn't have turned His back on the Empire.

Touched to the quick by the general metamorphosis, Helium lapsed into irony—that is, into a state of constant, drunken jeering at reality. That was hardly a problem, since his means to support a long-term binge—even considering for inflation, the progressive dimwittedness of the premier, the verbal jousting of the economists and politicians and even the tragic drying-up of liquor sources—would probably last until the end of the century.

11

TOWARD THE END of December our disgraced scholar suddenly got a call from the Cuban Embassy, where he had often drunk to and at revolutionary parties.

They asked if he would be so kind as to agree to appear about three weeks after the Roman Catholic Christmas at a Latin American-style carnival-symposium in Havana. It would be devoted to problems of Scientific Atheism. The choice of mask is up to you. Among other thinking comrades and gentlemen, we are expecting that great friend of the Soviet Union, Nobel laureate García Marquez, who has made a big pile of taboos on his Muse until the day socialism is declared victorious on Cuba, Island of Freedom.

"There," they added, awkwardly adapting to the idiom and folklore of our great Russian language, "it won't be too close for comfortable, but is warm, bright, and two cigars are better than one, and there are no flies on us, and Comrade Rum is a gentleman but the thinking sugarcane reed is our ergo sum."

Helium realized that the source of the invitation was none other than that distinguished foe of the Vatican, Fidel himself, and that for him, Helium, underneath the imposing mask, a leading scientific-carnival role was being prepared.

He thanked the embassy official and agreed to appear on one of the panels at this exceedingly prestigious and imposing forum.

He decided that on his way back he would stop over in the States to make some "rock-solid" investments with a former colleague now living in New York under the aegis of the UN.

Thanks to his old connections he soon got all his documents and visa in order. He got himself a first-class ticket after doling out a couple thousand "wooden rubles" to a certain atheist African ambassador's masseuse.

When everything was all set, he phoned Beria's old clandestine mistress (who had been seduced by that headsman practically at her school dance, and who had lived to see him dance out of life in most instructive fashion—atop a chopping block beslimed with the brains and neckbones of his Party cronies).

This woman was already past sixty, but she—like all women who, from an early age, mystically gravitate toward men and valuables (and besides, she had spent her entire life in idle comradely ease)—looked devilishly beautiful.

Helium had never been in bed with the lady, though it wasn't her age that bothered him, but rather her protruding teeth. They didn't even seem to be human at all, but more like the enormous prongs of two implanted antique ivory combs gone yellow with age.

So it was hard to understand just what had attracted Beria to this lady delightful of course in all other respects. If Helium liked everything in a woman—face, form, disposition, skin, shoe size, intimate details—then he couldn't dislike any one thing taken separately, but if he didn't like some trifling detail—whether it was her manner of drinking tea, of greasing her scaly hands with expensive creams, of coyly widening her eyes at whatever she didn't understand, of reading *Krokodil* jokes at supper, smoking in bed or falling asleep in the sorry pose of a broody hen who has mixed up which nest is which— then unfortunately he couldn't deal with her remaining charms. . . .

Helium had more than once smuggled K's family heirlooms (at least that's what she called them) out of the country. He'd surmised that many of those lovely "trinkets" had been presented to the lady by the all-powerful headsman himself who, after executions, loved to rummage around in his sad confiscated haul.

Helium had long been using the Sheremetevo customs line reserved for VIPs, whom the ridiculous government had always trusted so highly that any one of them might have walked off with a national reliquary stuffed in his homely traveling satchel—the most revolutionary part, i.e., the hypothalamus of Lenin's formaldehyde-soaked gray matter, or Stalin's freeze-dried prick, ready for top-secret introduction into the hospitable womb of a certain Hollywood star, a longtime Communist sympathizer; or Grand Prince Monomakh's sable-trimmed crown, or just about anything else on that order.

So why make a big deal over the necklace of some ancient Scythian beauty, which Helium had smuggled out to be melted down by the gentlemen brokers of some oil-field prince, or over an antique brooch that once belonged to the wife of that foolish liberal tycoon Savva Morozov, who fawned himself out of a fortune with his barefoot geniuses, and guess who had to pay.

But for quite understandable reasons, Helium most eagerly smuggled out miniature, antique cult-objects. Sometimes, on the plane, he'd pull a little portable icon that had belonged to, who knows, maybe the Lady Morozova out of his pocket and vindictively shove the "artifact" at a goonlet who, for equally understandable reasons, had suddenly popped up on the armrest and begun chuckling evilly.

The panicky goonlet would start thrashing around and the plane, to its pilots' surprise, would start shuddering horribly.

"What a frigging mess," thinks melancholy Helium for the nth time. "*He* doesn't exist, but they do. Why? What for? Can't we really, can't we somehow get along without all this devilry and just make do with the cozy semidarkness of global agnosticism and the delightful two-step of higher math and formal logic? . . . Wouldn't it be great to just explode right now, in one big boom over the ocean, and sink to the bottom, to join the sturgeon long gone from our shop counters? Yes and together with that tasty and intelligent fish say to everyone—you can all go to hell in a handbasket, you and all the folk psychics and that awful jingle-writing jurist, that double-domed Oseniev-Lukyanov, and that lunkhead Poloskov, and K, and scientific atheism and that pissantibody Nina Andreeva's means of (foolish on principle) existence."

And suddenly the plane rights the strange trembling in its wings. And Helium realizes that the goonlets won't let him croak. They won't let him. God forbid, he says with a melancholy slip of the tongue, this should be just a taste of some variety of eternal hellish torment—but then such brutality would run counter to all the fundamental laws of science. . . . Why me?

In short, some time before his upcoming flight to Cuba, K had entrusted Helium with an artifact wrapped in a piece of old flannel and firmly tied with a silk cord. She told him that this handwrought thing was worth more than his life and hers combined. And they had negotiated his courier's cut in this latest transaction.

We should note that K placed boundless trust in Helium and that he also flattered himself that he naturally possessed a certain sense of financial rectitude, which, in his opinion, irrefutably testified to the utter needlessness of a well-known number of holy-moly commandments.

Helium made a mental note that his share of the greenbacks would last him for years to come, even given his frequent dips into his foreign currency fund for cognac, lemons, filets, pâté de foie gras, prosciutto, pantyhose, and other small gifts for his ladies of the hotel-room sort.

Having decided to put off looking at the precious thing he was transporting until he was in the air, it occurred to him that while such a life as his was perhaps more nauseating than no life at all, it was still incomparably more exciting than those of the rank-and-file victims of perestroika who were whiling their time away in huge lines for some unbelievably insulting travesty of alcohol.

He'd been carrying this thing in his pocket for days. He hadn't packed any suits, shirts, or ties, since he'd decided to redo his whole wardrobe in New York. There was something magical—in the purely sociological sense, of course—about flying off this way, traveling light, practically half-dressed, with nothing but the package under his arm and the charming prospect of shopping for everything in southern Italy where you can slip your tired dogs into what aren't really shoes but homey little kennels, and where you get sudden goosebumps from just the texture and the look of a shirt, as if you weren't in that nice little shop at all but were reclining on the sensuous table of your

Filipina former-communist-terrorist masseuse. You recline, you lounge, and you think that despite the obvious senselessness of the phenomenon of random life on Earth, a whole bevy of first-class pleasures are quite capable of balancing out the morose boredom of personal existence and all the inept absurdity of the world around you. Quite capable . . . there are still some little gold medallions of fat, subtle possibility floating on the surface of our souring, polluted primordial soup. . . .

Helium had been more or less in this state of anticipation of the douce delights and happy accomplishments of Western civilization for a couple of weeks.

And the less time that remained before his departure from Moscow, the more acutely and childishly impatient he became—to unload the thing, to be done, maybe once and for all, with his little deals; to make his haul and then kick back in some little pensione in Naples or Florence; to cut loose, drink to his haul; to shop, shop for NN, . . . there *is* a subtle something in all this making of arrangements, in the comfortable flow of days, that amazingly reconciles you to all the unholy vermin and the lowest blows of fate. There *is!*

He picked up (for foreign currency) two kilos of grade-A pressed caviar—to keep up his own strength and to take to the half-starved Komsomol corps-de-ballet girls in Havana—from his father's heir to the Party pantry on Old Square.

In the text of his presentation at the prestigious forum Helium had concealed (like a little terrorist bomb planted on an airplane) an elegant, it seemed to him, and not at all trivial (given the crude, numbskull schemas of scientific atheism) theoretical innovation.

It was a crushing proof that the two things were mutually exclusive: that is, He doesn't exist, and *they* are the negative portion of that objective reality acessible to all our senses (save the olfactory).

The only thing left to get was his carnival-symposium mask. On the Old Arbat, while standing in front of the booth of a slightly tipsy folk-craftsman—obviously a defrocked agitprop instructor from deep in the heart of Mother Russia—Helium was wondering which of the numerous masks (each, we should note, distinguished by a genuine respect for the revived craft) he could wear to amaze the pillars of global godlessness as well as that great friend of the Motherland of Socialism, naive Trotskyite García Marquez, as well as the Cuban Party crowd.

"Castro would probably consider a Gorbachev mask with a red Cuba on its forehead some kind of Party-instigated attack. How about Lenin? Stalin? Beria? Bo-ring!! Khrushchev's mug somehow looked too much like the snout of a ridiculous piggy who didn't quite have time, unfortunately, to pig out on Suslov. . . . Chernenko, that acute case of emphysema of the imperial lungs. . . . Maybe I'll get old Lyonya Brezhnev himself. . . . In Lyonya's day, Fidel was sitting pretty, Fidel was rocking in the bosom of Lyuda Zykina—or maybe under her fancy peasant, ha-ha-ha, sarafan. . . . How is it those paranoids in *Pamyat* never caught on that 'sara-fan' is obviously Yid-Freemasonry in Russian clothing. . . . Cretins, numbskulls . . . one fiend pursues another, leaving night but half an hour. . . . If there's a power on earth capable of destroying Mother Russia, it's without a doubt that putrid-patriotic creepshow. Just like der Führer and Goebbels—they won't be content until they wipe out everything around them, women and children first. . . ."

At that moment, shabby little imps and demons began hopping almost too furiously all over the phiz of the renowned leader of Russia's rabid "saviors." . . .

Helium inquired whether that gentleman's wavy locks were real hair.

"Don't doubt it for a minute, sir. My sister-in-law's two kids went completely bald overnight as a result of Zionist plots against the environment. No sense wasting good merchandise. So I had to fill in the back of this notable contemporary figure's scalp . . . " was the vendor's courteous and businesslike reply.

Reluctant to haggle, Helium asked distastefully, "And what, actually, are Brezhnev's eyebrows done in?"

"Stiffened-reinforced cat, and the hairdo itself—a heavy-duty sheepskin coat treated with relaxing and straightening agents. . . . That's why old Nikita's cheaper, sir. We also have a selection of mechanical figures—a windup Chernenko with lifelike cough, and a battery-powered Lenin with authentic accent (but that's something I'd have to sell you under the table, sir). The new just can't quite break through the old yet, I'll tell you, sir. Too many folks trying to squeeze through the narrow gates of the free market."

"Why are these prices so outrageous?"

"Well, you just try finding egg cartons, soaking them into a gluey papier-mâché solution, sculpting wooden forms, skinning enough cats—and all that in a period of initial capital-accumulation when you're trying to balance your honest labor against unlimited capital and the social pluralism of prices," pissed the first-generation private entrepeneur.

"Do you have any more of these cretins?"

"I'm sorry, sir, I've just sold you the only original, so to speak. The rest of them are still soaking in the VIP tub."

12 THE MASK PURCHASED, Helium took a general staff "Chaika" (whose driver was moonlighting while the marshal himself was in the company of his strategist colleagues, assessing old miscalculations in the logistics of boldly capturing one of those damned—but, chiefly, still besiegable—White Houses) and made the rounds of several shady enterprises where he replenished his supplies. He never liked to show up anywhere empty-handed, even on visits to ladies of the hotel-room sort.

But on this night, the 6th of January, the person waiting for him was someone absolutely remarkable. This person was the enchanting NN.

Later we'll have occasion to speak of her, and of the fateful role she played in Helium's life.

But what goodies *didn't* he have, a stockpiled feast for them both, all in two cardboard boxes that had held cheap imported Christian Brothers brandy. Those goodies would have set Professor Pavlov himself to drooling . . . not to speak of the purebred but tragically homeless, miserable, and hungry hounds who, as Helium trudged from the Chaika to the street entrance of NN's building, were drawn to the aromas wafting out of the boxes—to the whiffs of cheese, rolls, ham, sausage, and smoked fish—like iron filings to a magnet.

Maybe it was only a certain nobility of bloodline, not yet

drained out of these well-schooled creatures even by murderous, bestial appetite, that kept them from flinging themselves, wolflike, at Helium, ripping the hell out of the packages and dragging the fabulous delicacies through the depressingly seedy back alleys and porches of the capital.

The dogs, with tears in their eyes, saw the boxes all the way to the door, and then lay down hopelessly next to an enormous heating pipe that was generously and irresponsibly sharing—that is, plundering—state-owned heat.

Helium, in anticipation of the soon-to-come, blissful, crowning moment of existence, was feeling so well-disposed toward himself—and also toward the world of other beings and things—that he also felt a sudden rush of fondness for the hot pipe vainly wrapped in ragged asbestos, and for the frostbitten dogs too.

"Stay warm, doggies," he thought with genuine sympathy, "and you, pipe, you just go ahead and plunder that heat. If nobody's got time for us, then we've got no time for anybody else, and we're not about to let the idiot fecklessness of the stupid Politburo do us in. Everyone plunders everything, so you go on and help yourselves to those official caloric units—for the salvation and evolution of those little dumplings of life cooked up in oozy primordial bouillon. . . ha-ha-ha . . . when blind Mr. Chance slipped horny Miss Probability his stick."

By the way, this fact of new-world-order types' inspired conformity to the categorical imperative "plunder" had long and meaningfully suggested to observant individuals with an aggravated sense of the metaphysical that, in nature, there did indeed exist a villainously covert, universal, and all-encompassing conspiracy against the Soviet System, masterminded not only by energetically larcenous residents but also by inanimate material objects.

Helium was of course no master metaphysician intensely attuned to otherwordly matters, but more than once, while leaving his office, he had caught himself automatically and despondently casting around for something to filch.

Sometimes he (who had no need of paper clips, carbon paper, lightbulbs, water glasses, or carafe stoppers) was simply amazed and exceedingly depressed by state property's nagging desire to be plundered.

It wasn't that this desire somehow monstrously increased his impulse to snatch something, since he had never been prone to anything of the sort, but that this desire would somehow ravish his will, his logical objections, and the sense of distaste that a certain type of irascible person sometimes takes for a sense of honor.

It was as if, in some strange fashion, he would fall under the hypnotic influence of some pathetic writing-paper and somnambulistically carry off thirty or forty sheets, who knows what for. At the same time, he sensed that the paper was doing everything in its power not only to be plundered but also to be exceedingly gray, coarse grained, and chapped as the face of a bought-off traffic cop—in a word, revoltingly and criminally shoddy.

Evidently there were many other down-and-out Soviet objects and articles in that same state of vagrant fecklessness or resistance to the divine notion of the comeliness of all creation. And they had sunk to that state and mood purely as a sign of protest against the inept destruction of the natural order by the makers of brave new worlds. . . .

For lack of a better place, Helium had to shop for all his household stuff at the excruciating store Thousands of Things.

At times it occurred to him that, for example, his recently-purchased table lamp had, by virtue of its exquisite slipshoddi-ness, fallen to such depths of masochistic self-humiliation, and driven its manufacturers to such frenzied hatred of it, that the overall ugliness of this item, its malicious aversion to all sources of electrical current and to the sheer physical marvel of a burn-ing bulb—that is, this item's obvious contempt for its sole pur-pose in life—could be coherently understood solely in terms of sabotage and conspiracy—a conspiracy hatched against the So-viet Seal of Quality by the basic matter of this hideous freak.

At times he thought that perhaps, really, somewhere in the invisibility of the micro-world the Platonic eidos—the ideas of each thing—did exist, and that these very ideas had gone all skinch-eyed in sheer offence at the Soviet regime. And it was *their* deformed appearance that made a Soviet wallet look as if it was designed to hold Brezhnev's phlegm instead of money or documents, and made a soup bowl, squashed by some glum manufacturing error or else by Gosplan pressure from above, stand before you in the shape of a bedpan. It was quite possible that the majority of manufactured goods simply couldn't help reflecting our long-term social insanity—and so what a galosh or a high-heeled shoe, let's say, presents to you when you first glance at these items of primary historical necessity is not its essential or expedient features but instead some sort of phan-tasmagorical mask covering the remarkable idea of a skinch-eyed galosh or a long-suffering shoe.

"So," our far-from-stupid Helium once soberly thought, "our idiot leaders, unhinged by incomprehensible outbreaks of collective resistance among certain material objects, shouldn't have been putting wreckers or saboteurs or scapegoats on trial back in the thirties. They should have been indicting all those Platonic eidoses and raw materials that, while still in a state of embryonic design, were assuming the saboteur-shapes of tubercular factories, gangrenous mines, Red Downs weather balloons, paralyzed icebreakers, Parkinson landrovers, ruinous canals, suicidal hydrostations, locomotives jumping their dystrophic tracks, Alzheimer bicycles, and so on. . . . You blew your chance, comrades. All you Lenino-Stalinist degenerates should have brought the cause of practical theomachy to a victorious conclusion and forcibly Bolshevized the entire hostile natural environment, so that not one single, shitty little atom— not one, mind you—would ever dare contest the sacred principles of democratic centralism in the sphere of quality control. And then toilet paper wouldn't outweigh meat in the hellish sausage of these apocalyptic times. And ladies' lingerie wouldn't chafe poor Russian women's tender creases so painfully that their sweet faces develop tics in the effort to maintain an outwardly gracious demeanor. . . . But anyway . . . anything Soviet is by definition a deviation from the norm, and there's not a frigging thing you can do about this bold riddle of nature. . . ."

Could it really be, Helium once thought in a terrible moment of insight, that inanimate matter had somehow cheated the Cheka and devilishly duped Vladimir Ilyich himself in that long-ago October, in reaction to the abrupt severing of its honorable, private-proprietary ties with the consumer?

Isn't that why the crummy toilet paper in an institutional john, the humblest but most useful product in the whole wide world, simply begs you to tear off just a few sheets—if you're too straitlaced to snag the whole roll all at once—and turn them into your own private property, just for a while? But no, you fight off that crass, typically Soviet temptation and manage to balance your own excretory need for deficit toilet paper against the needs of your colleagues and coworkers (who, we must note, do not always respond to your hygiene habits with the same old-fashioned delicacy, dignity, or empathy).

Could it be that things had managed to impress upon consumers en masse that in that October, one-sixth of the earth's surface had begun its grimly irreversible progress toward the fateful day when it wasn't just that men's briefs and women's bras, say, were sickening to wear, but that they would, along with other consumer goods, vanish for entire generations?

They would vanish, evaporate, retreat into some obscure underground and start jacking up their own prices because now everything was permitted. Public property—no sin in shamelessly plundering *that*, in personally privatizing it, in recklessly letting the plunder rate overtake the replacement rate of everything so voluptuously plundered.

Once he had imagined the ripe fruits of this sort of full-blown consumer-and-goods conspiracy on an all-Russian pseudosocialist-statewide scale—the aim of which plot was complete and total shortfall in all consumer goods plus the discrediting of the mystically all-powerful Gosplan—and had multiplied these fruits by long years of struggle, victories, and the forces of implacably increasing entropy in the state commercial network, Helium was horrified at just how close the unavoidable collapse of the whole System, and perhaps the whole Empire, really was.

13

HE HAD BEEN marking its passing for some months now, with a strange feeling that he was somehow cheering it on, and yet was also absolutely and frighteningly indifferent toward the fate of the Soviet monster.

And here he was again thinking about the monster's fate on his way to NN's—he decided to spit on it, to say the hell with it once and for all, the hell with all the squalid crap of contemporary life. To hawk up all the sludge that had seeped into his soul all these foul years and in general just dive headfirst into a quiet, private life. Good thing there'll be more than enough money for that once I hand over K's little thing and get my cut of the greenbacks. Yes, you demon bastards, *green*backs. . . .

There was a feeling in his soul that something wonderful, something singular was about to happen between him and NN today, and this feeling grew and grew. And to quash a strange inner agitation, long missing from his melancholy existence, Helium deliberately forced himself to reflect on the terminal stench of Soviet history.

Usually, thoughts of this sort didn't dare peep, didn't dare hint that they even existed, but just cowered as usual in the stale little crannies of his brain. Although sometime back he'd become convinced that in the life and times of his native land, just as in his own life, the unholy vermin had no doubt left their little pile of shit at every important turn.

"The monster of course has contrived to drink up, gobble down, plunder, and mutilate just about everything it had grabbed from the Tsarist Empire and imperial society, but you did have to admit that relative order reigned on the streets, that the President of the United States kept one foot in the White House and the other in a fallout shelter . . . the genius Gabriel García Marquez (even if it was out of incredible foolishness) thought of our monster as the lodestar of social equality and the balance wheel of social justice . . . and Graham Greene, one hell of a smart guy, though I did personally see him practically swinging from one of the chandeliers in the Great Georgievsky Hall, because in the magical sheen of those crystal facets he saw visions of an earthly paradise, or maybe his own innermost, deeply private Catholic ideal . . . then again neither Marquez nor Greene . . . damn it, that green slime is starting to squirm all over me again, scat . . . you little bastard, scat! . . . there's no getting away from this vermin . . . nervy little critters . . . anyway the International Section never did recruit either Marquez or Greene to stage public displays of respect for the monster, or to genuflect and kiss its putrid sphinx I mean sphincter. . . ."

With these unpleasant thoughts in mind, Helium reached NN's floor. Just an instant before he pressed the doorbell, they were swept away by a gust of freshness, by a wondrous change in internal weather, and his heart flip-flopped with the sweet, agitated feeling that that singular something would flatly cancel out everything that had come before. He couldn't stand being alone with this feeling grabbing him by the shirtfront. He rang the bell.

14 NN OPENED THE DOOR. Helium's heart, gently pricked by the scent of pine, was finally freed of the welter of civic passions that, as it turned out, were hardly essential to his love (that is, private) life, and retreated into a sweet, childish melancholy.

Helium stood on the threshold, dazed. In the dining room gleamed a Christmas tree. Right there on the threshold, the spellbinding beginning of the "*Eine-kleine-Nachtmusik* serenade" (which, we repeat, is what he called his favorite Mozart composition) washed over him like a warm wave.

What had aroused him in the music (besides the very music itself) was a noble seasoning of womanly concern and a friendly, genuinely sincere desire to please—which, in his opinion, were as much a basis of marital sentiments as was sex.

For with the passage of years, they say, it's easy enough to get used to a wife's beloved beauty and nearness, but this rush of gratitude for the trueness of her knowledge of you and of herself, in long years of living under one roof, is always new and astonishly unexpected. And so, say the lucky few, a wave of passion set loose by everyday trifles imperceptible to the outsider's eye may engulf one spouse or the other, or else both of them, in the most inconvenient places: at a table in a restaurant, in an airplane, a museum, on the street—in a word, in any part of that shared space of life.

His heart began to ache sweetly and impatiently. Aroused, he suddenly remembered one of NN's best lines: "Marriage is a feeling of ownership—of what you don't own." He set down all the provisions he'd brought.

"Today . . . today . . . whatever it is has to happen today, how long can it drag on without happening? Until a breakup?"

The glad hostess planted a kiss on her guest's cheek and then moved away as if he weren't there at all—to apply the finishing touches to her culinary artistry.

Who gave a damn for Hollywood faces and centerfold figures in comparison to the rare (in our day, anyway) womanliness that informed her every movement and gesture? The wrist of the hand that had playfully tossed Helium's fur hat onto the floor smelled deliciously of risen dough, and gave off a heady promise of mind-boggling desserts in all possible senses of that word.

"Since when have you had any Christian brothers?" NN laughed, looking over the boxes.

"That's just some winery or other in the States," answered Helium with an ominous shudder which, however, was still powerless to darken his glowing mood.

The hostess, meanwhile, was spicing up the picture of this intimate wintertime feast with a little parsley-sage-rosemary-and-thyme. Helium took the edge off with a hefty shot of whiskey and, munching on some smoked sturgeon and bread, communed with the Christmas tree.

And suddenly he spied a little emerald papier-mâché devil swinging on a gold crescent moon. Helium surreptitiously took the devil off the tree, threw it on the floor, and shoved it under the sofa with the toe of his shoe. He looked around irritably. There didn't seem to be any more vermin.

But just in case, knowing that the sign of the cross would infuriate them, he blessed the entire space of the room in gleeful malice. He blessed it with the sadistic appetite that a hangman brings to his work after being starved for it all vacation long.

Then, foretasting a great spread, a few drinks, a few laughs, and, after, the very thing he'd come for, he turned his gaze to NN.

The mosaic of her genes aroused a previously unknown feeling in the interesting-looking but only moderately lusty Helium.

In her sleek body Helium seemed to sense a remarkable, indivisible, imperial wholeness. And in general, when he looked closely at NN, he once again felt an irrepressible nostalgia for the superpower status of the first-among-nations and even for the Old Square clowns' awful capers in the dirty international arena.

Sometimes, afterward, still lying in bed, they would peruse NN's family tree, which had been traced by the geneaology-genies of a little co-op called Root and Branch.

So NN's body was home to at least a dozen legations of those nations comprising the Russian Empire. In fact, what exotic genes *weren't* there in both the willful spiritual ornament and the bodily collage of Helium's friend . . . and all of them traceable to the most distant of ancestors, let alone the closest!

There was a German, a Gypsy, a Tatar; there was a Georgian, an Uzbek, Lithuanian, Cossack, Tadzhik, Chinese, another German, Azerbaijani, Armenian, Hungarian—truly, one couldn't begin to count all the marvelous tribal combinations.

And the fact that in this precious and rarest of live assortments there was not a single Jewish vein represented seemed to

Helium some strange, anecdotally Judeophobic riddle in the history of that race.

And the fact that for some incomprehensible reason, on this woman's resplendent family tree there was not a single Russian branch, not even a random Russian twig, to be found, that this could happen in our time and, in our definitively cohabited, so to speak, imperial space, struck Helium as "veiled Russophobia"—in the current parlance of the allegedly persecuted pseudopatriots who had resolved, apparently out of mindless envy, to overtake-take over-and-take-down the championship for humiliation, despair, and insult heretofore held by the genuinely harassed and persecuted Jews.

"Amazing, really, how ungrandly," Helium went back to his idée fixe, "the grandiose Empire is croaking, how grossly it's going belly up! All kinds of former Party bigwigs are rearing their ugly topknots. . . . Ukraine's hoist with its own petliura. . . . The Vatican's already hooked that fat eel Latvia and the mimosas of the captive of the Caucasus are getting nervier than ever on Trubnoy. . . . And in general the whole Caucasus is galloping away from us at about 300 Shamiles an hour. . . . we're pissing everything away, on borrowed time. And the Tatars have set up their own raiding Party to pay off that running debt to Donskoy. . . .

"Next thing you know the whole Jewish Autonomous Region'll be giving Moscow the sovereign, circumcised shaft. . . . In a word, they've all got us by the decurled, chemically relaxed short hairs. Inept, disgraceful bankruptcy. . . . This isn't history, it's a whole communo-enema-panama-White-Sea-Canalorama, a trip up the Issyk-Kul-de-sac-o-shit without a paddle and bye-bye Bai-ka-ka-et-al. The Empire couldn't just crumble like Greece or Rome, no-o-o, to the avalanche tune of ancient ruins, every chip of which would someday be more precious than gold. . . . What'll you leave behind for all peoples and museums, my feeblebrained gomer Empire? Mock-ups of purge-packed barracks or the floorboards from Komsomol saunas, all slimed over with Yanaev's sperm? Senile slogans? The tin gulag bowl I bought for a bunch of greenbacks from some old-timer by the Lubyanka, at the memorial stone, the bowl with its single line probably scratched out by a spoon held in the shaky hand of some poor prisoner at the point of utter desperation 'damn you to hell you red cannibals'? Ye-e-s. . . . I believed in you. I didn't believe in Him but in you, you sorry bastard. And now you can drop dead, since they're already divvying up your politico-administrative corpse, and you've got no life and won't let other nations have a life either, including my own poor falling-down-drunk Russian one. . . . You're nothing but a nutless wonder, you haven't got colossal clay feet, you've got perma-shit ones, and now they're starting to thaw . . . and flood the whole world with their crap. Like that crazy beggar sings in the underpass between socialism and capitalism, 'Citizens, please hold your noses,' and the main thing is, there's nobody to put on trial for it. Who's there to try?"

Helium knocked back another slug of whiskey without even the usual sniff of bread—so potent and bitter was his gall at the obvious hyperabsurdity of these last seven decades forcibly pounding the notion of their trailblazing, storm-the-gates grandeur into the historical consciousness.

"Yeah . . . drop dead . . . let people live their own private lives . . . personally I'm tired of yammering over a daisy-faced omelette like some limp Hamlet—a yegg or not a yegg, that is, to love or not to love. . . . Surely the presence of love is just as provable—and unprovable—as the existence of the lord god.

That's right—no capital letters for *him* until the second coming. Perestroika is just the coming of Gorby and his demi-angels and semi-demons. Their little winglets are smeared with Russian blood and their smeary faces with slops from the Party trough. As for you, you Suslov bacillae-rods and Andropov kidneys, I'll take my Revolver memoirs to Italy and publish them there, just to watch you squirm a little in the sound-and-light . . . special effects like a whole damn Sveta Allilueva chorus. The stubborn poet was right to publish his Zhivago outside, although personally that name-business, that Dr. Living, Dr. Life, irritates the hell out of me. The bloody hell. . . . But he was a thousand times right to publish it *outside*. . . . Here, nothing survives—history or its chronicles, either one. . . . On the other hand, you try and figure out this 'banana-lemon-Singapore-love' all on your own. . . . Can you really tell the difference, can you really understand—is your love true, or is it just romanticized lust slipping on the mask of loftier sentiments? What can serve as hard evidence that you feel love rather than just a hankering (since you've practically gone numb for want of a woman) for natural satisfaction? You can always fuck without loving, of course, but to love without loving—? Impossible! . . . Now with *him* things are a lot more complicated . . . because, little fishy, if you swallow some phony love-bait and get yourself hooked into marriage, then sooner or later it will all float to the surface with horribly persuasive clarity and appropriately scandalous stink. Divorce. Sayonara. But what precisely could serve as evidence of *his* existence? Your own self-established criteria of happiness, success, pleasure or—like the rock-solid fanatics—just the opposite, linking it all to a chain of misfortunes, failures, sufferings, disappointments? . . . But if we don't believe, what happens? We still live, carry a bunch of genes with us to the grave, get a few kicks out of life—if not here, then there, one way or another—without giving a damn for either the axioms of scientific atheism or the cloudy hypotheses of theology. . . . It's even strange that you can still live a remarkable existence without believing, but that sharing life with a woman, without loving her—that's a whole lot worse than hell. . . . And no matter what they say, trying to prove that he does not and cannot exist is a whole lot more interesting than repeating, with no proof at all—does too, does too, does! Our axioms can be proven every step of the way, and as for the 'heaven hypothesis'—at least, in any analysis of the history of our sleazy human race—well what can you say? Nothing! Pure, absolute Nothing. It's charming, by the way, this openmouthed awe with which . . . anyway, right now you've got to get the jump but not jump the gun, as Chapayev once said. You've got to love, love, love and not just yammer about it . . . this is life's gift to my sorry self . . . they're right to say—if you don't believe, then go ahead and risk trying, for you take the risk *in order to* believe . . . and in general, why not just flood the coils of damned, eternally doubting reason with some epoxy, so this Hamlet in gray aspic would have something to prop it up, support . . . or even pound some kind of support into it . . . it's hyperbizarre when our reason's got literally nothing to prop it up in times of doubt and hesitation. . . . Believe just because it *is* absurd? Sorry, that's not for me. . . . I can just picture what kind of wife I'd have if I let myself be guided by that marvelous principle in marriage. . . . " Helium was suddenly distracted from all these unresolvable things, downed another drink, and rubbed his hands together; he couldn't keep his eyes off the ellipse of the gravy boat, out of which a pair of fried-egg eyes—bright yellow, yolky irises beautifully set in bluish whites—were peering.

". . . That's it, it's decided, this minute I'll declare my intentions, I'll offer, I mean, I'll ask for her hand in marriage," he rubbed his hands together again, "and little Helium will sprout himself a little leaf, gentlemen, your precautions be damned, he'll graft himself, homeless Russian that he is, onto this delightful, mysterious International, and the child will learn to play the accordion over his grave, and to sing 'let there always be Mama, let there always be Papa' or better yet—'the incessant ringing of the harness bells / and the ro-o-oad. . . .'"

And as soon as he'd thought this, with devil-may-care, happy Russian melancholy, and had made up his mind and, half-buzzed on Scottish hooch and the genius of Russian folksong, risen from the sofa intending, first of all, to press his lips to her dark collarbone (its tan not yet faded) in whose bright hollow a little coolness always lingered however long its stint at a hot stove or in the heat of lovemaking—the doorbell rang.

The hostess led the apparently unexpected visitor into the dining room and introduced the men. The visitor, glancing at Helium, didn't proffer his hand. In this gesture, however, there was none of the intentional affectation that always fussily compromises an already sufficiently frank sentiment.

"Zelenkov," he dryly introduced himself, looking somewhere past Helium and addressing NN. "Sorry. I just dropped by for a second. Here's the rest of the paperwork. Sorry."

Helium, who had just stuck out his hand, demonstrated (in plebeian, i.e., shitass fashion, which made him even madder) what was supposed to be lordly disdain and turned his back on the visitor.

True, the arm instinctively extended in greeting somehow refused to drop and, burning with awkward indignation, continued to stick stumplike out of his jacket sleeve.

He poked it hatefully into one of the tree's prickly green paws. Everything seemed to go black, in a sudden darkening of the general mood and a deepening of his ominous forebodings. His arm still didn't want to bend at the elbow.

NN was a bit flustered. She offered her visitor a drink for the road, but he again very guiltily begged her pardon and said that someone was waiting for him downstairs, handed her some papers from his bag and left.

The lovers, who, we should note, had not yet reached the point of truly close friendship and instantaneous mutual understanding, sat down to eat. Helium, still bedeviled by petty emotion, splashed some more whiskey into his glass. The arm had finally gotten itself under control.

Still, realizing the absurdity of such an intimate meal in such a grim atmosphere, he genuinely tried to force a smile. He wanted to propose a silly toast to ease NN's growing embarrassment which, Helium knew, sensed, would soon turn into quite logical hurt and (given her remarkable willfulness) chilly, unbreachable, irritable aloofness.

And he'd just opened his mouth to say something conciliatory, to raise a glass to NN, to her beauty, to the warmth, the comfort, to their lighthearted and free love affair, when instead he furiously blurted out,

"Shi-i-t-head! Ze-e-e-ro! Assho-o-ole!"

With a cry of "Forward march!" the grime-green little devil re-emerged atop the golden crescent moon on the tree and propped one hoof on the other.

Helium's heart sank at the approach of this specter of the irreparable. But even mustering all his strength, he couldn't take himself in hand, and he bellowed out crudely:

"Your new fuck?"

"My fictive husband. He and his family are taking off for South Africa. The collapse of his career and all that. He's flat broke. He gets a good chunk of money, and we supposedly move into his apartment together. I want to have a baby and this little place is too small."

NN spoke coldly, into a void, but seemed to be leaving Helium a chance to salvage their relationship.

And again he tried to write off his rudeness and crudeness to a perfectly understandable flash of jealousy reinforced by the cat . . . cat? . . . what cat? . . . that is, reinforced by the fact that he *knew* this Zelenkov. He was a well-known biophysicist, who glorified the role of chaos in the natural order and preached the existence of a Creator by making uncivil use of the infamous data of quantum physics, and I had no choice but to (uncharacteristically of course) broach the matter there at Old Square, and also before the Academy presidium . . . not that I was ratting on him, of course, I always operate strictly above board. . . .

Helium wanted to tell her all this and add that it was a downright sin not to have shared all her day-to-day plans with him, that she shouldn't masochistically nurse her injured feminine pride, that he wasn't a jealous man, wasn't a snitch, as apparently that king of cats thought he was, but rather a paladin of Scientific Atheism whom even the Vatican considered the most cultured, *most* cultured, of opponents . . . that he, in fatherly fashion, would have gladly bought her not only an apartment but a dacha . . . actually, he already had a dacha . . . over my grave . . . preferably a boy . . .

He wanted to tell her all this, he did, he did! And he wanted to add some declaration of love, and a lot more.

But suddenly, realizing in horror that, just as in the swimming pool right before the awful moment his love died, not a single bubble of his own will was left him; suddenly, with an almost childlike whimper at his total inability to cope with the whole gaggle of devils glowing green against the red caviar and the golden salmon, he pounded his fists on the table and then hoarsely, boorishly, mockingly, in some other man's voice, wailed—or rather howled:

"A ba-a-a-by?!!! So I'll be forking over the child support instead of your Zelenkov?!!!! Is that it?!!!"

"Get out of here. Now. Out!" said NN, rising sharply and turning to the window, her back to Helium.

He went deathly pale. In his breast there was an oppressive emptiness. His hands were shaking. His lips were quivering in dismay.

If NN had turned around for an instant, if she had taken a single look at his pain-contorted face and trapped, sick, pleading eyes, then a feeling of unhesitating sympathy for someone who was obviously undergoing some sort of crisis and strange misfortune would have instantly overcome the feeling (one unknown to men) of insult, of injury to her womanly desire to conceive a child.

"I thought I told you to take a flying leap—straight to hell . . . get out!" she repeated—not hysterically, but starting to lose her temper.

Helium thought he was going to drop to his knees and beg her to forgive him and protect him from the demons. "Can't you see it's not me doing it? Darling, save me, it's them, it's them again . . . save . . . "

And indeed he nearly upended table and food both as he lunged across the room toward her, toward the window, but instead of falling on his knees, he grabbed her by the blouse,

shook the dazed woman furiously and belched such unbelievably filthy things in her face that they in themselves killed off any
power he might have had to stop, to come to his senses, to hide
his face and eyes, crazed by the recurrence of that old horror, in
her bosom.

Then he let her go as unexpectedly as he'd attacked, threw
on his overcoat, and with a clearly suicidal grin fixed his gaze
on an expensive carving knife he'd brought NN from Munich.
Actually it wasn't the blade itself that held his gaze, but two
little goonlets, greener than ever in the tree's reflection on the
red trademark, flapping their arms and legs.

And it wasn't villainous intent, as NN assumed, that had
drawn Helium's diabolical gaze to the knife; it was the knife's
handle, cast in the shape of a mountain-goat foot, with a little
cloven hoof just like the Christmas-tree devil's.

NN couldn't help but catch that grin and that look. And then
began something which defies description.

15 HOWEVER, THERE'S NO WAY I can *not* attempt to describe
what happened, at least briefly.

NN shagged the first thing that came to hand (it
was a bottle of champagne standing in an ice bucket on a side
table) at the unspeakable lout and caught him right on the
cheekbone, just below the temple. Helium staggered and thrust
his arms out in self-defense, but it was too late.

Evidently the resplendent genes of all those inherited national characters were just getting started. Furiously, she hurled
plates with hors d'oeuvres and slices of aspic. She smeared the
beets-with-prunes-and-mayonnaise all over his face and favor-

ite shirt. She smashed the plate of meat pies over his head. She splashed something-or-other-with-sour-cream in his face. She swung at him with an enormous juicy cut of what was practically the last Kremlin ham to leave the stage of Party history. She smacked him in the ear with cold red caviar from a crystal dish shaped like a hockey puck.

But suddenly Helium was hardly aware of the blows, the splashing and flinging of multicolored mush, the tangy slime of heady marinades and sauces and aromatic liquids, of spicy rusks redolent of garlic sauteed in genuine Provencal olive oil, Caucasian cloves, and Moldavian chrysanthemums.

He was no more aware of any of it than NN was aware of his dazed state, for his eyes were riveted to the edge of the table where, as if on the edge of an abyss, stood an enormous platter with a roast pig blissfully nestled in its warm china embrace.

The stuffing, handily and tastefully prepared by NN from a recipe Helium had brought from a village in Tuscany, had burst through the seam on its belly, and through a rip just barely held closed by a crusty, appetizing cord, he could see bits of tripe languishing in the steam heat, mixing with pinches of dill, parsley, coriander, with arrows of leek, young hothouse garlic, and Provençal herbs.

But it wasn't at all the temptation to eat, or the animal hunger that arises in us at the sight of such a seductively primeval dish, that had drawn Helium's gaze, magnetlike, to the pig.

Forgetting everything else, forgetting NN's raging movements, Helium, in amazement and fear that he was losing his mind, noticed that all the imps present in the room—all the imps, demons, devils and goons and goonlets—had suddenly stepped (or rather oozed) into line at all the various entrances, so to speak, to the pig.

There were familiar figures and unfamiliar ones too, ones he was seeing for the first time. One column of these plasmalike, dirty-green blobs and spinners were heading for the rip in the belly, while the more prominently diabolical figures of the Russian revolution—no doubt the most important in rank and position—were already sedately parting the roast-cord fence with their loathsome extremities, climbing over it, then disappearing into the exceedingly appetizing darkness within.

Some of the unholy vermin crowding the VIP entrance wore—like marathoners—white bibs with black letters back and front, informing the astonished Helium that they were the imps and demons of The Dictatorship of the Proletariat, The Monolithic Unity of Party and People, Free Medical Care, Friendship of Nations, Confidence in Tomorrow, The Communist and Unaffiliated Solidarity Blok, Developed Socialism, On the Horizon, The Most Democratic Justice System in the World, A Steady Growth in the Wellbeing of Working People (this last lie-encrusted little goon was locked in an embrace with the fat and sluttish Food Program) and of course Gosplan and other chimerical Soviet slime.

The other two less imposing columns—in which could be observed a certain voluptuous, barely-restrained exasperation of the kind you see when vacationing families of higher-and-middle-ranking service sector personnel assigned to the no-menclature's red bedbugs are boarding one of those little Crimean excursion boats—were moving in the direction of the pig's snout, heading toward both nostrils.

It was there that an unseemly scuffle seemed about to begin, but in general, since the ripply demons were sliding into both, you might say, burrows, a relative order still reigned.

But something positively ugly was going on near the triangular funnels of the pig's ears, which had by some culinary miracle escaped being charred to blackness in the oven, and were sticking up from its bald, greasy dome, their unsinged little whitish-red hairs even sparkling in the candlelight.

The devils, petty demons, imps, and goons were shoving their way deep into the ears, pushing one another, mercilessly flinging their fellow demons aside—all, however, without the slightest sound. The revolting spectacle reminded Helium of those mocking cinematic parodies of the flight of wretched Russian civilians and Wrangel's troops as they boarded steamers to Constantinople.

And there in front of the genially grinning jaws of the pig whose teeth were nipping its tongue ever so slightly something unimaginable was happening. The unholy vermin, all distinguishing features gone (and even before that they had been hard enough to distinguish from one another), were simply swarming all over the pig's snout—hopping into the mouth, hanging on the lower teeth as if they were wrought-iron fence spikes; they were climbing the upper ones and sliding down them, kicking, elbowing, reaching the point they'd been so indecently clambering to reach, finally making room for those remaining, who had all suddenly responded to some imperceptible marching order.

But what was most repulsive of all, what had riveted Helium's gaze and distracted him from the general flow of time and reality, was the spectacle of a whole party of insignificant, nasty, but terrifically pretentious morons from our inept Party underworld proceeding into a rather wide opening under the overcooked pigtail (which was obscured by a thick stalk of pasternip . . . parsnak? . . . no, celery! . . . celery! . . .).

It was clear that their embarkation into the porcine deeps

was proceeding in orderly fashion, on a strict timetable, in accordance with some obviously bogus directives and phony guarantees. The group's looks were obviously synthesized, but within its overall demonic, purulent, viscous reddish-greenish mass certain features could be distinguished, in part:

—the brainless wood louse bloat of the fanatical madame who crawled out from under the chemical stench of the St. Petersburg dike;

—the unpunished, servile insolence of the greasy little descendant of "jurists";

—something avian, owl-eyed, colonel-of-engineerish that looked like it had swallowed the black box of a derailed train hauling, as the simple folk put it, shit;

—the olfactorily-challenged sleaziness of a certain no-talent twittering brownnosed nightingale of the imperial back door;

—the scrotumesque outlines of a certain ambitious but frigid writer totally lacking any notion of decent style or capacity for free expression, an imported lemon squeezed dry and flabby by his own rabblerousing streetwalking oral fixations.*

All that aside, this demon-mob had the look of hard-luck paratroopers waiting to be dropped in the enemy's rear, doomed by history to that terrible leap into nothingness and stoically resigned to the inevitable kick in the ass.

Of course, Helium's perceptions had their own time frame, which in no way corresponded to the time frame of NN's furious indignation. She continued lobbing not only things he'd

*All these demon-properties suggest (by puns on names, in part) certain characters on the Russian political scene of the early 90s: Nina Andreeva, science teacher and notorious letter-writer; Vladimir Zhirinovsky (zhir = fat, grease); Alexander Rutskoy, Alexander Prokhanov, ultrapatriotic poet; Eduard Limonov, returned writer-in-exile.—TRANS.

brought with him this time, but also things he'd brought her long before.

But suddenly it occurred to her that this monstrous, heartless lout might be planning on having a little snack, after all he'd said and done (no sense good food going to waste), and that's why he was staring like that, wondering if he should tear a big old hunk off this side of the pig, or the other. . . . She was so incensed by this suspicion that she grabbed the roast pig by its hind trotters and began whacking Helium with it, driving him to the door.

He backed dazedly toward the door, fearing that the devils who had dived into the pig's belly would fall out again, out through the suture and all the orifices, and he tried to recall just what this whole demon evacuation (so to speak) reminded him of. . . . And what actually was *Eine-kleine-Nachtmusik Serenade* trying to say, skipping there on the same spot . . . what did it mean . . . where was it he'd previously encountered a mythical porcine fuselage straining to fly? How closely did the metaphysical parameters of this loutish embarkation match those of the other nastiest moment in his absurd life? What did it all mean? What was it hinting at? What ominous sense was the hideous vision concealing?

This was trial by memory. Something known, something familiar was openly, mockingly eluding him just around the corner, holding out just the very edge of some scrawl or straggling letter. But just as awful and tormenting for Helium at that instant was the fear that he'd gone mad and was about to lose the sole thing remaining to him—his sense of himself. "Like they say, Oh Lord, don't let me lose my mind. . . ."

He tried to relax the way his mother had taught him, to distract himself from the sadistic jokes of fickle memory, to hide around a corner like a boy with a butterfly net and then suddenly swoop down on the vermin, squash it underfoot and throw it the hell out of sight; he tried to make his hearing cling to the thin edge of his favorite theme from *Eine kleine Nachtmusik,* to help him hold on to that edge while madness yawned before him. . . .

For no particular reason, the inconceivably sorrowful, suffering image of his beloved Bulgakov rose up in his imagination, and for an instant took Helium's mind off what was happening. . . . "I get it," he thought. "I finally understand. . . . I understand why you flattered the unholy vermin, master, and painted them in carnival colors and what I consider impermissible romanticism, why you assigned them certain honorable functions. . . . I understand that in comparison with our third-rate Soviet excuse for hell, with our half-ass Soviet Hades, any genuine devilry might seem to be the work of Grade-A-prime evil. . . . I get it now, I understand . . . but you also, master, sold yourself too cheap when you started believing the actual earthly existence of all manner of imposing charlatan bastards like Woland and his circus of flunkeys . . . believe me, genuine vermin are so putrid and disgusting that one whiff of their awful miasmas is so . . . well personally my poor nostrils don't have the opportunity right now . . . and won't . . . I don't want. . . ."

NN was in no condition to analyze the reasons for Helium's somnambulistic, exceedingly dazed look or his strange smile, in which she saw only hatred, menace and, it seemed, a readiness for yet another loutish outburst expressing all his essential pettiness and lewdness. Though she kept on pounding away at the "villain," she wasn't frothing at the mouth or screaming out anything stunningly illogical, as is sometimes the case with intelligent but exultantly infuriated women. Instead, she spoke surprisingly calmly:

"Out! Out! How could I get involved with such scum? I'd poke your pig-eye out with a fork, but I don't want to have a baby in prison. Oh, not yours! Not yours! Somebody, anybody else's! Thank God nothing happened! Thank God!"

In the front hall Helium grabbed his attaché case, where Brezhnev's death mask lay nestled, and used it to defend himself from the half-shredded pig whose roast hide was splitting in the hands of a genuine Fury and pleaded,

"I'm going . . . please . . . just give me a little whiskey. . . . "

His face was hardly visible under the slops of sauerkraut blended with three colors of caviar (rich man's and poor man's both), under the globs of mayonnaise, the dabs of horseradish, the lilac streams of grated beets, but there was such pleading, such hopelessness in his beaten voice that NN dashed back in for a bottle of White Horse, shoved it into his coat pocket, and flung open the door. Then, since both her hands were limp with disgust, she slammed it shut with her foot.

16 HE WAS ALONE in the foyer. He collapsed onto a stairstep. He pressed his palms to his temples, inside which a dull pain pounded as if trying to break out. He discovered he could see out of one eye only—the other had already swollen shut from the bottle-blow to his cheekbone. "Perfectly clear," he thought, "that there's no way I can go walking around downtown Moscow with a shiner, and looking like this in general. No way. It's perfectly clear also that my life . . . lawful matrimony . . . Cuba . . . banquet . . . ."

From his breast there burst a groan of total exhaustion and terminal suffocation in the crap of life and fate. And at the word banquet and the accidental touch of a slimy mushroom on his tie—on top of everything else, its smell of cloves, cinnamon, and vinegar was hitting him right in the nose—the bile rose convulsively in his throat.

His pulse quickened at the opportunity to take a drink and he unscrewed the imported bottlecap and applied his swollen lips to the bottle's mouth. His brain, irrigated by the lifesaving poison, suddenly raised its head the way a wildflower placed in a jar of water raises its head after drooping the whole way home. His brain suddenly (but surreptitiously, to prevent those devious goons from reading his thoughts) thirsted to put an end to his whole loathsome existence.

In general, this urge to croak as soon as possible perked Helium up, since it was the one goal he had left in life. But remembering how handily his attempt at hanging himself after the pool had been thwarted, he was sure that the demon brood had just accomplished some kind of double-edged maneuver, and he decided this time to make sure nothing went wrong.

He got out the mask with its huge black "reinforced cat" eyebrows. . . . He disgustedly tossed his attaché case aside, like a suddenly worthless thing. . . . "I've got to dupe those hellish little geeks no matter what or else the bastards will keep me from chucking a gob at this earthly mess the way I used to spit at the heavens. . . . Damn, my head is swimming . . . "

This verb maliciously plunged Helium into the same—if not worse—despair he'd felt when, defeated and drained, he crawled out of the vaporous stench of the Moscow pool.

It was as if something was churning up all the sediment that had long ago settled to the bottom of his soul. And the murderous reek in the foyer—the stale urine of young men and stray cats—recalled in that churned-up memory the spectral stench of the House of Writers' toilet.

"That was just stupid of me back then, taking off my belt right in front of those putrid little torturers posing as my guardians. . . . As if taking it off weren't bad enough—there I was, mumbling curses on my shitcan existence—out loud. This time I'll be smarter. . . . It could be that those infamous old church fathers weren't so far off the mark when they clouded medieval minds with their warnings that demons and imps can hear our words and the audible stirrings of our will, but that they can't read our thoughts; that devils haven't learned how to penetrate the meaning of secret plans . . . just one more swig and we'll see. . . . "

He might have acted differently had he been able to cope with his general confusion and recall the Gospel story of the devils that Dostoevsky had used for the epigraph to his novel prophecy. He might have remembered the novel itself, which he'd warily glanced through when he first took an interest in demonology. He had tossed it aside without finishing it because he couldn't understand a word and got terribly exasperated at not finding any genuine demons in it.

But the very thing was—he couldn't even conceive of anyone or anything suddenly (however inexplicably) exorcising the demons from the grim reality of his life. And since at the moment he couldn't possibly disbelieve in the demons' existence, so he was dependent on them in both thought and deed.

With relish, Helium took his swig, and sat up a little. He happened to glance out the nearest window, and saw circlets of sausage, slices of tongue, boxes with Christian Brothers labels, smoked fish, steaming potatoes, cookies, bits of cheese, a bouquet of white chrysanthemums, salad, herring, and finally, the swarthy carcass of the suckling pig, disfigured by direct contact with Helium's own person, all come flying out NN's window and land on the ground. Everything, in a word, that he "respected" and that NN had once regaled him with, with such artistry and gusto, was getting shitcanned.

"Just like some old-time highrolling merchant, dammit, here taking it out on deficit goods," he thought to himself, once again shuddering inwardly at the melancholy ruin and loss of his dinner-table fortunes as well his bedroom pleasures.

Then he loudly and clearly announced, "Like they say, 'farewell, free element,' this is it, here I stand before you passing the gas and snot of ontological ennui for the very last time. . . ."

Then, still wary of some final treacherous maneuver on the demons' part, he made as if to dive headfirst into the stairwell.

And he might well have done it. But at the very second he spoke the impulse aloud, he slipped on a bit of aspic that had dripped from his own shoulder, and he put his butt on the stairstep so hard that his one good eye saw a whole skyful of stars. He even let out a yelp as a terrible pain shot through his tailbone.

Up a flight, some pathological activist was already rattling on in his hallway voice:

"Police, comrades? What good are the police? The police are in league with the local mafia, they've sold out to Tel Aviv. God knows I've been rallying our floor to take up the ax and patrol without mercy!"

Helium, quickly donning the doubtlessly frightening Brezhnev mask, clearly remembered the scene at his private audience in the Kremlin. The alleged author, twitching his reinforced cats, was autographing his trilogy for Helium. "To our Soviet life," said the openly senile dedication, "I cannot help being painfully boring honestly to dear Comrade Seriouso shamefully with all the best marshal's is it Brezhnev . . . ?"

And so, in the guise of the late general secretary of the mind-honor-and-conscience of our epoch, Helium speedily left the building.

17

THE SNOWY WHITENESS blinded him completely. It even somehow got under his swollen eyelid into his closed eye. Judging by the touch of flakes against the mask of the pseudoauthor–commander-in-chief, snow was still falling hard.

It was so quiet in the courtyard that the only sound to be heard was the snowfall itself. You couldn't put a name to this sound, which resembled the uninterrupted—no inhale or exhale—breathing of some live, fantastic, cosmic being; it seemed to console and soften all the numerous other sounds of urban space.

And the snow, without the slightest distaste, blanketed the squalor of the courtyard and the chronic ulcers of all the various excavations that suggested to the observant mind some mindless game of "funeral" and "graves" played by city authorities with themselves and their weary citizens.

His single eye wide open, Helium saw nothing before him save the blinding whiteness that had wiped even the windows' reflections from the slushy asphalt. The demons—vanished without a trace. Not a single one to be seen.

The silence scared him. He needed the street and its growling stream of cars, or actually, just *a* car, preferably one exceeding the speed limit.

So he began to hurry, and at that instant the courtyard, the silence, the breathing of the cosmic snowfall was ripped wide open by an expressive canine howl, torn apart by the indescribable, gut-deep growl with which excited—or else terrified—cats turn their highly mystical insides out.

Adding to the cacophony were the no less bestial cries of the humans who had entered into some life-and-death contest with their animal cousins.

Helium couldn't help being distracted from his lethal melancholy by the spectacle of living beings who stand on what would seem to be different levels of development and who occupy totally disparate positions in society fighting on equal terms for the food that NN had flung out after him—this incomparable spectacle amazed him, confirmed him in a certain sort of scepticism and spurred his resolution to break it the hell off with this lousy reality.

Like spotted lightning, a homeless pointer with an amazingly sculpted, not-yet-ruined frame dashed past him. The hungry hunter's jaws had a death grip on a stick of Ukrainian-brand kielbasa from the Kremlin's VIP meat lockers. The joy of good fortune and the hope of continued life gleamed in its eyes.

In pursuit, barefoot and clad in nothing but undershorts, raced a grayhaired individual bearing a slight resemblance to Kravchuk, with whom Helium had more than once plotted devious strikes against both of the Ukraine's official churches. The citizen's face was twisted in disagreement (with fate) and surprise (at this latest trick of social chaos), and might, in the sensitive person's soul, have aroused both sympathy and disgusted contempt. He was chanting something that sounded almost Japanese—"ahgitchubitchahgitchubitchu!"

Faint with primordial disappointment, he was forced to resign himself to the difference in his speed and the gitchubitchi's. He fell back and began furiously yanking the pickets out of the fence around the children's play-yard.

Another individual nonetheless managed, right in front of Helium, to wrest something obviously porcine from the teeth of an old, patchy shepherd. But then the shepherd, evidently unwilling to part with the wondrous hunk of meat so lately in her mouth, turned into an absolute fiend from hell. She knocked the man down in the snow with her front paws. There was such fearsome and resolute rage in her bared teeth and throaty growl that the fallen man howled out to his fellow humans for aid. He must have gone limp with terror, because the shepherd stripped the ham from his hands—but then all of a sudden the character who'd let the Ukrainian get by him thwacked her on the spine with a picket.

Fortunately for the mutt, the slat just skidded down her gaunt ribs and she took off running without so much as a yelp, inasmuch as her jaws were gainfully occupied at the moment and too busy for righteous snarls.

True, a good-sized hunk of the unfortunate pig who had found himself in such a hellish posthumous fix did fall to the ground. The barefoot character in shorts scooped it up—the one who had lost the contest with the pointer.

The other individual, popping up from the snow, began protesting, using expressions like "you could choke on that bone" and "what do you know about existence anyway" and "that's absurd, who do you think you're talking to" and "in a crisis situation anybody can shit their pants."

Barefoot-shorts contemptuously stalked off, holding his nose with his free fingers. Helium, dazed, was trying to figure out what had become of the suckling pig's demonic stuffing, but nothing natural or for that matter supernatural occurred to him.

Off to one side about seven of the building's residents— acting, as Helium understood it, in concert—were trying to fling the cats and dogs aside. But the battle was clearly going the animals' way, "our way" noted Helium to himself with heartfelt sympathy and a fan's passion.

There was literally not a single cat or dog who hadn't managed to drag off some edible trophy. Even a gaunt kitten, whose overall pitifulness had reached heartbreaking apotheosis, had a little golden sprat sticking out of its mouth.

The residents, embarrassed by the whole event, suddenly huddled together, transformed themselves into an instant political rally and resolved to organize the last Leninist overtime of this unforeseen perestroika in human-animal relations and, axes in hand, unanimously take all these stray bastards prisoner.

Helium felt a sinking in his soul after this temporary respite. He realized the residents had noticed him, and quickly headed through the archway out onto the street. But no one even thought to pursue him, because a sudden blizzard had loosed its snowy whirlwinds and begun to howl.

Its vortex was particularly fearsome in the courtyard. The wind howled through all the drainpipes, rattled the windowpanes, banged the building directory, ripped down people's stupid ads and announcements, slammed doors and with a certain sadistic enjoyment tore off some terminally ownerless hooks and latches, and drove a stray Christian Brothers carton in Helium's wake.

He glanced round to see if anyone was pursuing him, and

somehow his one good eye managed to make out the words which had been persecuting him all day, the words Christian Brothers, and he stiffened in anger.

He completely forgot that the mask covered his whole face and from time to time he took a drink to ease the orphan loneliness racking his whole being; he stuck the bottleneck right into the Brezhnev's mouth, still gaping wide in a marasmatic Mayday call to Party and People.

It was late. The storm had chased nearly everyone home. And the few passersby who hadn't yet found a place to take shelter were either walking hunched over against the wind, faces hidden in their collars, scarves, mufflers, or else with it at their backs, mockingly flapping their coattails. They didn't bother with Helium. Nor did he, for that matter, with them.

"Just who *is* on our side? The luckless cats and dogs and birds, that's who, because all us humans are just shit, because it's one against all and all against one," he thought listlessly. This circumstance stood forth in his imagination as virtually the one last cosmic, cold, and exceedingly painful truth of human existence.

He stopped and sat down on the sidewalk's edge, if in fact one can even say that city geometry still has an edge against such a snowfall and such a storm.

Then he took one more swig, and with spiteful, fearless challenge repeated aloud the feeling the sad truth had revealed to him, then loudly added in English:

"Good-bye, my disgusting shitass life!"

Switching to a foreign language seemed to him, aside from everything else, a necessary part of furthering his plan to croak proudly, resentfully, fearlessly and with absolutely no regrets.

He repeated the English phrase in order to "scan the area for lice," that is, for the presence of demons who were no doubt out there maneuvering somewhere, but also to fool them once and for all by concealing his final intentions in the words of an alien language.

But everything around him was white-on-white, and the streetlights had gone out completely, as if conserving what was left of state energy and the e-lec-tri-fi-ca-tion-ary ideal from the stubborn surges of unrestrained plundering and general entropy pushing in through every crack.

There was not a single demon or devil, not a single scrawny imp as far as the eye could see, which left him feeling strangely orphaned and abandoned.

A gust of wind brought a far-off roar of motors and the pitilessly steely gnash of scrapers on the asphalt's frozen hide.

At the other end of the street he saw two pairs of headlights at once—some fuzzy yellow ones and a blinding distant glare. There was a car apparently racing along at high speed; it was swerving side to side, either for kicks or because of the ice.

"Well," Helium said quite drunkenly but exclusively for himself, "good-bye, my disgusting, shitass life! I hate and despise you."

18 THE CAR, still swerving, was getting closer now. He swallowed a little more whiskey, thinking to himself that this swig would be the very last one he ever took, but not really regretting it.

He tossed the bottle down, and drunkenly smirking at the thought that for once he had "the objective reality of these vermin" wrapped round his little finger, he lurched toward the four headlights racing to meet him—"just try not to think about what happened, just shed, here in the present, all the burden of past and future . . . "

At the very last instant, who knows why, something connected with Dostoevsky or with some scriptural text he himself had personally ripped to shreds flashed through his brain, but it barely flashed and then he seemed to go completely blind in the light of the speeding headlights.

If the posh new black Mercedes belonging to a certain fairly-soused father of our economic renaissance hadn't been swerving all over the road from too little visibility and too much horsepower, its elegant, gleaming front end would have instantly knocked—head-on—the life out of the would-be suicide.

But once he noticed a bottle glinting dangerously in his headlights, and an awful figure heading straight under his wheels, the soused Mercedes owner cranked the steering wheel sharply to the left; he cranked hard, and the right-hand side of the car tossed Helium, with terrible force, into a snowdrift.

The drift was fresh and fluffy, like white bread that hadn't had time yet to go stale. Helium tumbled deep into it, and snow covered him immediately, head and all.

The Mercedes whirled, spun around, slammed into the base of a streetlight and mutilated its brand-new snout. All its lights blew out at once.

But the crumpled metal of the bumper didn't seem to be wedged against the front wheels, and the drunken owner didn't give a damn for helping his victim, so he sped—this time suprisingly observant of all the remaining rules of traffic safety—off into the distance, away from the scene of the accident.

There were no witnesses to his crime. At the other end of the street, tearing through the quiet of the snowfall, five nocturnal auto-monsters were approaching. Their curved blades were shoveling snow from the roadway onto the curb and their steel brushes were scrabbling the icy glaze from the asphalt.

It's hard to say whether the nearest driver even saw anything human sticking up out of the snow—a hand or a foot, for example. Most likely he didn't see, because what with the fine swirling snow coating their windshields the drivers work their plows practically blind, and besides they don't give a damn about anything either, as long as they don't shear off any street-lights with their wide scraper blades or score the already carious sidewalk curb.

Helium, though in a near-faint from the blow and the pain, could hear the ever-nearer, ever-louder gnashing of the snow-removal monster.

He might even have been able to move a little and give some sign to the drivers that there was a man down; he could have avoided being hit, but instead he just kept waiting, with a combination of curiosity and growing resentment, for the whole scraping, rattling, growling mass to chew him up, mash the hell out of him and drag his unfeeling, done-with rag of a body on down the street. "Dragged far, chewed up small, so that all that's left in place of my unrecognizable face is a bloody mask and the immortal papier-mâché of stagnation's old swamp-gas gomer . . . on the other hand, in his day my life wasn't all that bad. . . . "

In the midst of these absurd thoughts he somehow lost consciousness.

The wide angle of the nearest machine's scraper brutally—but not fatally—tossed him, his bottle, and some snow off the road and onto the sidewalk, and the whole clattering cavalcade moved on.

For a while Helium actually must have been unconscious. In any case, he felt neither cold, nor pain, nor heartache. Though a little snow had sifted in, his face was mostly shielded from the storm by the mask of the late General Secretary whose immortal scowl was just barely peeking out of the snowbank.

Perhaps he might never have come to, but instead lay there drunk oblivious and fresh-frozen until somebody finally found him, if a pair of drunks hadn't stopped right near the spot where he lay sprawled.

 19 THEY WERE BOTH plastered to the gills, and therefore were both strenuously philosophizing, their unruly tongues barely under control.

Helium heard the sound of drunken human voices—one of which he, with absolute indifference, recognized as that of the ill-fated Zelenkov, the unexpected visitor and fictive spouse of NN.

"Mister Chaos, Granat Granatych, is more substantive and more, so to speak, form-bearing than is Cosmos, more than it might seem to a lot of intellectuals, that is, idiots . . . present company excluded . . . you think those taxicrappers will notice us here?"

"The taxicab is chaos's most unpredictable particle. . . . I'm sincerely glad, Ivan Yurievich, that we went ahead and got ourselves stinking drunk at a wake for a bunch of theoretical-physics postulates. . . . I swear to—paragraph . . . paragraph."

"D'you believe that when I saw that what derives from chaos equations is uh-h-h the very person of the Supreme Being and that without him all things visible and invisible—existentially, and purely mathematically too—simply grow faint with terminal despair at all the unresolvables of the universal absurd. . . . Thanks, I won't fall . . . I ordered them to crack open the whole month's supply of liquor . . . you, I thought, can all go to fucking hell with your limits, begging your pardon, we're celebrating a triumph of scientific nativity, I mean creativity, here."

"I am stunned and con-cep-tu-ally deconstruc-ted by your ingenious slip of the tongue. . . . It pains me, though, it truly pains me . . . why was I trying for ages to prove that He didn't exist, and why did He refuse to fight back when a whole world of formulas were in his hands, so to speak: 'No, gentlemen,' says He, 'I AM. . . . ' . . . you have all Descartes in your hands, so to speak, but you sorry assholes wasted, that is, offed all your Trumpovs and fluffed the game. . . ."

"Mind if I . . . "

"A noble thing—draining off a pint for bruderschaft. . . . I love nonlinear friendship, as we used to say back in first-year . . . just watch you don't piss all over my coat. . . . Taxi! . . . Sadists! . . . you'd think that the Science Section bureaucrats on Old Square were driving . . . led by . . . "

Two streams of urine shot toward the snow, drilling through right where it powdered Brezhnev's mask; as they drummed on the mask and bared one edge, an eyebrow showed black as a reinforced cat, and the marshal-and-author's cheek pinkened beneath the parasol of dim light.

"Listen, have we just pissed all over somebody here . . . on some homo sap-iens who can *be* but not necessarily *think*, as Descartes might have said in our place . . . you don't think so?"

"It's a mask. Somebody probably threw it out . . . it's all covered with salad and red-caviar puke. . . . I sent two just like it to France . . . of our Leonitwit Ilyich . . . there can't be anybody underneath."

"Well, fine, let's suppose I agree, although I do not yet conclusively not agree. Have I gotten tangled up in my nots? . . . But what about evil: You can't avoid that question so easily, my friend."

"I'm no expert on these things, but . . . ta-a-a-xi-i-!! do you know what, in my entirely unscientific view, is the principal difference between good and evil?"

"You'd think it would be obvious to two decent, upstanding people . . . "

"To us, maybe, but not to two . . . taxi! three or even four taxidrivers. So, it's merely that evil can be reckoned in advance. That realization hit me a while back. I'll bet you a bottle that the fifth cab doesn't stop either. Taxi! But good—or let's put it more concretely, true art as a *form* of good—is unpredictable even in hindsight . . . take music if you like—absolutely improbable. In other words—divine. . . . Just exactly like the phenomenon of life itself . . . or Language . . . or have I gotten myself tangled up with formal logic here? . . . The hell with it . . . Taxi!"

The two drunken specialists on the physics of chaos zipped up on the run and dashed toward a vehicle standing miraculously stock-still.

Again, Helium might well have bestirred himself and let them know that there really was a person buried there, but at that moment he hadn't the slightest desire to show any signs of life whatsoever.

He was simply waiting for that last little life-supporting vein inside him to burst. After the blow he'd taken, he would die, and that was that. And he couldn't care less about being peed on. " . . . and besides it didn't even trickle down under my collar, it ran past, it actually warmed up the mask over my cheek a bit . . . the last bit of warmth . . . but still . . . warmth . . . life. . . . "

Strangely, there wasn't a single demon around. "It's got to be one of two things—either they can't penetrate thoughts, can only snatch at our words (crummy little snatchers) . . . I shouldn't have said that even in English . . . should have just made my move and everything would be over with by now . . . or else they've all vanished with the pig . . . and they really arranged a shit-fest there at the end, the little buggers, they put me in a holiday mood, a lighthearted mood, got me primed to propose to her, like a jerk . . . candles, happiness, and I did love her, I really did . . . I could finally love, it was all healed up . . . and then, then I saw something hopeless and ruinous on your ugly little pusses while you were climbing the stalk of paster— . . . parsnip again? no, no it was celery . . . into the roasted porthole of that pig . . . I saw something . . . "

20 HE WAS GETTING colder and colder. But he wasn't so much cold as he was uncomfortable and miserable lying there waiting his last earthly wait, waiting for death, and never knowing just when the whole cooling process would come to an end.

And a familiar but wordless intonation began ringing through his mind, a certain grumpiness and irritability at having to wait in line, so to speak, for that final cool-down.

He waved these thoughts away—waved them away like

pesky mosquitoes on a summer's evening on the dacha veranda, and he seemed to be succeeding, but then there they were, breaking through to his conscious mind, pestering and buzzing, try to batten themselves onto him and bite as hard as they could.

"So the Supreme Being came out of the brackets of a mathematical formula . . . appeared to them out of chaos . . . dickbrains . . . and so where was he headed when he came out? Maybe over to my place? I'd tell him right now what I personally think of him . . . *He* didn't come out of the brackets, you dickbrains, *they* did . . . *they* are what Luther and I saw, not *him* . . . thank-you-Mamochka-for-my-name . . . I'm cooling down to where those proteins just stop dead in their tracks, Mamochka . . . but you know gentlemen they used to put people in jail for insulting Descartes. . . . I wouldn't have, but our men-of-iron did. . . . I remember Papa Revolver yelling at someone over the phone that any denigration of Descartes was tantamount to a personal attack on a Politburo member or on a top-level commercial-sector administrator. . . . 'I'll show you smart-asses that I'm the one who gets to *think* ergo you bastards will cease to *be* in about twenty-four hours.' . . . ah Papa, Papa . . . "

And that's when his ill-fated conversation with his father Revolver Fomich in the private room at the Prague came to mind.

That evening he'd been listening to his father quite absentmindedly. With marvelous irresponsibility, he was feeling the unusually intoxicating relief of transferring his onerous feeling of dread at the future—the feeling that he had a singular fate in store—to his father's experienced, long-suffering shoulders. And it seemed to him then that the social success his father could guarantee was indeed the most pragmatic version of earthly happiness—Pushkin's "peace and liberty" . . .

"You, Helium, are a third-generation theomachist, a god-wrestler from way back," said Revolver Fomich. "Your grand-dad was a Marxist and, by the way, a better apostle of the revolutionary verities than that mummified smart-ass . . . that dried apricot in marble marmelade . . . . He was an atheist by God's grace, was your granddad. Be proud. True, I myself have always combined antireligious activism with my work in the commercial sector, where everything serves as the best proof that there is no demiurge, nor can there be. There are Party and people's control commissions, and likewise a multibranched network of inspectors, seen and unseen. In short—God does not exist but religion does, and (this is just between us) we'd be better off if it were the other way around. So, well, these days the war on Opiates of the People is a far more promising busi-ness than chemistry or rocket science or Party activism—that's something to bear in mind while choosing a profession or carv-ing out the profile of your future career. Because everything in a person should be Party: private life, and eyes and thoughts, and spiritual activism under the aegis of militant godlessness—that's according to Chekhov, who was our seagull and, by anal-ogy, the Uncle Vanya in the cherry orchard of the Russian Revo-lution. With your wimp character you've got no business in the commerce network, where homo homini lupus and also cobra, tapeworm, swine and rat. Whereas the war on narco-religion brings the clever warrior nothing but respect from the procura-tor's office, a respectable income and the social envy of our whole damned society. What you've got here, Helium, is not a fight with the RSFSR Criminal Code but a call on the Turkoman carpet of Higher Authority. Atheism, of course, is limping a bit ever since that Biblical Zionist Yakovlev (if I'm not mistaken) got his leg hurt in the first round of our match with God, but these days such outrageously baldfaced militance, well, it's profitable business. And that's not cynicism, it's a clear-eyed look at one of life's realities. Something strange has been going on lately, ideals have shrunk, gotten as puny as our apartments, citizens' private contributions to the unavoidably bright common future, and Antonov apples, while prison terms and dissent just keep getting bigger all the time. So you need to know how to cover your ass but not rock the boat. Got it? Study history and I'll personally take you before the Committee." The naturally indolent and easygoing Helium gave a shudder, but Revolver Fomich explained, "Not that Committee. Not the Lubyanka. Don't get all pucker-assed. The Committee on all those religions and churches, I mean. I've got some people there . . . on the inside, smack in the middle of the Orthodox leadership, which is subordinate in the highest sense to the plans of the Party, which is to say the plans of the People. *Everybody's* happy to belly up to what's left of the Tsar's table. Even during Lent. You should just see them, all our church hierarchs, snitching and slurping and screwing. They eat and fornicate so much you'd think they'd been given a top-secret Party assignment to act counter to *his* interests in every possible way. To give him no peace, not for a minute, to becloud his starry-eyed celestiality with their petty little sins, to make mischief, mischief, mischief, understand, in the sense of one step forward, two steps back.

"By the way, Suslov, who back then was still in a covert state of tuberculosis, calls me in one time and says: 'Revolver, we've come to the conclusion that you should grow a beard, conjointly with mustache and other hair, around the perimeter of your foolhardy head. The Politburo has decided to assign you an important role in a controlled experiment to revive the Orthodox Church. We'll assign it a clerical job as our moral and budgetary assistant, and you'll be in charge, because you've outdone everyone else in Party ranks in renouncing the norms of the old morality. Go, and fulfill the mandate of the mind, honor, and conscience of our epoch.'

"I don't shave for two months, I don't cut my hair. Suslov hauls me in again, praises my hairy growth, orders me to keep a sharp eye out for dandruff, like they say in a certain gangster ditty, and announces, 'Bring in all your papers and personal data. You're going to enroll in the seminary and whiz all over, I mean right through, all the courses. Then we'll gradually get you elected Metropolitan, with an eye to a speedy nomination to the Patriarchate of All the Russ—I mean the USSR.'

"I'm having some trouble taking this all in and faint dead away right there in his office. I come to, plop myself down at Suslov's feet and beg for a shave and a haircut, that is, for him to groom somebody else equally amoral and devoted for that responsible and nomenclatured church office, but I, I tell him, I'm dying from all those smells and bells, and besides pressure from a mole planted in a highly sensitive position makes me positively horny, and besides, I say, I drink too much . . . at Party seminars I mix up sphinxes and sphincters and phenomenclatures with noumenclatures. . . . I possess a whole number of other fundamental weaknesses and fidget lewdly in the presence of foreign guests. . . . I've got a Gorkom reprimand on my record for trying to drag Dolores Ibarurri by her Hispano-Communist clit into the men's toilet at a banquet at the Georgievsky Hall. . . . Suslov (and this was somebody I looked up to as the thinking rod, I mean reed and living corpse of the Russian Revolution) starts to cough, spit blood, and patiently try to convince me that blah-blah-blah the Party and its organs had already grown at least two generations-worth of pheno . . . I mean noumo . . . why can't I . . . Martelium, I mean Helium, pour us some more Martell . . . anyway the Party has trained its own religion corpse I mean corps which also—like Budyonny and Zhdanov—drinks, eats, fornicates, thieves, et cetera, but many of them, judging from our agents' communiques, have begun (for some mysterious reason inexplicable to the security organs themselves) to fall under the influence of the damned Opiate of the People itself. One scoundrel set up a whole harem in his residence, and we have reliable information that during Holy Week he eats rare steaks on the sly and makes his driver beat him on the back—and lower down—with a mechanical hand. He carries on as shamelessly as if he knows he'll have to pay in hell anyway. . . . But the one thing he won't do is violate the secrecy of confession. He won't record confessions with his listening devices and refuses to hand over the results of his investigation into the clandestine relationship between covertly devout intellectuals and their inner selves in conditions of absolute internal solitude. And whose confessions *doesn't* he hear! Wives of Obkom and Raikom secretaries, a whole gang of People's Artists, the children and mistresses of ministers, cellists (damn them and their divas, anyway), all sorts of philologizing academicians and Moscow Circus jugglers . . . there's even one General Staff marshal who goes to confession regularly all tricked out as a civilian . . . all of them go to this man who was trained by the Party and dropped behind Church lines. We organized a Confessional Research Institute at the Lubyanka under the auspices of the Public Opinion Section, so as to get the spiritual life of the people on the Gosplan track as well, but here our blasphemer friend, this reprobate, this drunk, this avaricious glutton, this incestuous despoiler of innocent cleaning girls and penitent ladies of the demimonde, this reckless snitch, this pederast of practically metaphysical proportions (although that's probably an unreliable tip from someone with a grudge, and I personally believe that there's got to be something saintly in a nice rare steak) . . . anyway, our hierarch suddenly balked. 'I,' he says, 'am unworthy to encroach upon the sacrament of confession.' 'That is . . . what do you mean?' I ask him again. 'Unworthy? Are you crazy?' 'It's very simple,' he answers. 'I lack the grand, outrageous rottenness this devilish and tawdry business requires, and I should not be invested with the black office of the Antichrist. I have a wealth of personal vices. Every blessed day I add to them wonderfully and fearlessly. I'll answer for each of them on Judgment Day, if the archangels trumpet it in all the circles of hell and the peripheries of life. And at that Judgment I will ask the Supreme Judge for one indulgence and one indulgence only: that He not even think of absolving me, louse that I am, of even one little peccadillo, not even the smallest, humblest, least provocatively shameful one—which request is nobly heroic payment on my part for the pleasures of the belly and the exceedingly debauched flesh under the utterly thankless conditions of imperfect earthly life. I'm answerable for all my sins. I stand guilty—before the Party, the People, and the Omniscient Heavens—of delusions of the grandeur of my own immoral inferiority. But in the meantime, my sinful comrade-brother Suslov, declares this candidate for bishop, in my time off (from sinning) I continue to dutifully perform church offices: I bless and christen, marry, confirm, hear confession, serve communion, and at that listening post I stand fast, a staunch pillar of the Holy Canon, which nourishes the souls of the many and the few with the Word of God, and I am also the transmitter and relay passing Heaven all the secrets of people's lives. Off duty I sin without ceasing. However, I cannot betray the secrets of confession. Never. Military secrets I might bump your way, and use my earnings to take the edge off a hangover or pat a sweet thing's cheeks in chaste spiritual delight and fleshly weakness—and after a swig of mulled wine I would certainly unselfishly hand over some hypergrim classified info in exchange for the prospect of unrepeatable (to my immense regret) services to be performed by sinful ladies in the Next World. After all, I can fornicate without being defrocked (or disrobed, even), but scribble police reports on the content of confessions? Disbar me, defrock me and leave me to rot, deprive my sinful body of its daily bread and pleasure—but that's something I won't do. I will suffer loftily, that is deservedly. Forgive me, Mikhail Andreevich, but I can't violate that sweetly fearful, grandly celestial silence of confession, for it's not the torments of hell that I myself fear, but something more awful and insurmountable, the meaning of which my foul mouth can neither say nor even attempt to pronounce. So if you like, I'm ready to shed my cassock in a Party striptease right there at any Obkom meeting and hand you my slippery wine-red serpent— my Party card, I mean—right on the table, on a platter . . . '

" 'The bastard,' fretted Suslov, 'and here I'm practically spitting blood into his lecherous beard telling him that the Party has access to information on the mysteries of universal matter, and he, the drunken whoremongering asshole, who stinks of undercover work, he's here singing the praises of the mysteries of the Church? Of confession? Is that it? . . . Well,' says Suslov, 'we'll defrock him back in two shakes and pack him off to be personnel manager at the top-secret Institute for Moral Beauty Research where he can try and turn freaks into Party functionaries.

Let him screw *their* personal lives—instead of cleaning women or the conscience-stricken wives of embezzlers of state funds. Strip yourself of your high church office in twenty-four hours! That's an order! About face—forward march into wordly life, you villain!'

"Helium, I'm still on my knees, digging in my heels, so to speak. 'Mikhail Andreevich,' I say, 'I do hate religion, hate it so much that I'd ruin the Church's international reputation in a minute! Putting me into high church office and religious circles would be like putting a tiger into a cage with an antelope! I'd rip them to shreds! But on my honor, I don't want to have any relations with a demiurge who after all doesn't exist. What does exist is the commerce network, and its closed supply bases which are being magically infiltrated by shortages as we speak. Containing those shortages as the Central Committee's bon appetit systematically develops and expands—that is my job. Mikhail Andreevich, without me, who'll supply you with gourmet badger fat to make those little Koch-rods curl up and die? Who'll send expeditions to Africa to get orangutan eggs for the flabby scrota of Politburo members, atomic academicians, marshalls of all manner of troops and those same pious People's Artists of the USSR?' The latter arguments had some effect. 'Fine,' he says, 'go shave your chin, Serious, and get yourself your old indomitable crewcut, our official state parody of Kerensky's. We'll deal with religious confessions without you. We'll just call it all testimony given under interrogation. You'll take over Minorov's paperwork—he just got caught with his pants down while his dentist friend was supposedly drilling, plugging his cavity with an imported filling . . . .'

"In short, Helium, I can see the general line of your fate right here in front of me so clearly that I'd like to propose a toast to it.

I'll do a little groundwork at your institute and in the meantime you tell the Komsomols that you're joining the frontlines of the battle to undermine the Church's influence among our dirty rotten intellectuals. We'll have you specialize in, say, writers. By all indications they've got some problems with atheism. Still they are workers of the word, so to speak, which was in the beginning and was god, by the way. This unfortunate circumstance can't help telling on the level of workplace hazard in that writing shop of theirs—for which the Party does in fact pay them weekly pie-in-the-sky. Gotten fat and besotted lately, the wordsmiths have. . . . So anyway we'll turn your thesis and dissertation over to a certain needy defrocked priest who's already blown ungodly amounts on women and booze. This character would love the chance to aim one more gob at the heavens, for appropriate remuneration of course. . . ."

This whole bizarre conversation with his father—bizarre because his father was the only one talking, and Helium sat fatefully silent—was repeating itself in Helium's brain to an insinuating musical accompaniment, to the insistent sounds of his favorite composition . . . ta, ta-ta, tata-tata-tata . . . and he felt like a homeless blind man who'd caught the livesaving scent of a dwelling but who couldn't, in the cold void of darkness, find the road that led there. . . .

21 THE IMAGE of NN, by the way, had almost stopped coming to mind. Helium had reconciled himself to the fact that this was it—the end of the road, the end of the line, the end. True, a shadow of terrible suspicion had crept into his mind that *she* (the other one, the one who had seemed to swim off into nonbeing) had somehow set up this whole fantasmagorical ending—she, not his own acquiescence to the calling his father had imposed upon him. But he listlessly waved the suspicion away.

And as for his friend's artifact, the precious thing he'd been carrying these last few days, switching it from pocket to pocket—he'd forgotten it completely. And so he never checked to see if it was there, and consequently never imagined to himself how somebody would find it on him either right there or at the morgue; they'd find the lovely thing, go crazy at their luck, unload it on some dealers, they'd drink up, eat up and blow the money on whores. . . .

Maybe if he'd imagined all that for a split second, the force of cupidity (which is no small part of the life force itself) might have nudged him into some move to save himself.

But what he was recalling, in place of his little package, were all the famous literary examples of various freezings, all of them ending in cold, pristine sleep. He was surprised at how insistently "the freeze motif" recurred in his native literature and at how unfeelingly the whole world with all its absurd problems and hopeless tangle of affairs shrinks inside the body of a freezing man—shrinks to the point from which, if you believed all the rotten quantum-and-chaos experts, this frigging unecessary Universe had sprung. And the entire Universe, presumably still utterly horrified at its own emergence, is still expanding the hell away from itself . . . "and doing exactly the right thing at that. . . . "

He was scared that "if I don't croak right off, if there's some sudden twenty-degree-or-so change in the weather, if it starts to thaw, then all these bruises will start aching and my bumps start throbbing and scratches prickling. . . ." . . . the pain would become his body and his body would become the pain . . . and the whole thing would start all over again . . . he would want to take drink . . . to choke . . . to warm up . . . to be saved . . . no . . . no . . . no . . .

The snowplows, their blades rumbling along the other side of the street, turned a corner and moved off into the distance.

Helium lay stock-still beneath the snow. He'd decided he would just croak—no lifting a finger, toe, hand, foot, no sniffing, no blinking—just lie there on his right side and let himself cool down . . . just listen distantly to the last shushing sounds of his heart, which right now was either pounding madly or skipping in sharp pain and melancholy silence. . . . Why don't you just croak, all of you, from despair over the absurd world's unresolvable . . . .

He was wearing his watch but the very thought of time turned his stomach. He didn't know why, but there was perhaps nothing more hateful to him in those minutes, and the terror at its soulless, self-willed, frighteningly irreversible flow that maliciously hangs back just when we want to speed it up and, by the same token, always outraces our passion to stop it even for an instant. His revulsion for time was even greater than his revulsion for the unholy vermin. Time was more odious than the chill, the snow, the pain, the torments of remembrance, and there was reason enough for Helium to think that in this reality he had nothing left *but* time. He was swaddled in a snowy shroud like a fly in a spiderweb. . . . Time had already begun odiously sucking away these long final hours (or maybe short minutes) of his existence. . . . "And now it's going to sit back and make the whole thing last as long as possible, and all the dirty bloodsucking tricks of Sove bureaucracy will seem like the very spirit of angelic consideration and courtesy to you, Hal. . . ."

If he hadn't been freezing but simply perishing on the street in drunken solitude, he might have been enchanted by the astounding silence, distributed equally to all the expanse of snowy darkness, and almost unbroken at that hour by the roar of passenger cars or the voices of passersby.

He might have been jealous as hell, desperately envious of the flow of other lives in the kick-back comfort of warm little apartments where, like them, he too could have been, not only enjoying NN's charms but also "getting a kick out of creating a new life, with a long distance shot at ordinary old-age . . . "

It might well have driven him to civic fury that Christmas Eve was apparently being celebrated not only by the unreasoning crowd but also by the new lords and masters of life, eagerly truckling to that crowd after pissing away not just the Aral Sea but the whole sorry Empire (but an Empire nonetheless) and, lawful candles in hand, frequenting churches they themselves had once trashed.

But there in the cold snow that seemed to swaddle his body

twice round, it was a different sort of anger that frozen Helium felt, something like hundred-proof childish hurt that the former sovereigns had "led him by the nose, down the primrose path, and then gone off and had a picnic without him" . . . outrageous, declaring Christmas a day off! Those lowlifes had burrowed down deep into the warmth of their homey nests, and there they were, the Party pricks, warming their chilled palms over the flickering little flames of myriads of suddenly brassy and legalized candles . . . how all that dark ignorance cups its little palms, patty-cake, patty-cake, and shields the little flame from air currents . . . and the hot wax flows down the slender necks of the candles into its fist, missing the white, I guess, paper ruffs . . . how they shield that flame with their palms . . . and she's probably shielding the candle on . . . I think it was the table . . . from the storm over all the earth . . . murmuring some poem . . . and hands really do glow pink in the candle-light . . . the sun used to shine right through hers too. . . .

22 NO DOUBT HELIUM had started drifting in and out of consciousness, wandering, but when the small, wavering flame of the vesper candle suddenly merged with the midday fire of the celestial Orb, something flared in his conscious mind, something which had never before even entered his head.

"That ill-fated element is more than just the absolute champion of deep-freeze, it's named for Helios, after all . . . and so am I, in my turn . . . how about that . . . to live your life, as her favorite poet said, like a country stroll and never make the connection even in late-night talks with your lady love . . . a life like that, you know, is nothing but one long hungover belch . . . and father or no, Revolver, why the frigging *hell* did you set up your idiot boy, as a scientific (now there's a joke) atheist. . . . I could have got through with a major in teaching methodology and then lived just fine, polishing the seat of an Old Square chair and picking at the putty in hotel windows the world over, Papa . . . your long view turned out nearsighted, with loss of vision in one eye taken individually. . . . "

He shrank into himself even more pitifully from inward cold and loathing, and was surprised that he couldn't feel the snow touching his bare hands. He shrank into himself, and, strangely enough, felt a certain dignity surge into his soul. . . . "It wouldn't cost me a thing to call up those shit-green fiends and cut some orders regarding contingency measures for the snowbank rescue of an inebriated, formerly Imperial citizen mugged by a roast pig . . . not a thing . . . those little flunkeys would hop to on the double . . . then all hell would break loose . . . sirens in the headlights glare . . . passersby . . . streets . . . faces, the paramedic swayed . . . it wouldn't cost me a thing . . . but you little buggers can just bite it, you stinking green little turds, you won't hear a word out of me. . . . I'll take my frostbitten foot and rub you out the way I'd rub out a spit gob on an parquet office floor. . . . "

Drifting off again, he so passionately desired an end to all thought, circulation, breathing, to his melancholy pain-racked heartbeat—a final dulling of feeling in every cell in his body—that his passion produced the opposite effect—the sort that always astonishes children who, frantic to blow out a tiny blaze, just fan the treacherous flame and then in absolute terror run to grownups for help.

Frightened by this surge of strength, he focused his inner

gaze on the trembling (and it was clear just what thoughts were causing that) flame of a candle so slender that its waxy slip of a body was almost melting away to nothing in the murk of his imagination, while the little vermilion tongue and the little blue shadow within (shaped like a goatee with its soft wedge pointing upward) flickered alone in the murk.

He was trying to keep from blowing it out, and his breath was growing fainter, weaker—as he was either falling asleep or actually dying—when his snow-blanketed body suddenly sensed pressure—a slight, almost weightless but still tangible tread. And he heard a weak, barely audible rasp, the huff-and-puff of something breathing. But he lay still.

Then . . . "This obviously isn't human . . . " then . . . "Has that green slime sniffed my death out after all, at the most critical point?"

Then some sort of creature started scrabbling at the snow on top of the mask and just under it, where it met Helium's neck, and Helium, with ever growing revulsion, began to sense someone or something's rapid, insistent, and quite intentional movements.

He was sure that a rat, or several rats, were scuffling all over him. . . . "When there was a strong hand at the helm (Gorby and his ilk be damned) for decades the only rat anybody saw was Suslov" . . . and suppressing a spasm of nausea, he was about to prepare himself the way people prepare themselves for the worst . . .

But suddenly the movements stopped and he heard greedy —low, lusty, broken only by a gurgling growl—chomping.

Helium immediately—and with unexpected joy—surmised that it was a hungry, freezing stray kitten shaking his whole body with its shivering, and that the little beastie was bolting down bits and pieces and globs of all the tasty stuff Helium's imperial beauty had furiously splattered all over his kisser— which had of course run down his collar, stuck to his clothes, wormed into the folds, clung . . . .

Oh Lord, how perfect are Thy . . . it wasn't clear where it came from, but for the first time in Helium's life, he heard himself give an involuntary wail of happiness and gratitude— to whom or what, he didn't know—"It *wasn't* a rat, no rats, it was a kitten, a kitty, the very one that stole the sprat from the Soviet rats . . . let him eat . . . eat up, little one, don't let good food get lost in the murk and snowbanks of shortfall . . . here, just left of my cheekbone, it smells of cold cuts, and my shirt is all covered with shreds of pork, though I bet the skin is going to be damn crunchy for your little choppers, it's so cold. . . . I suspect this will last your little belly for a couple of days any- way . . . try some smoked fish, kitty, here under the mask something smells of sturgeon too, or maybe it's that roquefort from the Central Committee's last reserves . . . chomp away, my accidental graveside friend . . . finish off the Empire's left- overs here in the snow . . . I'd have a little nosh with you, no, I'd have a snort and then we'd have ourselves a snack, just you and me together . . . I think there's a juicy chunk of ham here inside my jacket . . . chow down, brother . . . if cat is born—it soon meow, as Genghis Khan said over Dmitri Donskoy's cra- dle. . . . Ah, I could use a drink right now, and you could too!"

Helium didn't stir for fear of disturbing the kitten, who was choking but still furiously snapping up some scrap, just in case, and growling at some foe and swallowing it all without chew- ing, but then Helium pushed away some snow with his free hand, groped for his pocket and just managed to reach the asphalt with the stiffened fingers of the hand he was lying on;

he fumbled around, addressed a prayer to something or other, and at first couldn't quite believe that he'd happened on the rounded shape of a bottle.

He couldn't quite believe it, and figured that his melancholy sense of touch was having quite understandable delusions. But no, it *was* his bottle . . . Oh Lord, how perfect are Thy works . . . again his whole being, without making any connection between their music or their meaning or anything else, breathed out these words which had been gathering dust in his memory . . . it *was* his bottle, which the snowplow had tossed from the roadway along with him.

Sensing danger, the kitten suddenly went still. True, the hunger proved substantially stronger than the fear, or even the terror that bends any cat into a horse-collar arc with bulging, sparking eyes and makes it hiss at you in that surprising form.

It went on chewing, choking, and swallowing, as if it had already dismissed all of reality's alarming, muddled signals, and its behavior was intelligent in the highest degree, despite the risk now approaching critical levels.

Helium had taken all this in. Mentally he congratulated the kitten on its scorn for the usual instinctive fears as compared to the irresistible attraction to a pathetic scrap of lifesaving chow.

Wincing from pain, he raised the bottle to his lips. But before he could unscrew the cap with his teeth, the bottleneck clipped the stupid mask . . . . "So much for presenting this to some Gabriel García Márquez, friend of Trotskyism and Stalinism stupidtaneously—this reinforced-cat-chemically-straightened-sheepdip-Brezhnev coiffure . . . to think that a writer and genius could be such an idiot . . . I'm no genius, I'm just a cynic, but even I always knew just what all the cock-and-bull was worth. . . . " He accidently clipped the mask again and then disgustedly shoved its chin up onto his forehead, spitting out some snow that had wasted no time getting into his mouth.

He cautiously shifted from his side to his back, supporting the bottle and kitten with one hand so that the poor little beggar wouldn't tumble off his chest into the snow. Only then, never even feeling the tin's coldness, did he unscrew the cap with his teeth.

The kitten, however, was clinging securely to the fabric of his coat.

Helium unscrewed the cap, and without the slightest idea how much whiskey was left, allowed himself one more frantic prayer. He prayed unthinkingly, not at all bothered by his own conscious hostility toward all such things, prayed with the naked sincerity of a man rousted out of bed by a housefire and forced to jump out his window before a crowd of curious onlookers.

"Lord," prayed Helium, "let there be just seventeen, no twenty, no thirty, no Lord just thirty-seven grams, twenty plus seventeen. . . . "

His wooden lips were still whispering something as he tipped the bottle up, but he couldn't feel a single drop flowing from it into his mouth. Only after his throat clutched at the whiskey poured directly into it did he—trying not to cough, not to gag, not to choke—hold his breath, tense his throat muscles and, in three careful swallows, down the whole mouthful.

Then he hearkened to the rapid, weightless spread of an encouraging, profoundly native warmth filling every last one of his internal cavities—not just chest, abdomen, and lungs but the spaces between ribs where the drafts of existence had just been whistling their melancholy tune, and those bod ily provinces—his unbearably aching toetips, for example—particularly remote from the heart.

This strange heat was more than some let-your-body-hair-down alcohol buzz. It reminded him of the homely, native warmth of his grandma's breath, when she used to raise the funnel of Helium's handknit mittens to her lips, and breathe warm air into them, put one mitten back on her grandson's hand, then do the same with the other. . . . And both his palms would get prickly goosebumps of blessed, healing comfort, the way your throat feels after a spoonful of honey. . . .

The whiskey left in the bottle was even more than he'd prayed for. Trying not to think about his embarrassing prayer, he took another swig, and another. He felt bad for the kitten, who couldn't have even a drop to thaw out. The little beggar was lapping up something underneath Helium's collar, butting its icy button-nose against his neck, tickling his skin—almost making him laugh—with its hot, scaly tongue.

If he squinted, Helium could just make out the waif's skinny, dirty, black-and-white spine, every hair on it shaking and quivering. The shiver would seem to subside, then come back to hammer the little creature until its legs seemed on the verge of giving out.

23 HELIUM JUST COULDN'T lie there dumbly dying in the snow anymore. In general, it was as if he'd become detached from himself, although in his mind there lingered a certain embarrassment at the words he'd blurted out, the same words that had infuriated and bedeviled him so fatefully back in the pool.

Knowing that the awful pain was not dead, but just dormant deep in his side, under his ribs, waiting for the right moment to sink its claws into his nerves and flesh, he hesitated to get up.

He screwed on the cap and plunked the bottle one-handed into the snow. With the other hand he stroked the kitten.

Then he struggled to unbutton his coat, squirming at the villainous touch of clumps of snow stuck to his arms and legs. He pried away the kitten's tenacious paws and pushed its shivering body in deep under his coat, under his arm, to where his hand felt some traces of his own body heat.

The kitten immediately burrowed in deeper, tighter, into the coatsleeve where the fit was so close that it couldn't even open its eyes. It lay flush against arm and sleeve. It probably even got drunk right away on the relative warmth of this blessed place and on the near presence of living, benign flesh-and-blood, a primal, domestic trust of which had always flowed in its veins.

Soon Helium could feel a struggle going on in the kitten's body—shiver against purr.

The shivering went menacingly still, as if listening to the initial (so meek, so polite) purring rhythms, in which there sounded a clear invitation to neighborliness and compromise. Apparently the self-important shiver was rather stung by the infamous diplomacy of "dialogue" and gave the kitten such a jolt from eartips to pawtips that it took a minute for the animal to cope with it.

It seemed strange and, to Helium's shame, rather funny that the shiver somehow expanded the poor creature's puny body— as if that body were an inanimate sack being pumped up and inflated.

Still, the kitten managed to hold off the shiver, to calm it, and curled up in a ball once again. Once or twice the purr seemed about to catch, but stalled.

Helium had never felt for, never cheered on anyone or anything, although he *was* good-natured and responsive around children and dumb animals.

He had never owned an automobile, sheerly out of lack of interest in human reason's romantic discovery of its own technical potential and abilities, and he always felt a frank and malicious glee in wintertime, when right beneath his apartment windows car owners—faint with annoyance, despair, and hatred of the USSR Seal of Quality stamped on their listless engines and unfeeling batteries—suffered for hours trying to to start up their gelid engines.

But it was with a true fan's passion that he took in the kitten's efforts to crank up its chilled motor so that it could catnap serenely in the wilderness of this world. Helium's heart was practically banging on his ribs as he followed the dramatic action in this skirmish between the rude shiver and the courteous purr now raging inside the kitten's tiny body. Now the shiver had shut things down again. And again the kitten's tiny cylinders stubbornly began popping and chugging. . . . And again the damn thing that was, by the way, trying to sink its hooks into his body too, shut the purr down. . . . No, no . . . again the purr caught, it caught. The shiver was trying to throw its monkey wrench into the kitten's works, but the kitten rasped and huffed, sputtered out, hissed like wet kindling in a stove, sneezed, sparked, refused to turn over . . . put-put-purrrr-pop-purr-rrr-rr . . .

The kitten finally fought off the shiver and started purring, but there was less meekness and courtesy in what had initially been the softest of throaty little sounds. And now the cat was revving its purring motor, starting with one, then two, then three and finally four cylinders . . . put-put-put-poppop-purr-rr-rrurr—unfazed by the now clearly subdued and somewhat dazed shiver.

Finally the purr won out in all the kitten's extremities, except for eartips, paws, and tail, where the shiver had crawled in retreat and where, apparently, it had decided to hunker down and shudder to the last.

But by now the kitten couldn't have cared less. It had drifted off to sleep and providential respite from a cruel infancy.

And suddenly Helium realized he was crying. He wasn't sobbing. There was no catch in his throat. Both his eyes were already watery, most likely from the stormy darkness and blinding wind, but the salt of an unshed tear that, like in childhood, lent the mood of the moment a taste of sweetly unresolveable hurt and despair, stung the eye that was bruised and glued shut.

It was only his heart that was clenched in the dumb, wordless weeping that ravages the brain, hampers breathing, and informs the lonely person's entire organism with an insatiable pity for its own sorry self.

All Helium's thoughts, every single one, now huddled together in the narrow spaces of his heart. They were silent and appreciative, like refugees or exiles in a chance shelter who try not to be tiresome, not to pester their long-suffering hosts with one word too many, one request too many, one idle remark too many.

There was such shock in the forced silence of his thoughts— shock at their own indigence, bitter sorrow having to seek refuge under an alien roof, such unbearably clear understanding of how vain life's toils and troubles really were—but there was at the same time such a sense of salvation and deliverance from something so terrible that Helium's thoughts wept there within his heart the way survivors of a fire, fortunate in their misfortune, weep in remembrance of everything random chance has just turned to soot and ashes.

And his heart clenched and shrank the way the rest of him had clenched and shrunk from his own powerlessness and his inability to help (with anything other than encouragement and body heat) this other small being quiet the cruel shiver and hateful despair of abandonment.

Suddenly, just as it sometimes happens in the bodies and souls of sobbing children, a fit of laughter seized Helium. The kitten's motor stalled immediately, and this tickled Helium even more because what had made him laugh in the first place was this very waif—or rather, a thought directly related to it.

And this was the thought that seemed to soothe his weeping heart and to michievously whisper to the kitten, "Buddy, little cat, it's almost like you're resting in the bosom of Abraham, like you're taken under Jesus' wing."

Once upon a time, expressions like that would have been simply unthinkable for Helium, most legitimately and principally unthinkable.

To keep from bothering the sleeper, Helium tried to quash his laughing fit—something not everyone can do, and some people, as they get more and more wound up, are suddenly surprised by the unanticipated but firmly established fact of their own hysteria.

Then he rolled back on his side and tried to get up, but his hand, then his foot just plunged deeper into the snow, and floundering around in search of solid ground was something he wasn't up to at the moment. Pain shot through his side and his thigh.

Somehow he was certain that he wasn't bleeding, even though he'd taken a good knock and maybe even broken some bones. One hand was no use at all, since it was supporting the kitten inside his coat.

Still, the liquor had perked him up, distracted him thanks to his newfound love for his feline neighbor, and fighting off the the pain and chill, and he was about to scramble—cautiously— out of the snowbank . . .

24

BUT SUDDENLY he heard the sound of young, boozy mobster voices.

These were clearly urban punks of the new, post-perestroika ilk who would think nothing of slashing your lights out or (out of nothing but dark curiosity or perverted passion for felonious innovation) stripping some helpless person bare in subzero weather and raping her—or him, whichever.

Helium knew that the only language these punks would understand was bravado and cruelly preventive force, but he was completely unarmed, and the street was deserted.

"I guess I could break the bottleneck off, just in case, and slash the first one that gets close with the jagged edge, and the rest of them would turn tail, but I probably haven't got the strength left, and besides it would be a shame to waste good liquor . . . . "

He drew his collar in even tighter, covered his face with the Brezhnev mask and flopped back sideways into the snowbank so that the kitten would be as comfortable as possible. And then he settled down to wait for the punks—que sera, sera.

A couple of days back, he'd never have doubted that, in a similar situation, the demons and imps would have concocted some stunning maneuver and dealt with the punks in the most (for the punks) unexpected fashion.

But on this uncanny evening, late on Christmas Eve, Helium's hatred for the unholy vermin who had first befouled his whole life and then dutifully watched the hell over him, seemed to turned to insurmountable revulsion, and he would rather have meekly let himself be robbed or maybe even murdered than summon a single demon for help. If he'd never before stooped to ask them to get involved in any of his business, then he wasn't going to start now.

In the meantime there was an insistent little itch somewhere in his brain, something painfully trying to place that "pig plot," but by now he was in no mood to try and calmly root around in his memory.

For an instant he remembered how, five years earlier, while literally writhing in hungover despair at his loveless existence, he almost fell to his knees, almost prayed to a demon—a little

gobbet enthusiastically fussing around a Veuve Cliquot cork—
to grant his lost soul just one molecule of genuine love for some
modest personage, someone as exhausted as he was by the
useless procession of nights and days. He might have prayed,
prayed out of sheerest despair, and that unholy crew would
probably have started stitching together some sweet, sentimental plot for him. But now, who knows why, it occurred to him
that it was *another* power—not that green scum—he should be
asking to grant him love, if of course that power did obtain, and
even if it obtained in a form highly mysterious yet suggestive of
its omnipotent and miraculous involvement in the lives of unhappy humans as well as the depressingly unclear purposes of
history. . . . Helium even gave a chuckle at the thought of what
fateful outrages and perversions these demon recruits to his
innocent matchmaking efforts toward capital improvement of
his unbearable life might have had in store.

"But maybe I should pray to . . . but what could I pray
for . . . Love? . . . Too late . . . Salvation . . . Gentlemen, let's be
serious. . . . I may be a half-frozen turd here, but I'm not that
peabrain Nina Andreeva either, with a mind as frigid as dry ice,
measure it Celsius or Reaumur either one. . . . I don't give a
damn for the principles and honor of a service career . . . or a
rat's ass for how bankrupt scientific atheism in-a-single-country-
taken-individually really is . . . that prayer popped out of my
mouth that one time—pure accident, nerves . . . after all, the
archetype of primitive horror does force an instinctive cry for
help out of the breast and into the empty heavens . . . it's nothing
but psychology, pure and simple . . . and it wasn't salvation I
prayed for anyway, I just needed a drink . . . praying for a second
time, true, would be ridiculous . . . we don't attend youth fel-

lowship at the House of Religious Renaissance, Brezhnev District, thank you very much . . . and besides after everything that's happened between us it would hardly be civil to keep asking with such unprincipled insolence . . . I wasn't born in a barn, after all . . . ehh, if it weren't for the kitten and the bruises I'd carve these jackals' belly buttons out with a bottleneck . . . "

So thought Helium, hoping that the drunken punks wouldn't notice a body lying there in the snowbank. But one of the young men suddenly yelled out:

"Hey! There's some stiff here in a sweet coat! Looks dead as a fuckin' doornail!"

The others came up and stood silent for a minute, apparently checking him out—was it a half-buried corpse there in the snowbank or a passed-out wino?

One of the modern youths suggested they boost the dead man's coat and haul ass so they wouldn't end up taking the rap for somebody else's stiff like that dipshit Kolya who got sent up on robbery and murder both.

Another one nudged Helium with one foot, then touched him with a hand, only to jump back and yell:

"Sumbitch! The stupid faggot's drunk! He's all over puke and there's some mush with eyebrows coming out his nose!"

"Yeah but that won't keep these rats from murdering me and gnawing on the bones . . . " thought Helium.

"Sweartagodnoshit I'll shake him down if you slip me a grand plus a can of sweetened condensed milk—hazard pay. We'll take the coat to a dry cleaner—not a state one, to Monya's, where they owe us. They won't rat . . . "

"Mr. Suit's got import trou and kickers too. Can't be retired, maybe a writer suckin' union tit."

"Nah, they never get this shitass drunk. They're all business-men."

"So if he's dying for real and kicks off?"

"Well who the fuck cares—let him croak! All the more hu-manitarian sweet milk and salt pretzels for you!

"Ha-ha-ha!"

"Hah, fuckin' ay! Busolya said something bright! We've got a regular fuckin' Einstein here!"

"Busolya, you're the one we oughtta off, you stupid asshole. After all that here we are stuck without wheels and you're cutting deals, faggot, with your faggot head up your ass."

"You try figuring out when the stinking cunt's gonna start up and when she isn't," Busolya snarled back. "All that heap's good for is standing in line . . . it's worthless for jobs. . . . "

He took a step closer to Helium and plunged into deep snow. His comrades pulled him out, joking and cursing, and decided to go round to the street side of the snowbank to get at the freezing man.

But even at this critical moment Helium for some reason didn't remember that he had anything of value hidden in his pocket. Feeling neither pain nor fear, he lay perfectly still, wait-ing his chance.

If there were any thoughts at all still running through his mind, there were no longer thoughts of himself—he didn't give a damn about anything—but of the sleeping kitten's peace-and-quiet. And since he had nothing else to lose, he was mustering all his strength, waiting for the thugs to take one last step before he leaped to his feet with a terrible, headsplitting bellow and broke the bottle against the streetlight's iron base. . . . these douchebags won't get off cheap, sending me to the next world. That's for sure. . . .

Helium had just enough time to think that if it hadn't been for the kitten he might have tried provoking the punks himself, tried asking for a bullet or a knife but forcing them to do him in such a way that the cops could track them down and the specter of a murdered man would follow the assholes all the way into prison and out again. . . . "Now there's a little black humor for the posthumous comedy of my worthless life. . . . but then again, how to get the cops onto the scent. . . . Jagged cuts on their rat-nose faces maybe . . . You can't stitch up tears like that by yourself. . . . They'd have to roust out the whole Sklifasov-sky Emergency Clinic . . . and pay them overtime . . . but what a boring, stupid hassle . . . who needs it . . . dirty, bloody, damned. . . . a frigging mess . . . He's personally damned to hell because there's practically no one else left to damn us. . . . In the end there isn't any proof that He doesn't exist, if you consider it scientifically and civilly rather than in the categories of my Sove godlessness and the over-the-edge license of this scum . . . I should admit this like a gentleman, but then what sort of gentleman can be a scientific atheist? . . . as far as these restructured slugs go . . . well, my fellow citizens, you should have used a flamethrower on this stinking back-water toilet of a system, re-fucking-structured it so that the shit—along with your ass-wipe teachings—would flood the whole, yes the *whole* globe our president's out there trotting . . . and how *would* Mik-hail row that little boat ashore . . . ?"

Helium was saved from the various options his situation presented—that is, a fight, mugging, death—by that very same lit-up Mercedes owner who had knocked him down and then, like a jerk, left the scene of vehicular assault on a decidedly dead-drunk individual.

Apparently the driver's conscience had been bothering him

and, when he'd sobered up some, come to his senses and consulted with sensible friends, he had decided to come back—just in case, or maybe for some reason unknown even to himself—to the scene of the unfortunate incident.

He certainly wasn't planning on foolishly sticking his neck out for a breath test or a legal smack upside the head, but he was at least behaving more or less like a person sincerely distressed by the incident, one with enough self-respect that, for decency's sake, he couldn't help but take a risk and try to seek out, in this deadly situation, at least some tiny possibility of assuaging his guilt by taking independent action.

It's just too bad that there wasn't a single casual onlooker there to idly notice this person's behavior.

What that onlooker might have seen in that behavior was a touching challenge by independent, human, individual conscience (even the most rumpled and bedraggled excuse for it) to the petty, daily fear which—more than anything else—has for decades quashed and continues to quash in the teeming mass of the frayed and frazzled, indignant Russian people any effective objections to the mustached, hog-jowled or bushy-browed demon-face of their ridiculous regime.

And how could an onlooker with at least some mind and taste not rejoice and delight in this weirdly marvelous (albeit small) sign of hope that the beautiful and ugly human race hasn't been terminally befouled by its history of disease, that unseen, celestial birds of conscience continue to weave their oft-ruined, burnt-out, spat-upon nests in human souls; that one by one each unseen bird, miraculously delivered from traps, snares, and cages, hatches the unseen but enterprising chicks of all our inevitable impulses and acts; she flutters over them, feeds them—sometimes with the last of her strength—feeds all this timid and vulnerable, easily cowable fledgling guard with celestial food, right under the nose of the stunningly shameless specter of our epoch's "collective reason" hanging grimly over them—that is, over all of us.

So the man who had "in his cups" run down Helium had returned to the scene of his not-so-accidental-crime, but not in his damaged imported beauty. He was in another foreign make.

He braked a little when he noticed the pack of midnight jackals obviously creeping up on what might be a still-living person—since the blow that had tossed his victim into the snow-bank might have been, God willing, a fairly benign one, in which case the drunk, as a rule, has to deal with a few bruises and breaks rather than Madame Pathologica Anatomica Morgue.

Helium didn't see the approaching "chariot," nor did he yet comprehend or sense the shape of what was approaching—which (it would not be superfluous to note) when embodied in some incomprehensible incident, is more often than not frag-mented into any number of parts, and it takes a great poet or clairvoyant to gather these fragments and imagine—whether on paper or in the madness of inspiration—the shape in all its wholeness.

In the meantime the cold, hungry, not-quite-dead-drunk jackals, scenting fabulous (given the foul weather) prey, con-forming perfectly to a pack instinct, without consulting one another, instantaneously restructured their rapacious plans, their allocation of hunting territory and sequence of action.

What frigging good was a puke-covered overcoat when there was the scent of real loot in the snowy midnight air—this fancy set of nouveau riche wheels! And they had to act on the run, animal-like, instinctively dividing up the various tasks of the hunt, giving the prey no time to think, surrounding it on all sides.

They'd been taught all this long ago, as children, by the purely ecologically-minded camera safaris on TV's *Travel Club* as well as by the perverse promptings of those of our own brutish natural origins that stand a gloomy lookout deep inside certain lumbering types, especially when those types are drawn into extremist mobs and criminal gangs.

In times of general chaos and hostility, like these, all this morose brutishness is aroused, possessed to act, to maim and maul, to make mischief, to make good all the losses suffered over its long hibernation in the dens of wild natures, snowed in, so to speak, by fear and forced obedience to rule of law.

Helium was lying face down in the snow. When he heard their quick, wolfish, snow-muffled flight, he knew that the punks must have retreated and were speeding toward some other prey.

He couldn't seem to move his head enough to match his only good eye to the slit in the mask. Then when his almost totally numb and frostbitten nose landed in an indentation on the inside of the mask, he realized that both eyeholes were plugged with snow.

Then, like it or not, he had to discard all caution. With one benumbed finger he first felt for the shaggy "reinforced cat," then poked through one of the eyeholes, shrinking from the cold that seared his tender eyelid and seemed the piercing kiss of Death itself.

But the snow on his eyelid melted immediately, flowed round the lid, and a droplet of water slid from his eyelashes onto his cheekbone and from there to the flare of one nostril, from which it plopped into the corner of his mouth; he licked off the droplet with the tip of a clumsy tongue and suddenly felt this unimaginable trifle drawing a generous warmth from somewhere in the region of his heart right up to his iced-over head.

This wave of warmth, which in its turn heated up the edges of his despondent (with good cause) brain, again evoked in the freezing man's entire being the same, unfamiliar state that had inexplicably arisen in him once before—not merely with the miraculous appearance of the kitten or the disappearance of thirty-seven grams of whiskey down his thirsty throat.

If it hadn't been for his passion to see what would happen next, then again that line which had suddenly floated up from memory and been forced out by his whole being—"Oh Lord, how perfect are Thy works!"—would have expressed and formulated his inner amazement at the indisputable existence of a certain Higher Order, into which even he had been fitted.

Fitted, fit, and therefore by virtue of the status granted him by existence, entitled to a vital ration of divine good. Which meant he hadn't been passed over, for all the unimaginable incongruity of his paltry prayer for a drop of liquor and deliverance from the rats when compared to the countless cares of the boundless Universe—if this drop had trickled down into his chilled gullet and a little chunk of ice melted on his solitary eyelid, then indeed he too still had a particle of universal warmth, applicable also to private individuals.

This state had already taken root in his soul and the only reason he didn't cry out the words of the poem was that he was struck dumb by joy that the warmth inside him hadn't faded entirely, that in the depths of his flesh the emergency distribution of lifesaving body heat—hoarded with kindly fellow feeling by his eye, for example, for the thinskinned eyelid not swollen into a shiner—was in progress.

In general, Helium's conscious mind couldn't help but feel stirrings of gratitude to "that gomer"—that is, not to the marshal-and-author himself, but to the mask—for at least partially protecting the defenseless skin on his face from the blizzard's blasts, from the cruel touch of the wintry elements and the chilly breath of the street, so murderously indifferent to the fate of an injured, freezing man.

The cold was beginning to pluck at his wet eyelashes. He rubbed away the tiny ice pellets on their tips; kept, as they say, his eye peeled, and suddenly that one eye (all alone and feeling a certain melancholy and genuine awkwardness at the unaccustomed absence of its partner) took in a scene made totally absurd by its utter unpredictability, which had been ripening in the weird greenery of Chance and now dropped unexpectedly right in Helium's lap.

The driver of the foreign car saw, of course, several jackals running out into the roadway and signaling, as if pleading for him to stop and help their comrade. The comrade himself was faking either illness or injury and he lay sprawled artistically in the street, while another jackal was dragging his supposedly insensible body by one foot, in the direction of the approaching car.

The driver anxiously flashed his dazzling brights, and flipped on his yellow fog lights. He must have sensed some obviously threatening intent in their playacting, or else he had simply had time to catch some expression of jackal-like brutality in the figures spilling out onto the street, and see in their faces a lobo readiness for the most unspeakable acts.

The driver didn't honk as he slowed, because he didn't want to attract attention. As it was, he himself was already floundering in the grip of danger and an already committed crime. There was no way to maneuver at any speed on the drifted-over, windblown street.

He could of course ram one of the stalking jackals with his

bumper and then peel away, the way he'd just peeled away from the would-be suicide, but he wasn't quite rotten enough for such a decisive way out of the brutal ambush.

That he was being ambushed by these feral, thoroughly chilled and probably liquor-starved jackals—this he didn't doubt. And he didn't have time to scan the snowbanks along the street for his incidental victim. Stopping and opening the door to clarify the situation would mean, in the best of cases, being mugged and tossed out of his car into the cold.

He braked tentatively, as if to double-check his suspicions by looking into the faces and forms of the jackals encircling him. The car continued moving. The more cautiously, quietly, and sneakily it tried to roll by, the more audible was the innocent, trusting squeak of newfallen snow under its tires.

And now two pairs of lobo paws had latched onto the door handles. And the punk who had been lying down in his sick-man act jumped up and launched himself at the hood of the car.

The street, by the way, wasn't entirely deserted at that moment, but neither of the two passing vehicles—a taxi and a private car—even thought of braking or stopping to see what was happening. On the contrary—as if trying to save themselves from something horrible and loathesome, they were putting as much distance as possible between them and the putrid place.

The "sick man" flung himself onto the hood, managed to get a grip on the upper ridge of the hood, between the madly flapping windshield wipers, and everything concerning this gang's intentions became terminally clear to the driver. The car's motor let out a roar. The car itself bucked as it skidded forward, though the jolt was cushioned slightly by the snow on the asphalt. It dragged two of the lobos down the street with it, one of whom was already trying to smash out the side window with his pistol butt, to get at that uncooperative pigeon, that asshole, who'd get no mercy from . . . none . . . none . . . not after pulling this shit. . . .

He didn't shoot, for fear of the noise, the risk, or maybe for another reason altogether—that they'd used up all their bullets on an earlier job.

Like a living being, the car tried to shake off those clinging to it, but at first it dragged them cautiously, with obvious decency, trying not to hurt anyone, trying just to escape from everyone and everything into the protection of the night and storm. It was as if the car were still hoping that the jackals' bare paws would soon lose their grip, that the metal's searing cold would soon throw them off their treasure hunt.

But once the car sensed that that play wasn't going to work, it let out a howl of rage and spun 360 degrees; the right-hand jackal flew sideways but managed to grab the door handle again. The left-hand jackal was still holding on. First they were both running, then being dragged in the snow, then the car leaped forward, braked sharply and flipped around in such a way that the jackal pounding his pistol butt against the window was thrown under the back wheels. There was the crunch of bone. In his shock and pain he probably didn't even have time to scream. The car bumped and bounced over him as if it were crossing a punky log bridge.

The jackal on the other side couldn't keep hold either. He flew off and tumbled head over heels once or twice. But the one who lay plastered to the hood was still holding on by the ridge. The driver stepped on the gas, the car roared again and skidded diagonally from one side of the street to the other, directly at Helium, who at that instant was scared not so much for himself as for the kitten.

His savior turned the wheel sharply, apparently hoping that the creep sprawled on his hood would have to let go and would fly the hell off into a snowbank. And he did let go, as the car jerked so forcefully and abruptly that it jolted his body from the hood, tossed it up, flipped it over in the air and slammed it headfirst against the streetlight's iron base.

And it was these last few words that started jingling insistently in Helium's brain, just like the words of some stupid song that lands deep in the folds, in between the convolutions of the brain, like a bug in a rug . . . against the streetlight's iron base . . . against the streetlight's iron base. . . .

In general, we should note that Helium, a music lover all his life, was at times sensitive to some musical meaning in events. It always manifested itself in his inner hearing either rhythmically or melodically, and, naturally, in moments of self-willed harmonic development of these essential qualities which are characteristic not only of music—this he understood—but also of all noisily extant nature and the world of people living throughout history at nature's expense.

Therefore what he sensed in what had just happened was a corrosive air of ugly, criminalized reality—the air of a gangster opus bursting through time like the stinking flow from rusted-out sewer pipes. It had burst out, and was slowly flooding all spheres of human contact—without exception—with the foul-smelling liquid of our own excrement, rising even to the bars of the Imperial Anthem, and down into this sludge what would seem to be the most important notes ever to exist in the Russian historical atmosphere were pathetically and squeamishly dipping their drowning, delicate black-heeled feet—these rhythms of empire in a dark alleyway . . . did I not groom your chestnut mane . . . against the streetlight's iron base . . . .

Helium heard no departing groan come from the jackal-soul, no death rattle from the body. Perhaps the whine of the tires and the roar of the motor had drowned them out, as the car, breaking out of ambush, vanished in clouds of snow into the gloomy underbrush of the city.

The one jackal left unmaimed by the hunt didn't even think to look out for his comrade who, legs fractured, was lying in the street in silent convulsions, or to find out what had happened to stupid Busolya, whose foolhardy head had slammed against the streetlight's base.

The car disappeared from view, just as if Helium's observing eye had never seen its skirmish with the jackals, as if the whole turn of events had been part of some strange dream rather than the fantastical ravings of "jazzed" reality itself, the roof of which had suddenly been blown off by time-gone-crazy, time singing a jingling gangland song.

25 SUDDENLY HE EITHER thought, or felt, that the storm and cold were about to blow what was left of his strength right out of his body, that in another minute or two the vertiginous emptiness which had formed underneath him would turn even more gelid and bottomless, and that he wouldn't be able to fight off the strange temptations of overall weakness and would surrender to it, closing his seeing eye too. . . . "This cat is fucked, no more warm shits for him . . . "

The instinct for self-preservation that instantly turns a human being into an intelligent animal whose every movement is informed with lightning-fast purpose probably is just this—a moment of union between thought and feeling.

His comparison of himself and the kitten, the despairing wail of that cynical, cruel saying which had instantly washed away the gangland sludge of events just past and suddenly acquired the most the most compassionate of all possible meanings, set off in Helium another wave of vital gaiety.

The purring kitten itself, asleep on the left-hand side of his breast, its paw ticklishly stretched into his armpit, simply added a certain gay, almost comically feverish enthusiasm to that wave. If it hadn't been for the regular purr-purr of the little bodily motor's revolutions, the man's own heart might have up and stopped out of weakness, despair, and the pain he felt for everything in his body that was bruised, battered, aching and chilled to the marrow. But as it was—as it was, it was almost funny, his weakened organism having a tiny twin and sidekick there shuddering—knocking, vibrating for all it was worth, to the beat, to the beat, the beat . . . of his friend of his friend in need. . . .

Helium never even pondered what sort of brute strength had suddenly given him breath, had forced him to his feet, and—for all his absolute reluctance to move at all—raised him up, led him out of the snowbank, outright blunted the pain and simply carried him over the snow-swept street, directing him almost blindly to the nearest doorway.

His eye was in no condition to observe much of anything, but it did manage at the last minute to take in the street scene where the wind and storm were still running amok. One injured man was crawling off somewhere, anywhere, just off the street, his hands scrabbling at the street, shoveling the snow and ice out from under himself. Beneath the streetlight sprawled an unnaturally twisted body with a smashed-in skull. The snow underneath it was black. The single unhurt jackal had already taken off.

Helium shuddered in fleeting empathy with the two victims whose run-in with chance had—no getting round it—served them right.

But then he was distracted from them both by that all-powerful, animal (honorable person or no), reaction which, as it leads (who knows, perhaps not without regret) the wolf, the deer, the goose, the monkey out of the hunter's reach, forces the fleeing creature to leave its wounded and fallen—but not yet finished-off—fellow creatures behind.

26

HE HAD TROUBLE opening the door of the nearest entry-way, which a spiteful wind was stubbornly pushing shut. There was an awful rumbling and groaning and cracking as behind him the wind slammed shut this door into another life, and itself stayed outside to work its spite.

And so he tumbled into the gloomy, stagnant reek of half-lit public space—toward which, for all the insignificance of the occasion, he felt an enormous gratitude. At the same time he realized straight away that this feeling of limited protection and sudden warmth would immediately turn to one of even greater homelessness and listlessness in the chill that would no doubt sniff him out here too and pounce on him before he'd even had a chance to thaw out and then. . . .

" . . . truly, Helium Revolverovich, the irreversibility of the everyday vileness of all that is shameful before eternity *is* our reality of hell-on-earth . . . " . . . a certain father made a direct hit with that one, in one debate . . . now *those* are the fathers I should have trusted myself to . . . well, and whose shameful stupidity and low-down tricks set up (under somebody's else's byline of course) that sleazy sensation in our prostitute press over the "opportunistically obscurantist exercises of a certain pseudo-scholar who is attempting to foist his own interpreptation of the word 'obogret' on our innately secular-materialist Russian etymology," what goes around comes around, here's what I get for his "obogret"* and the voluptuous sin of a fall to the lowest depths, into a bucket of my own warm spit . . . that's the way it's been my whole life, my whole life . . . well well, looks like a shit-sweeper or a homeless dumpster rat are aristocrats in starched collars compared to old Helium . . .

The kitten started tossing and turning in discomfort. This utterly distracted Helium from his stumbling about in the fusty corners of his private hell, which had suddenly (but, it would seem, not accidentally) declared its presence at what was perhaps the most pitiful, vulnerable, and difficult moment of the errant man's existence.

He groped blindly for a radiator, the sort you might find in the foyer of an old building. One hand found it, but there'd been no hint of decent heat there in ages—probably not since one of the recent winters still janitored by our damned-doomed low-rent-but-still-imperiously-wheezing-on-its-deathbed System. "All the same, I should stay a while, warm up as best I can . . . catch my breath, though there's not much left, my fingers haven't got any feeling in them, my teeth are chattering, lips trembling, knees buckling, heart'd be sputtering if it weren't for the kitten . . . lucky I stuck that whiskey in my pocket . . . Oh Lord how perfect are thy . . . "

Then he thought about the vermin, and still believing in its invulnerability and omnipotence, said, or rather (since his

*The word "obogret" means to warm up, but happens to contain "bog"—God.—TRANS.

tongue had gone dumb from something other than drink) mooed out: "Come on out, you little buggers I'll squash you all over the walls you heathen sons of bitches!!! . . . "

And although the half-light of the foyer was somehow even grimmer and more impenetrable than its mother-darkness, Helium scouted round for the plasma-spinners and plumes that had had a habit of materializing even in absolute blackness. Then he shoved the furry-browed mask up onto his forehead, struggled to unscrew, with his teeth, the cap which his own saliva had frozen to the mouth of the bottle and, taking a gulp of liquor, waited with sinfully passionate anticipation for some active support for his chilled-through body.

He swallowed, held his breath and felt a rush of bitter warmth moving from his palate, larynx, and esophagus down into his hoarfrosted lungs, down into his heart. For some reason the warmth stopped at his heart.

Then he started worrying about his lonely stomach, found a shred of cabbage frozen into the angle between the lapel and collar of his coat, raised it with two fingers to a snot-packed (just like when he was little) nostril, raised it in dashing Russian fashion to chase the sacred swig with a whiff of some lifesaving trash, but instead both eyes went black from the ice-bound misery of his nose, and something like smelling salts rocketed into his brain . . . passersby, the street, faces . . . flashed by . . . again the words darted back and forth, restoring themselves line by line, rhyme by rhyme . . . piece by ragged piece of the poem that for some reason was resolved to survive inside this dying man.

Grimacing from pain, he tossed the frozen shred of cabbage into his mouth and started chewing this chance bite, for his stomach's sake, all with the same feeling—tears, agitation— with which he'd taken shelter here from the merciless elements.

He chewed for a while, than squatted down underneath the staircase . . . they gave him a bed near the entrance . . . he then cast a grateful glance . . . he couldn't help thinking, or rather feeling . . . that . . . that . . .

This is what he felt. It suddenly came to Helium with a clarity behind which stood nothing other than the darkness it itself illuminated, the dark pit, irrevocability—it suddenly came to him that this *was* happiness—this gratitude for some pathetic trifle, like this practically glacial shelter, this warming swig, this shred of cabbage, this phenomenon of another small life plumped up against his own faltering heart.

"But how can it be," he thought first detachedly, then with growing excitement, "that some existential truth reveals itself to you only on the very edge of an abyss of clarity, in that last-minute cliffhanger over irrevocability, instead of when you're first given freedom to move toward all of that? What kind of Destiny is it that would deprive you of grateful vision at the reckless beginning of your lonesome road? I mean you passed blindly by all those countless little things that might have hourly, daily, yearly, made up your happiness, and you just now succeeded in seizing that priceless moment on . . . the death-night, the night city . . . just barely succeeded . . . but success is success . . . it's sweet in the dim light just barely falling on the bed . . . well, so what I had to lay down a whole life for such butterfly success . . . if I hadn't succeeded . . . but then I did . . . you might say it just up and threw me out of bed, out of the luxury of those arms . . . into the wind, the storm, the cold, some crazy car, right into those punks' clutches . . . but I didn't miss out, I didn't . . . it'd have been better of course if I'd succeeded in fathering some continuation of myself first, but . . . "

Suddenly the image of NN, of her form, her self, seemed to bring a timid, weak but clearly lifesaving warmth to somewhere in the region of his heart.

In the sweet smallness of a moment remembered from another life, she was quickly and deftly chopping a head of cabbage and he was slowly, slowly rolling the sleeve of her white sweater up to the shoulder while the sharp knife in that hand was playfully going zhik-zhik-zhik . . . and then he rolled the other sleeve up from the other hand, the one holding the sturdy cranium of the white cabbage on the cutting board just like a head on a block, rolled it up, and for the first time in his life was pierced by a flesh-and-blood yearning to see an oh-so-tender likeness between the skin of a child's, *his* child's, cheeks, and the skin of NN's dizzyingly feminine, overheated shoulders. . . . Then she took her fists and forced the entire cabbage, with a crunch, into a small antique oak barrel, and her hands sank silently into the coolness of the light-orange brine. . . . I've taken a sedative dose . . . and cry as I tug at my kerchief . . . now there's someone who knows how to pickle . . . ohhh, she did quite the number on my face . . . there they slice and chop and pepper . . . and put cloves in the marinade . . . that was another of his poems she liked to recite . . . I should have drowned back in that chlorinated hellhole . . . and under the cupola of that last bubble there would have been nothing left of unlucky Helium but one stinking little atom . . . and on top of it some plasmoid goonlet would have been balancing and dancing a jig. . . .

Helium, peeling open his glued-shut eye with some difficulty, again tried scanning the surrounding space "for lice," but again, nothing showed up in that eye except a droplet of moisture, quivering in the foreboding half-light.

The kitten had stopped purring and slept the sleep of the dead, twitching occasionally—but probably from the sweet dreams of childhood rather than the bone-chilling cold of life.

The pain in his bruised side and the pricking sensation all over his body had either left Helium, or else he was leaving them. It was starting to seem as if he and the rest of the world (and he and something inside him too) were fast moving apart.

Then he again shut his eye tightly, as if to keep his very soul from leaving its cool but cozy refuge for the outside, from crossing the ice-glazed threshold into reality, where there was nothing left for it, and where he personally had not one damn thing, not one person . . . nobody, nothing, damned. . . .

He couldn't tell how much time he'd spent half-adrift like that, and when he heard voices he felt a little disgruntled and annoyed, like someone suddenly jostled for no reason—and he also felt and recognized the repulsive shiver creeping directly from the kitten's body into his own.

This rotten little shiver started restructuring everything right off: it made the guts feel all the impossiblity of untying life's awful knot, it reduced the liver to a pathetic groan, smacked the heart around a few more times, sandpapered the left temple and squeezed the right one in a vise, mercilessly pinioned the groin and all its husbandry—which was already in a state of extreme dejection and utter delirium—in its icy grip.

"But most likely he'll kick off out on the street," said, not very confidently, an elderly and—judging by her voice— simple woman, continuing a discussion the beginning of which Helium had missed.

"That's his problem. One of them croaks—maybe the others won't be coming round again. They've smeared up the whole foyer top to bottom and now? We're supposed to shovel out all this crap? Yeah? Stinking winos," a younger individual spite-fully shrieked. "What is this, an apartment building or a brick shithouse?"

"And what if sometime they take your Mishka and drag him out feet first into the cold like the Armenians and Azeris were doing to each other, you dimwit, what then?"

"Well, Ma she doesn't give a shit for a living soul, me included," drunkenly blurted someone who was probably the inhuman individual's husband. "But vote against yanking Lenin's stiff out of its marble R&R and burying it in the clay of our new cultural—I mean lethal—space, well, fu-u-u-, well n-o-o problem, we'll just toss our greasy little washtubs high as the rooftops . . . most likely he'll ki-i-ick off out on the stre-e-e-t . . . and over one dark e-e-ey-y-yelash . . . a lock of gra-a-a-ay will fa-a-alllll."

"Shut your yap, you brainless hick. You're no better than the rest of these popeyed winos, drinkin' up our refrigerator coupon money. A cross between a lousebit faggot and a rotten rubber, that's all you are," hissed the spiteful one, practically fainting from absolutely sincere hatred.

Enjoying the laugh at his spiteful dearly-beloved and going on—out of drunken inertia—with his little number, the man objected:

"Whaddya need a fridge in the winter for anyway, huh? String some bologna from the veranda. . . . "

In the charming sound of this not entirely senseless phrase, which seemed to come from far, far away, Helium heard all the charm of Italian, which he'd once studied at the behest of a certain aggressive government agency, as part of preliminary Old Square plans for the latest hopeless psychic assault on the Vatican. . . . "I remember—on the steps of a Venetian palazzo where Vivaldi once lived—sharing a flask of Irish whiskey with a certain remarkable Leningra . . . with a Petersburg poet . . . he flew the editorial coop to chirp away at liberty. . . . I wouldn't mind downing a shot or two with him right here, right now. . . . we'd have a few laughs . . . I'd say to him: look, Lyosha, isn't it funny about Russian that all you have to do is add one sorry letter to the word zamer and there you have it zamer—zamerz. He stopped still—he froze. . . . "

"A fridge? What do I need a fridge for? 'Cause the food gets cut off the string, you ugly sonofabitch shit-for-brains. . . . "

"Misha, take a look, maybe the cops haven't hauled off the corpse and the crippled one yet? This'un over there—he's probably a stiff himself by now, we'll turn him over to the cops. We're not animals, are we? My Lord, Misha, you must have had your head up a certain place when you married this piece of trash."

"To my great regret, Ma, my head was drunk under the table along with the rest of me. And as far as the cops go—Mama, are you crazy? This suit's still got his tic-toc on and decent clothes. They'll roust him and shake him down, spit right in his bare belly button—and stick a kopeck in it like they did Filatkin. Here Filatkin went on TV, on *Man and the Law,* to show everybody his insulted-and-injured belly button, put it on display at the Manezh—but that didn't do shit. So there he is at every demonstration with his kopeck sticking out tails up. A man looks for justice in this world and what does he get? Squat— and the Procurator-General! Let the guy snooze—at least he had a merry Christmas."

"This is like something out of a jailhouse romance," thought Helium almost sentimentally.

"You can all go to hell! Scum! You've ruined the country!"

again shrieked the younger woman and then bawled at the top of her lungs, "Oh Lord, why hast Thou sent these damn democrats down upon us?"

"Why are believers forever pestering Him in vain, tugging at His sleeve with all their stupid little problems? Do they really suppose that He's got nothing better to do than hang around here in subzero weather and settle all their personal gripes on all counts, including the daily cartoon of our ridiculous political life? . . . But then again, if even a Serious unbeliever can appeal to him. . . . "

"Mish, let's go, dear, it's bedtime, I'll call the ambulance."

"Ha! HA! Ambulance! Well, Mama, you crack me up. You've tickled me right down to the belly button. . . . Sure, you just ring up the boys and say the liquor store's got a new shipment of rotgut—and they'll be screaming down here, sirens wailing—probably even forget to pull their uniforms on their fat asses . . . cracks me up. . . . "

"Let's go, Mish, don't make a scene, it's late. The activists are spouting off again. Guess the stupid faggots can't sleep. . . . "

From upstairs came the sound of resolute, just-awakened (or else insomniac) male voices. The words "police" and "arrest" came up more and more often in their debate, which had turned spitefully indignant, given the impossibility of turning into a growling order or an commanding bark.

Helium closed in on himself more snugly than ever. He was indifferent to it all. Of course he might have roused himself and explained that he wasn't some derelict wino, that he'd been hit by a car and that he and the kitten had just been saved from both rampaging hoodlums and unobliging cops. But he decided, with obstinate, hardy resentment, that since he'd dodged his demon helpers, he could just as well dodge the human ones, all the more because nobody here seemed the slightest bit inclined to help him out.

"On the contrary," he found strength enough for a smirk, "this whole crew's been bred on the sulphurous fumes of contempt for any kind of charity (not without my personal assistance, and let it be on my head), and they'll toss me and this starving orphan right the hell out of here. Expect this bunch to show the same mercy and sympathy for a crapped-out stranger that they would for themselves? . . . After all, I knew what pile of bullshit I was handing them, but, no, I kept on hammering away at these boobs that the problem of 'I and thou' was a crock of bourgeois scholasticism and the egotistical isolation of self from society, while 'I and we' was the indestructible, monolithic basis of our forward-looking Soviet morality. We need, I'd say, to pull the enormous, warm quilted blanket of *We* over the lonely, shivering *I*. Our blanket gives us *all* a feeling of sturdy shelter and inner peace. Gave us, rather. Now who's left to say a bardzo gracias, señores, for this piss-soaked, shit-caked blanket? Just me . . . 'I and We' . . . wee wee all the way home, except this little piggy has none . . . just hellholes and foundation pits. . . . So, Helium, these staunch Sovactivists are your own trained animal act, and you're just dead meat . . . you knew what you were covering yourself with, up to the ears— not that blanket, but the chill of an anthropological catastrophe, that's what you were covering yourself up with. . . . Even Genka Yanaev—who's the numbest of numbnuts—is warmer in his cell in Matroskaya Tishina than you are right now. I repent. I'm done for. But you, my fellow citizens and boobs, be damned yourselves for swallowing my line. Why didn't you just belch and heave all that shameless nonsense back at me, señores? After all, your papas weren't all very-revolutionary Revolvers, were they."

Judging from the building-activists remarks, they were all firmly and vengefully resolved to call in the police, inasmuch as their foyer had become a source of unforeseeable contagion, where "for example old-lady Mimzikova broke her hip last week when she slipped on a puddle of hooligan sperm."

After things in the foyer itself grew quiet again, Helium started imagining the police, the medics . . . the ambulance, passing by pavement and doorways and idlers, the bustle of night on the street, dived headlights first into the dark . . . but chiefly, what flashed through his mind was a revolting image of salvation, of this life continued . . . The floors of a state hospital . . . pneumonia . . . a pitiful gray hospital gown . . . a hell-ishly despairing gown migrating from one set of shoulders to another, and another . . . then his own . . . there and back again, heigh-ho, from the ward to the morgue we go we go from the morgue to the ward heigh-ho heigh-ho. . . .

A shudder of revulsion and loathing shook him so violently that the marshal-and-author mask slid down over his forehead. He tossed it to one side.

The minute he felt some signs of energy in his body, his nerves began to respond, and his whole body started throbbing and smarting from the bruising and the frostbite.

He stuck his hand under his coat lapel to borrow a little warmth from the kitten, "just until payday." But it gave a yowl at the touch of his cold fingers, growled in irritation and started tossing and turning, and Helium felt a certain irrational alarm for the sleepy creature.

Or rather, Helium was instantly transformed into the normal, intelligent animal for whom life is a series of necessary responses to the business of maintaining and preserving life itself, rather than idle—shall we say academic—timeserving in some featherbed department of the Scientific Research Institute for the Survival of Flora and Fauna of the (Former) USSR.

He could tell the poor creature was in for it, that they'd toss it the hell out by the scruff of its neck if they found it on him after he'd croaked or been taken in . . . "under Jesus' wing" . . . they'd toss it out to freeze, starve, die all alone, because that was what society was headed for anyway . . . the liberalization of shock privatization, the idiotic vacillation of a new leadership crazed with wolfish appetite, the murk of state ignorance, the new cannibal generation of jackal-hyenas—"kitty and me, we don't hold out much hope for any sudden improvement in the new man's brutal nature or the sanitary inspections of public toilets either one. . . . "

He quickly crawled out from under the staircase, and, to his great luck, didn't smell that most utterly depressing of all earthly smells—the whiff of frozen, stagnant urine.

Still on his knees, he began rubbing his palms together forcefully, not so much to warm them as to more equitably distribute their monstrous (damn-damn-damn) pain and sting to other parts of his body. Then, holding the bottle with difficulty, he lapped up the last few drops of whiskey and almost burst into sobs at the pitifulness of what was probably his farewell to alcohol—at the sorrowful, end-of-a-lifetime pitifulness of it all.

27 HE ALREADY KNEW what he had to do. And although the very thought of going out to face the cold, the wind, the snow, and the trouble skulking around practically every streetcorner threw him into absolute terror, and the regret that today, like a fool, he'd forgotten to cover his idiot head with his otterskin hat, a souvenir from a certain Kremlin reception, was just unbearable, but despite all this he somehow fought off his sickness at heart, leaned one shoulder against the door, poked his nose outside—and then quickly popped back in, away from the whistle and bite of the hostile weather standing guard, on duty, outside.

He realized right away that he'd be much more comfortable and protected walking in such windchill with the Brezhnev mask on. He went back to where it was lying under the staircase and donned it one more time.

Then, frowning, he dived into the murk and cold as if they were icy absinthe. He staggered down the deserted street, passionately hoping he'd chosen the right direction—to NN's house.

And again, for an instant, he felt a flash of gratitude to the ridiculous father . . . "that is, to papa-mâché, so to speak . . . " of Russia's fateful stagnation, gratitude for the indentations inside the mask that protected his nose, cheeks, and forehead from the spiteful wind's touch.

And the fact that, since the moment when the last of the demons—the greasy, squeezed-lemon aviator-owl-eyed demon with bifocals on his scrotum-shaped puss—had vanished into the pig's left nostril, not a single one had reappeared gave Helium a feeling of remarkable liberation.

This state of freedom made his loneliness even more acute, and even took it to some unbearable limit; strangely enough, it also seemed to help (as if they were in it together, sidekicks) the errant man bear his heavy load.

"She won't turn me away. I don't give a damn for pride. Well, what's pride in comparison to this cat's story, or my sores? This has nothing to do with it personally . . . what this has to do with is another living being who happens to be chilled to the bone. So let her do what she wants with the kitten, since she's so upstanding, so good, kind, thoughtful and I'm such a sack of shit. Yeah, I'm a sack of flophouse shit in a plague year. But she's not. I'll wake her up, drop the poor critter at her feet. . . . 'Save its life,' I'll say, 'keep it until springtime anyway, and by summer, who knows, maybe there'll be mice and rats and birds . . . maybe a few unclaimed table scraps will finally reappear in this damn country . . . sausage skins, cheese casings, chicken gristle, pork rinds . . . maybe even some native birds and beasts'll live to see them . . . and in general, even if you don't let him settle in, dying's an easier thing in the summertime than in this melancholy winter . . . he's just a baby, señora, just a baby, and not a roast pig stuffed with minced demon and chopped slogan . . . ' I'll say to her, 'hand me a piece of paper and I'll write my will, I'll leave everything to you if you aren't too disgusted to inherit my accidental guardianship . . . I'll be happy to write a will and I will! . . . you're one of those who tore me apart . . . I'll even sign my apartment over to you . . . I don't have long to live on this earth . . . what do I need a living room for . . . live in it, señora, with whomever you please, there's room for the fathers of your children and for hundreds of kittens. . . . Be fruitful, as it says in the supposedly Holy Scriptures, and multiply. . . . Whoa! Why should we be fruitful and multiply, after all? . . . That's a very curious little question. . . . Why and what for? So that after the Fall you can stick your Sovie shovels into the crap piled up at technology's dead end, just like in the West—or no, just like here at home, you can shoot proletarian cobblestones out of the people's battered kidneys through a narrow little urinary White-Sea canal? To what end, excuse-me-for-asking? . . . There's nothing about *that* in the Holy Scripture . . . but then if no clear secondary goal is indicated by the Creator and Founder and no direct general line, then it would seem that the continuation of life is for the sake of life itself, and not for the sake of some stinking communism-or-other, some nation-state notion—that the noble end-in-itself turns out to be all Creation's very existence? . . . Oh, if I didn't have to croak pretty soon I'd organize—either with my own money or else jointly with the Vatican (because who could possibly come to any agreement with our supreme pseudonyms—like a Filaret or Juvenal?)— I'd organize a quiet little intellectual workshop for the extrac- tion of the real practical meaning of this hyperobvious (and therefore incomprehensible to humans) parting Instruction: the ends are clear, the lines are defined . . . be fruitful, sirs and mesdames, grasses and birds, fish and giraffes, kitties and pups, and multiply! . . . it's too late . . . too late for you, Hal . . . no, I'll get to her place and say: look, here's written proof of my positive unwillingness to stay a minute longer in this foul pig- sty, with my (everything else aside) gangster family name, which is unthinkable to allow into any kind of public life . . . and my revolutionary patronymic? . . . absurdity . . . horror . . . zdarkness . . . well the time has come, ladies and gentlemen, for conceptions and executions of . . . the time . . . the storm covers the sky with darkness . . . I don't think I mixed up my directions . . . the demon isn't spinning us anymore . . . isn't leading us in circles, the bitch . . . let's drink, good friend of my poor youth . . . let's drink from sorrow . . . oh, no, I won't ask you for a drink . . . never . . . not a swallow, not a sip . . . not a drop . . . I'll croak cold-turkey in a deep-freeze before I sink to that. . . ."

With this prideful and self-denying mental step, Helium's pain-stricken soul contracted into a little lump. He stopped in his tracks, rooted to the spot, because for the first time in his life he felt sudden and acute compassion for himself.

And frightened by this mental step, and purely to calm his soul as quickly as possible, he ardently begged its pardon and assured it that he really didn't give a damn about his pride, he could spit on it a thousand times to the nth degree. . . . "The first thing she'll hear from me, even if she balks and won't open the door, will be an utterly abject request for just a little shot of Swedish Absolut . . . just a request . . . no dying pathos. Exactly three words. Not one letter more . . . one little nip. . . . Maybe 'nip' isn't the word I want here . . . wasn't likely to get out of this fix alive . . . Oh, she'll open the door . . . she won't let me in, but she *will* open the door and contemptuously hand me that shot, because she's better than I am . . . I'm a piece of shit."

Driven by such thoughts, he hurried, hunched over, toward NN's apartment building, which by now was not far at all.

28 ITS COURTYARD WAS filling up with snow which had already covered the site of that unseemly skirmish between the feral humans and their former pets.

Helium looked over his shoulder at his string of tracks in the virgin snow from the iron fence to the doorway, and again something snapped painfully within him, as if that string of tracks were a vision of steps through his life's last snow.

He had the sudden impression these tracks were moving independently of him, in the opposite direction—toes heading toward the street-side archway, heels heading this way, to the building's entrance.

And though it was the most senseless thing in the world for a person out freezing in the wind and the cold to further slow the already terribly slowed motion of his life and time, he looked back, and even bent over to investigate this unpleasant phenomenon. . . . No, things had just seemed that way. . . . The tracks were strung along behind him like a flock of dejected, docile creatures—not in front.

It was much warmer in NN's foyer than in the one where he and the kitten had rested. "Why it's a veritable little Cuba. As long as they haven't shut the elevator off for the night, the bastards," thought Helium, because his strength was flagging and he was having trouble breathing. "As long as it's working . . . "

And when the electrical device, asleep on its feet, shuddered like a resting horse and responded as he pressed the button, and began carrying Helium up to his floor, he recalled his childhood delight at the miracle of the little wooden cabin's ascent, at the mirrors on its four walls, going-up; he recalled the terror that, at the same time, would icily invade his shorts, going right for his balls, gripping his whole being. It would happen when he too vividly pictured the break in the steely, grease-black cable and too soon anticipated his strange fall within the little mirrored cabin, down into the abyss beneath his feet—at the bottom of which he, Mama, and Papa would all end up flat as pancakes . . . a-a-a-a-a!!!!

"I was a fool back then to blubber . . . now I'd laugh at my luck and dance a jig, that is, if I had time to dance it in free fall, and probably the kitten would be just fine . . . Amortiséz, marquise, tu est belle! If only we could twist like cats when we fall to the very bottom of somewhere, and land on all fours, if only . . . ."

The higher the elevator went, the more frightened Helium got, but it wasn't his old childhood fear of heights; it was the inevitably looming discussion with a rudely-awakened NN about at least a temporary refuge for the unlucky animal, and also about a little something to take the edge off. . . .

". . . and here I am looking like this at the crack of dawn . . . after my hellish, crude . . . Madame, you musn't think that this kitten is merely a beastly excuse for a sentimental journey back into our—that is, your—warm bed. . . . Jamais! . . . I'll just drop him inside the door, here in your front hall. . . . I'll say, 'such a death would be unthinkable . . . he's a complete innocent . . . ' and also—'not a gram, not a drop, not a swig . . . it's not worth sinking to such cheap dissonance between tragedy and alcohol even once in a lifetime . . . that won't save any of us now . . . '"

He almost burst into childish sobs after pronouncing this heartrending speech to himself. His heart was beating furiously as he stepped out of the elevator. He left the doors open so he could drop the kitten off in a warm place and quickly (to avoid any delaying chatter or pitiful gestures which would only add to the paltriness of his already ridiculous figure), quickly make his exit. It was dark on the landing, but the light from the elevator fell directly on NN's door.

Feeling out the doorbell with one hand, Helium mustered all his strength—to quiet his pounding heart, to ring the bell and positively, once and for all put an end to the whole business. He had completely forgotten that he was still masked.

The doorbell, too, was masked by something; apparently it wasn't working. So Helium pounded a fist on the door padding, so that the sound would be muffled, directed into the apartment. He immediately put his ear to the padding. Neither step nor rustle was to be heard. Inside, strangely, a single passage from *Eine kleine Nachtmusik* was playing, over and over.

A strange conjecture returned him to his youth, to the times when he would gaze into the mysterious musical meaning of this composition which had so portentously hinted at something essential, something which bore a relation—either past or future—to himself.

In later life he had despaired of reaching its beguiling depths, he had gotten used to its annoying inaccessibility. He persuaded himself that he had been intellectualizing, aestheticizing, mania-izing, mysticizing. . . . "On the other hand, to whom is it given to contemplate the result without first master-

ing the beginnings and meanings of intermediate states? . . .
Nobody . . . "

And suddenly what pierced him, on the dark landing, at
the very door through which he'd been shoved, was not so
much his own conjecture as something like the frankness of
the music itself, which had decided that the time had finally
come to reveal to him the secret of their relationship. "Fate!"
Helium gasped. "Fate! . . . Nothing in this world just happens. . . . This is my end . . . but not its result. . . . I'm stuck in
one spot, that means something is waiting to happen . . . but
what? Death, for sure, but what else? I can't just run in place
forever. . . . "

As the needle kept landing in the pit—as if in a ditch—and
being tossed back out again, it just, in helpless solitude, started
digging at the same beloved and tasty musical bit all over
again . . . "And once upon a time she would wait here by the
window, and her door would be half-open. . . . it was all
there. . . . Lord, Lord. . . ."

He knocked again a few times—stubborn, quick, muffled
knocks—but then his good eye adjusted to the darkness and
made out, just above the doorbell, a hastily folded sheet of
paper. Something snapped inside him.

"She's not here! . . . She left! . . . and why should she sit
around in the middle of that gastronomic disaster! In her place I
would have gone out too—but where?"

Without understanding just why he was flouting one of his
firmest rules (it never entered his head NN would be writing
him after all that) he took the note from the bell, unfolded it,
moved closer to the elevator and began to read. It took him a
moment to realize that the somewhat jumbled, nervous text,

clearly written hurriedly, even breathlessly, was indeed addressed to him, Helium.

But when he did begin to realize it, he squatted, or rather sank helplessly onto the pitted floor tiling, and read and reread the note, as if doubting his heart's first impression, as of thinking that impression was just some delusion of a poor mind traumatized by the night's events.

"If you did have enough sense to come back, then forgive me my lapse of conscience—I'm a swine, if only for, well, not considering the time of night and the cold. Oh Lord . . . you're a jerk, a jerk, a complete jerk, but I'm something worse, forgive me, wait . . . I called your place, I'm going to look for you at the church, too, it's right next door, but it would have been unthinkable to leave a key out, you know that. . . . I can't change what happened, but forgive me for the outrageousness and ugliness of my actions. . . . wait, and then you can take off for parts unknown, but, well, . . . just wait here. . . . "

It wasn't clear, as he read and reread the note, what sort of honey this was, delighting his mind and steeping his soul in the strange healing power of an unfamiliar state. After all there was nothing very encouraging about it. On the contrary, NN's contrite frankness and her guilt over what she thought unforgivable in her own behavior should have just rubbed Helium's nose in the crap of his own shameful stunt one more time. And (as had happened to him before) he should have been so mortified by the moral superiority of a fellow human that he would sincerely have considered the cold cruelty and pridefulness of such a position even greater boorishness than his own.

But Helium didn't feel anything of the sort. His attention was glued to the word "wait"; he kept repeating to himself, repeating . . . "wait, wait, wait . . . " Then, utterly dumb-founded by the hint of (possibly self-imposed) meanings contained in the unexpected missive he had just received in his wilderness, he pressed the note to the mask's stupid nose, to its picanthropic lips, to its reinforced-cat brows, quite oblivious to the fact that this was all just papier-mâché and not his own live flesh-and-blood.

His first thought was that the kitten would be OK, that in the very near future both room and board were guaranteed. Actually, he had never doubted that her nature was noble, nor-mal . . . "What I always did have my doubts about, dear one, was the foul mind, besmirched honor and missing conscience of our gasbag era, the moral superiority of the state-church hier-archy to its flocks and to all the denizens of this stagnant swamp, the writers whose grunting snouts were permanently stuck to the Soviet-Socialist trough, et cetera et cetera—but your lovely normality was something I never doubted, never . . . ."

He drew his hands back deeper into his sleeves. He didn't even try to take off the mask. Breathing under the mask had warmed his face, but maybe he left it on, too, because some forced poor-relation bond had sprung up between the two of them.

Strangely enough, this worthless, ridiculous, pathetically comic, soulless, homemade-pressed-egg-carton-stale-smelling-weird-stench-emitting *thing* had given the freezing man a feeling—perhaps illusory, but a feeling nonetheless—of some kind of comfortable distance from the hostile enormity of the world around.

Like a wood chip carried who knows where by time forever flowing, like a man locked into a cattle car, say, or the hold of a ship at sea, who surrenders himself entirely to the power of movement, the direction of which he knows himself powerless to change, Helium gave no thought to himself at all.

29 GIVEN SUCH A FEELING, it was quite natural that his mind's eye, glued to this ice-clad window, would follow everything floating past him outside. Just the same way, as a child, he would sit glued to the one ice-free patch left on the windowpane as if his very soul had breathed it clear, and with ardent, childish passion look out into the far-and-away, the through-the-windowglass-world that teased him from time to time with its strange inside-outness, that is, its mysteriously artful placement of a frosty landscape within the house's warmth instead of out in the frigid air.

How many of those pictures had floated past him, pictures forever abandoned, forever left behind by time and for that reason fixed in his memory, in his own eternity, in some unfathomable order!

The magnificent wholeness of that private eternity was such that this remained an order, despite the chaotic flashing of pictures which seemed to be set in the ornate gilt frames of years past, or in the less sturdy frames of months and days . . . pictures, mounted in the shabby fake-leather of hours, drawings shoved into the dog-eared passports of minutes . . . random sketches in the ragged cutouts of seconds, meaningless brushstrokes on the scraps of formless instants.

And all this flickered past his gaze like autumn foliage in the golden days of its noble dying. Either it had itself floated down from the Tree of Ages, or something had plucked it from there, who knows how, who knows why—but it fell and fell, burying him neck-deep. . . . "Maybe it's Grandma tiptoeing up to cover me with that raggedy blanket?"

Kaleidoscopically shifting, as if shuffled by someone's willful hand, the pictures, cutouts, snapshots, prints, drawings, scraps seemed to be trying to persuade Helium that not just they, but even their tiniest particles would preserve the memory of his life.

We all, they were saying, are fixed, are fitted into even the most insignificant fragment of time, and no matter how slyly you shuffle us, no matter what unreachable cubbyholes of invisible memory you stash us in, at the appointed time each one of us will render our own individual service to the sum total of all of us—the self-restoring (whether by chance or by will) Whole of your life.

"But what about all my, so to speak, good and evil, when I kick off? . . . What becomes of my own private memory? . . . Probably not a single molecule in nature goes to waste, and atoms themselves don't go dissolving without a trace. A law is a law. But then why do all these images long since vanished in time appear in my mind's eye? And actually, what *is it* all these pictures of my vainly-lived existence are printed on? What optical mechanics have the mysterious power to capture the images of this world on something completely invisible, so that right here in this fusty hallway I can feel the warmth of that hollow in her shoulder? How does the whole of this image and all the parts comprising it—all these outrageous molecules— where do they live, where do they stay, how could the winds of time *not* scatter them or mix them up—just a little—with the molecules in the leathery smell of my very first Czech shoes or in the hellish chlorine of the pool? . . . If I wanted, then, I could call all that greenwillow lightning down on me, the willow that used to pour its branches into my brook in the country, all summer long. . . . Or that joy to the ear, that Bach recording, all those quick insatiable little smacks of tiny gold-and-silver valves of flute, oboe and bassoon, all at odds and yet all in such passionate accord, kissing shut the marvelous bodies of the instruments, never hindering the sound but in fact laying the invisible flesh of the music so vividly bare that the heart practically leaps out of the ribs at the infinite impossibility of slaking its love for it. . . . Well, fine. There are fourteen billion neurons in my stupid skull. They tally up the images of reality, sniff around them, take in their sound, work out their quantities and poetically mix their qualities. But the skull—well, it's not a very reliable storehouse for the Whole of somebody's life. If He does exist, then it would be pure foolishness on His part to entrust us—exceedingly mortal and impossibly frivolous beings—with a mass of unique artifacts, a priceless spiritual treasure. . . . These are the most precious particles of the bottomless, all-encompassing memory of being itself! . . . Not one single speck of dirt accidentally fallen into the eye of some here-and-now moment has the right to get lost, because that speck too is borne by Time into its Otherworldly Nest and thriftily spackled to it with fond saliva . . . But what if, what if . . . ." Helium felt his breath catch in that strange, unfamiliar agitation, and again he sent up a prayer, "Just five minutes or so, just to think this feeling through to the end . . . maybe I can even do it in three. . . . "

What if this fireproof, all-encompassing vault isn't really inside me but is outside—outside all the living, outside everyone about to become, to be? And all I have to do is make a wish to find myself back in a baby tub, let's say, with its melancholy plastic-boat smell, or in some compromising position, or even to (who the hell knows why) hear the nauseating squeal of chalk in the tobacco-stained fingers of that sadistic schoolmaster one more time—and then with that wish I can withdraw from that heavenly savings bank practically all my voluntary (and involuntary) deposits; besides, sometimes, asleep, awake, it doesn't matter, I get something I never thought I deposited in the first place—and I can't believe that I ever encountered some ugly mug, or bit my lip munching on a carrot thirty years ago, or ever burst into drunken sobs and hugged a cherry-tree trunk when I heard a bird twittering away high up in its blossoming snow. . . . And sometimes I'll get something I never wanted back, something I tried to wipe out of my memory, like the taint of some excruciating embarrassment or torturous uncertainty or groundless shame or nagging hatred for somebody who did me wrong. . . . And essentially there's nothing surprising about any of this, if for just an instant you correlate the fantastic success of our suicidal technologies, the communications that link their instruments to the far reaches of the Universe, all of bottomless hyper-cyber-sniper-space and the data of damn theoretical physics with all the boundless possibilities of the One Whom humankind apparently cannot help imitating in its grandly vainglorious sciences and divine arts, especially music. . . . And so what if all this has long since been described or was known to Plato and scores of mystics? And her poet said the same thing, that he wanted to get to the very heart of everything, to get that far, go that far . . . well, here I am, far-gone all right . . . a real goner. . . . Of course memory is bound up with that place in which everything long since vanished from the face of the earth has its being, all the essences, every single stopped-moment of private and common time. . . . Oh Lord, can it be that your storehouse holds all the fullness of times past, everything which Was, including my own pathetic, shameful little stash? . . . Can it be that in it lies the past-now-and-past-yet-to-come, as well as your beloved, infinite forms of the singularly great Logos, the final Number, the Divine Person and Gender which will elude my joyful understanding until the time be fulfilled for the indescribable to be described. . . . Like a swallow's nest, the past-now-and-yet-to-come has been woven and shaped for millennia, the Boundlessness of this Eternity takes its shape from all beings and things . . . and there's room enough in it for all those now-vanished parts of the Creation and it's filled with the sounds and faces of immortal life. . . . So there's no need to restore Pompeii—and any tree, before you even finish making the wish, can burst into the flames of an obliging autumn or else steam in the sauna-mists of dawn or sleep, swaddled in snow. . . . There the dead, ready to spring instantly to mind, to life, await memories of themselves, memories that warm those hearts weary of separation . . . there, the past of everyone living lives as the present of everything future. . . . This soft snow is falling there, and will never stop falling . . . because there is the Great Simultaneity of birth-death-being-event as a Whole . . . and if I require something from *it* in discrete form, memory lends to all this the property called time until I've forgotten again . . . and these same soullessly omnipotent winds of Time that ever since the first day of Creation have borne everyone and everything into some dark Nothingness—these winds breathe soft in the Nest, as if they never were, still are not, and never shall be . . . ever . . . never. . . . They're like some invisibly existing, obedient hounds that turn into real demons once those inaudible paws pad over the threshold into the visible universe, over the threshold of their Master's house, beyond the bounds of that Nest which they themselves helped shape. . . . too bad I'm all alone here at my joyous-hideous celebration, my trash-heap wake for stepdad Scientific Damn Atheism . . . let's invite that madame exaltée who demons more solid and talented than mine have goaded into ass-kissing the Antichrist. . . . I'd say to her, now listen, Madame double-dome, it's me, the former nylon titan of global godlessness, talking to you now; quit slopping your irresponsible, analytical, self-inebriating thought all over the people's sideboard. Stop! Drinks all round! Stop harassing the millions of unfortunates already abused by our insane experiment with your draft for greatest project of all times and peoples, your plan for the resurrection of the dead! Another round. Your health. He, Whose work of creation you propose should be carried out by a starving, cold, ruined, harassed, maimed and humiliated people, has plenty of opportunities to carry it out Himself, at His own appointed hour. And He will resurrect to this unimaginably new Life all those he deems necessary to summon to its mysterious sources. He won't just gather up all the dead bit by unstable atomic bit—like your pug philosopher Fydorov (who himself couldn't be bothered to create a single teeny-tiny new life) planned on doing, crawling on hands and knees all over the Universe to dig up the graveyard dust dear to every self-respecting Russian's heart. All the dead and departed are, at any given moment, safe in His pocket, or under His wing. Not a single tiny wart, prideful sneer, or shy birthmark on a dead-and-gone face is ever lost, and as for the internal organs or affectations of each and every departed nature—that goes without saying. Got it now, you who believe in neither Design nor Providence, but were seduced by passionate diabolical fantasy? In the Creation everything is present. And

Death, if you really want to know, doesn't exist at all. Time sweeps in, blows in from Out There, scatters everything, scatters it and carries it back. That clear? So? How can Death exist there, when that's where Life comes from, where the seed is kept safe? What, you've gone so blind you can't even see the unseen? Or do you just assume that no one can exist honorably without your crippled obsession with prosthetic absolutes? Well we can! And how! But Life will start handing out our hyper-tasks when we start living as normal human beings and not as parasites or pimps at the court of Their Imperial Highnesses Speculation and Idea. Just don't toss any more ideological monkey wrenches into Life's works—we've been doing that the last century and a half. Lord keep us, finally, from your professional obsession with the happiness of the People As A Whole. Spear yourself another mushroom there, m'dear. . . . You're blind drunk with the pride of supposedly spiritual titanism and on shamelessly unrestrained, that is, rather hysterical, ecstasy. So please, don't try and destroy our love of life by shortsightedly, stupidly arousing our hatred of death. Don't try and take away from us poor blessed fools the one last thing the Soviet ruling demons couldn't. Faith in the Kingdom of Heaven, stupid, is what you shouldn't take away, for There every thing exists in the very form in which it existed here, each and every transient moment. Everything—every blessed face, every blessed sound—is there. And as far as your auto-castrato Fyodorov* goes, well . . . like in the joke, he may have risen, but

*Philosopher Nikolai Fyodorov (1828–1903) had and still has a certain following among Russian intellectuals. The "common task" of humans (whose natural home is not so much Earth as the whole of the Cosmos) is to combine belief and science in regulating nature. They do this by defying their greatest enemies, chaos and chance, and by overcoming death itself. One aspect of that common task is the literal resurrection of our dead ancestors.—TRANS.

who cares. . . . There's already Someone to look out for all that's meant to be resurrected . . . and probably Up There your teacher is a bit ashamed of you, since probably he's posthumously suffered aplenty for letting his irritable intellect get hooked by devilbait, and by now he's been persuaded that Design and Providence are quite remarkably arranged, beyond all his dreams and schemes. . . . As far as the resurrection of the dead is concerned, they'll all rise, and we'll rise with them—no sooner and I assure you no later—than when the Lord, calling on the services of His Divine Memory, deigns to remember us; we'll just up and arise, and that's as clear as day. Well, bye-bye, dear, go on, you're free as a bird. . . . "

Helium got scared—because he thought he was going out of his mind. Without even realizing it, he'd been using his old opponents' words, taking snatches of discussions, debates, and an argument between a children's writer, Genka Byrdin, and some follower of Fyodorov.

He had a funny thought. "It's simple—get up, go to your typewriter, type a letter to the *Independent* editor and grab that crazed Utopian by the arguments. And say, look—a, b, c, d, et cetera. . . . In comparison with these Fyodorovist-futurist architects, I'm . . . well, gentlemen, I'm just a harmless hack. I declare positively that any fool can love God for giving him life, but not just any fool can love God for giving him death. . . . I have, I have, come to believe by dying, and if you really want to know, I came to love Him for that swig of whiskey. I lived half a century and never loved Him—but for that swig, and this little creature shivering next to my heart, I'll love him like a son. . . . It's just that I'm a fool for not fathering a child, for continuing myself . . . what a fool . . . continuation *is* resurrection. . . . OK, OK . . . at least I can save the kitten. . . . "

The misfortune of a whole life wasted suddenly descended on him so heavily that he had no time to regret his fate or the music that was his blessed world of unseen essences, or even his other admittedly small earthly joys. He felt the sudden breath of a cold sterility that neither produced life nor added anything lasting to memory. . . . "Just a few hours ago I could have . . . we could have . . . there would have been a tiny he, or she . . . Oh Lord, how perfect are Thy works. . . . everything else is our fault. . . . "

Nostalgia for everything forever lost and wasted stabbed at his heart so painfully that, to save himself, he sank into reminiscence again. . . . In those visions was everything which had ever been, except once-omnipotent Time, which—and Helium sensed this once again—with each moment destroys only itself, affirming in such complete turns of divine events the indestructibility—in Eternity—of everything now existing. . . . "Our sense of Time, well, . . . it's the sense of its eternal bearing-forth of everything existing in the Next World. . . . " Helium had just time enough for that thought before he came down in the otherworlds of his own memory. . . .

30

. . . HE WAS in joyous bliss, convalescing from the flu and fooling his mother into thinking he was still sick. He contrived to break the thermometer while no one was looking; he held the blue tea saucer sprinkled with tiny, sticky raspberry seeds, and watched the mercury pour heavily (to the fluttering beat of a faltering heart) out into the dish and instantly shatter into fluid drops, and drops of drops of drops, and then, obedient to his hand as it changed the dish's orbit, again converge into a single trembling quicksilver puddle full of invisible power and the will of centripetal force, which left— oh miracle—the unloved seeds of healing raspberry (which had spitefully, corrosively roused a nagging, rotten pain in the cavity of one particular tooth) completely untouched, unconsumed by the magically streamlined heaviness of the drops.

His little heartbeat was quick, furious, as if in some hurry to match its sweet shortness to the enormous number of ridiculous boy-faces reflected in the mirror-arcs of even the very smallest drops that seemed to be furnishing his own, Heelie's very own, miniature funhouse. . . .

. . . then another feeling remembered itself, a feeling of strange, sweet agitation connected with his passionate anticipation of a theater curtain rising. . . . With insurmountable annoyance he separated the unquiet world with its houses, apartments, cars, its tiers of theater galleries resembling a bosomy lady Gulliver in lilac-and-gold, bedecked by Lilliputians; the world with his fellow-spectators, with the overall acute feeling of impatience which had become murmur and noise, with the Helium badgered by sterilely, softly whispered admonitions about good manners—all this visible world he set apart from what was behind the dark blue waves of curtain falling heavily from ceiling to floor.

At such moments he was so faint with impatience and anticipation—an anticipation he likened to a yearning to escape the staleness of prison, or the grave—that even the cold of a certain terrible notice his soul might have given in advance (disappointment in the stage show itself) couldn't stem or even slow the hot, passionate rush within his soul. . . .

31 HE WOKE UP in the foyer and, unafraid, waited for death—waited as children wait for the first ripple of the heavy curtain making its light, magical ascent, waited not for something to be presented, but instead to be presented to something.

There, one more time, something would happen that, in his grandma's words, never has been and never can be of this earth, or at least can be only partially, and moreover that never-can-be happens and keeps on happening for so long that two lifetimes wouldn't be enough to see it all the way through, to its end. . . . The lights would begin to dim, but as if it wasn't light fading but the whole world falling sweetly asleep along with you, still grasping the edge over the abyss of slumber, still clinging to a bit of evening with just the tip ends of drooping eyelashes. The eyelashes droop, and fall shut, but the curtain rises and suddenly—it's not clear what comes from where, or even what turns into what: either in the theater the fading light is transmuted into the sounds of soft music, or else the music rings out and then fades, and over all this something-from-nothing dart blue, green, yellow, white, silver-indigo, long-armed rays—they dart past, scattering handfuls of sparkling seed in your eyes; shaking off the remains of this world, shafts of light dart by, flash by as if to tease out everything still basking in the far reaches of the world beyond, too idle to appear to the eye of a boy: the gray stone of an old castle . . . at a diagonal, a forest path that in some incomprehensible fashion disappears beyond the horizon. . . . on it, so far far away is someone's rushing carriage, and you see neither the flashing legs of the horses nor the lashes of the coachman's furious whip, but only the indistinguishable spokes of the wheels, merging with the dust of the road; and the pounding of hooves gradually fades into that far distance along with the completely soundless light. And suddenly, like a random cloud—there appears a split-second, vague, almost intangible feeling of guilt toward everyone and everything, everything he's just left behind, inside this theater and out, but having once darkened the soul, the pure little cloud melts away as quickly as it appeared, and here, as if transplanted once and for all into the time and space of fairy tale, the little boy is in bliss, and forgets the curtain; he's a bird of the air, a celestial being, and is already urging on the story's end and the key to the magical riddle with pain and passion even greater than that with which he, tormented by expectation, anticipated the performance itself.

There was not a soul to be seen on any of the landings, on any of the stairways, during those minutes that Helium drifted through the timeless world of his own memory, through his own private eternity.

The life within him hung, you might say, in the balance, on scales so precise that they would react to the merest random instance of a random instant, that is, to something which cannot be referred to in the thick-skinned cause-and-effect terms that always insist on poking their boorish snouts into the incredible subtlety of events.

Helium, like a letter that the wind has torn from someone's grasp, was already absorbing the weight of the River of Time's waters, the silent superficial calm of Lethe, and was about to surrender to the undertow that bears whatever falls into it off into the Next World.

And in his half-conscious mind a silent, mirrorlike rain was falling. In literally each and every one of the weightless quicksilver droplets falling from who knows where, or why, was Helium's own image—wonderfully, precisely, almost holographically captured. But here's what was so strange: all of these snapshots, so to speak, of Helium at various ages . . . a distinguished gentleman with traveling papers . . . teenager with a lop-eared full-lipped face retailored in adult fashion by a shopful of hormones busy sowing mischief in the body's lower depths . . . the suave, imposing tribune of the Executive Congress of African and Asian Atheist Movements . . . a newborn babe . . . a graduate student . . . a sleazy creature of the nomenclature, vacationing at Karlovy Vary . . . a pigeon-toed toddler . . . a well-known contributor to *Science and Religion* . . . . The large, warm drops of mercury with his iridescent portraits split into a countless number of small droplets on the surface of some kind of infinitely blue space. Its concavity was barely noticeable, seemingly minimal, but it had one locus, where a multitude of mirror-droplets were converging, converging into a single, great puddlelike drop. They eventually filled it up and out, and Helium, half-dreaming, half-conscious, waited in anticipation of this strange spectacle's final, crowning effect.

With an unfamiliar feeling of returning to something, he passionately thirsted for the moment when the truth of his instinct and the correctness of his mental reckonings would be confirmed. In the end he also desperately needed the support of his fanatic faith in the omnipotence of formal logic—to which he was honorably devoted, in the fashion of an unhappy but faithful husband devoted to his aged, paralysis-ridden wife. . . . And now, the multitudes of photos of various ages would merge into one general and whole portrait of Helium, and what emerged would be the very picture of himself—not in some frame bound in pathetic fake leather, but in the boundless final framework of Eternity and then whatever part of him was left outside that frame could just go to hell. . . . But what was this? What was this? . . . The drops and droplets were falling, merging, converging into something general and whole, but on its broad, mirrorsmooth surface there was nothing but pure and bottomless space, space unmuddied by anything visible or extraneous, and on the surface of the treacherously playful quicksilver wasteland there was not a trace to be seen of the image that just an instant ago had alighted from who knows where in unheard-of multiplicity—*his* image. . . . What kind of dirty theoretical trick was this? Was reality delirious, raving? How can it be, how can it seem that I don't exist, and in fact never did?

If it hadn't been for this accidental horror—one never before experienced in waking or the direst of nightmares or premonition or belated pangs of conscience—Helium might have tranquilly gone to sleep and died that very minute.

It was a horror in the face of some hideous, hellish incongruity that mocked not so much him personally as it did all the unfathomable foundations of the logic of natural existence.

Perhaps it wasn't even Helium personally who felt fear and trembling but rather the divine principle in the soul of every human—without exception—that rose up now in resistance to the incoherent ravings of a dying man's consciousness.

Something suddenly shook Helium. He awoke from the welter of marvelous and unbearable visions. In his soul there was fear: out in the snow and cold his lips hadn't been trembling, his teeth hadn't been pounding out a furious drum roll, but here in this shelter (not a particularly warm one, but still . . .)—he had such a case of the shakes that they seemed to be drilling right through the marrow of his bones.

He remembered neither the letter nor the kitten, for the solitude of his whole being had at that moment reached that unimaginable borderline beyond which loneliness exists all on its own, in disembodied, sorrowful form—in other words, in an idea that seems to remain outside any tangible connection with whatever may be doomed to it.

Helium's state at that instant was the exact equivalent of the naked "I"—the standard of absolute solitude which is of course kept not in the Paris Office of Weights and Measures, but under other skies, where there's nary a hint of the generally accepted notions of, say, a gram, a meter, a minute, the speed of light . . .

As if lashed by some elemental force rushing to put his business in order, Helium leapt to his feet without even noticing how hard it was for him to breathe. Coping with the overall pain was somehow easier than fighting off the sharp ache in one of his benumbed fingers, the clenched feeling round his heart or the dull nag of his suicidal contusion.

He didn't even understand why he suddenly stood up and, forgetting there was an elevator, walked down the stairs. Mechanically, he shoved NN's letter into one pocket without noticing that the pocket was full of melting snow. Mechanically he pressed one arm across his chest without remembering that under the coat, under the arm, was a kitten. Nor did he notice how revoltingly slimy was the coat collar touching his skin.

True, he leaned against the foyer walls as he walked, to support his weakened legs.

There was not a single thought in his head except for a

melancholy preoccupation with direction, the kind that always fills to overflowing those birds and animals who've fallen behind the flock or accidentally gone astray, far from home.

32 BACK OUT ON the street, where the wind had quieted but the snow exulted in the dead stillness of the night (having left not one single open spot on the surface of the ground, the bushes, the trees, the building, the wrought-iron railings, the wooden fences untouched)—Helium suddenly felt a simple, piercing desire to find NN and moreover felt that now, in the final stages of his life, this was—this had to be—his only goal.

He couldn't have explained for precisely what reason he needed to do this, as after all the only people who waste time seriously considering the causal formula of something hyperobviously necessary are either truly idle minds or impenetrable cretins and not, in any case, naive children or people trapped at life's dead ends.

Having felt this need to see NN, Helium welcomed his sudden power of locomotion, overcoming weakness, cold, fever-and-chills and, most important, an infinite and perhaps unresolvable lyric pity. This was pity unlike that he'd occasionally felt in childhood, which was for himself and inseparable from himself; this was pity for an absolutely unrelated and yet somehow kindred being, though no closer kin than, say, a kitten.

" . . . turn the kitten over to her of course . . . no problem . . . just a matter of getting there . . . if she's left . . . the church . . . don't want to miss her . . . if she's there I'll crawl up on my knees, no, maybe I'll walk . . . and that's that . . . but what'll I say? . . . nothing. . . . I don't know what to say. . . . I'm speechless. . . . then again who needs speech . . . what does she need a speech for. . . . I'll laugh. . . . I'll just start laughing my head off . . . start laughing . . . I'll use sign language . . . let her know she looked incomparable, beautiful, a wonder of natural genetic engineering, when she smacked shithead me in the chops with the roast pig . . . incomparable . . . and then when that one revolutionary demon got his hairy gray, red-officer-striped hind leg stuck, got it stuck tight in the piggy's nostril . . . and then his other leg got stuck in a little lemon-wheel . . . funniest thing in the world . . . like Kafka in a clinch with Bosch . . . I won't reproach her—not a word, not a look . . . how's she supposed to know when a person's not acting independently, when he's being controlled, that is corrupted, by a bunch of demonic little shitheels . . . some people *do* know, though . . . but then again the demons corrupt and cripple structures a good deal more complex than my sick little organism, as one late poet used to say . . . they've fouled the planet, knocked it out of orbit, the sons of bitches, cracked open the ozone layer . . . if I could just make it as far as my old enemy Father Alexander's place . . . what am I talking about . . . he was murdered . . . some lowlifes murdered him . . . on the other hand, I'll see him soon enough, and here's what I'll say to him, now that I know the the score, I'll say: so how come, padre, your cornerstone church has been going on about the devil and his legions of hell for a couple of millennia now, but in practice it hasn't really done a thing? . . . why aren't you, gentleman and holy fathers, out there exterminating these vermin the way people exterminate the bedbugs and roaches and green home-grown lice in their communal mattresses? . . . and yet I your humble servant, arrant, high-profile atheist, a doctor of sciences, excuse the expression, that I am, have—unless of course I'm not mistaken—just personally annihilated a large contingent of insects from that hell of yours, insects that were brazenly swarming all over reality in the guise of my personal benefactors . . . and I lost everything in the encounter . . . everything . . . my first wife . . . my second . . . a continuation of myself . . . and here I am trudging along, piss-soaked to the marrow of my bones, frozen stiff, and my poor little bladder has decided to shut down early, even before all those livers, spleens and whatever . . . I've put in my time, it says, that's it, the faucet's off . . . yes, Helium's trudging off to demi-points unknown, far from the bananas of Cuba and the succulent coconuts, dammit, of Fidel's corps de ballet . . . one hundred years of solitude at heaven's one-hundred-one-kilometer limit . . . wandering off with a dying mask, my gift for the writer-the-man-the-genius-the-Trotskyite, that is, the compleat idiot . . . conference, my ass . . . a stinking-rotten barnful of ungodly brutes . . . just like me . . . that's why I'm not sorry . . . I feel the warmth of Your hands . . . I'm trudging, by the way, on my very last legs . . . moving my soul with the help of my body, so that I can leave both this small shivering creature and my grateful last wheeze in that ama-a-a-zing woman's hands . . . sauerkraut in the kisser—splat . . . champagne upside the head—wham . . . ha-ha-ha—olives 'Olivier' stuffed with caviar . . . dark-rose twists of prosciutto . . . ah, Madame, Madame . . . mushrooms julienne . . . herring in grape leaves . . . cucumbers, sprats, pizza . . . flash by in the headlights' glare . . . anchovies in horseradish . . . ham . . . with a vial of smelling salts . . . Oh Lord, there's your *Eine kleine Nacht-musik* . . . thank you for this truly noble funereal sound in the flickering consciousness of a villain . . . except it keeps on skip-

ping . . . keeps grating . . . lay me in the grave . . . in an un-
marked grave . . . preferably alongside Mozart . . . he needs a
full house . . . and may the young thief we-e-e-p/o'er the cold
damp gra-a-ave . . . ."

33 IT WASN'T EXACTLY that Helium was delirious without
realizing it as, swaying, hands drawn back into his
coatsleeves, he dragged himself toward the church NN
sometimes attended; he'd simply set his eternally fettered consciousness free, the way you put an old, useless plug out to
pasture on some scrubland.

And that freed plug, indignantly snorting at the visions of its
own coltish youth flashing through flesh-and-blood memory,
and seemingly embarrassed by any likeness, at such a vener-
able age, to some unbridled young doofus, drooped its head; it
drooped its head, but couldn't maintain its respectably pluglike
stance for long, and kicked up all four heels as if trying to take
off and fly, and galloped in circles once or twice, flopped over,
blissfully rolled side and backbone in the dirt, grunting and
snorting like some old geezer, got to its feet, and suddenly,
blindly, ridiculously, dashed off to who knows where, with
nary a damn for the impression its death's-door antics were
making on the boozy stablehand who was at that very moment
sunk in melancholy, philosophical, morning-after contemplation of the unbearably heartbreaking lot of horses and men. . . .

Helium's unfettered consciousness eventually seemed to tire
of shying playfully, of rolling chaotically in various recollec-
tions, pleasant and shameful alike; of squealing at incautious
movements that unwittingly caused the soul some vexing,

unendurable pain . . . and also of furiously bucking, trying to throw off some terribly brazen, disgustingly persistent thing. . . .

It was getting harder and harder for Helium to walk, and so he slumped against a scrawny sidewalk tree to catch his breath. His consciousness, so sharply and unexpectedly roused, suddenly felt worn out; it stood calm, sunk into some sort of extended thought or in some final vision. There it stood, in that absolute wasteland, blissfully slumping against its fellow, against an equally pluglike, equally solitary, abandoned and perishing being.

There was no one walking at this late hour, and to the drivers of the few-and-far-between cars Helium gave the impression of some dead-drunk partygoer who'd lost any semblance of human form.

His becalmed consciousness took his fortuitous prop—the tree, that is—for a Christmas tree, scrawny, needleless, useless, thrown out of its warm abode into the snow and cold after a week of amazing triumph, ornate loveliness and general adulation, to now stand shivering pathetically in its shreds of tinsel, damp sparkles, dead, never-to-melt cotton snowflakes, sending a chill through the thoughtful heart of the sensitive observer with this image of rejection, of a useful plant so gracelessly freezing in the cold air of unfathomably absurd, fickle human soullessness.

He wasn't drunk at all. On the contrary, the night's events had put his whole being—especially his mind—into a state of free self-absorption and detachment from the visible world.

And yet there had been a time when scholarly or even purely social chitchat about states of being would make him furious, states of being which (so his kitchen-table mystic friends argued) could only be achieved by genuine holy fools, or by those grown wise in painstaking spiritual self-education, or else by those free birds of the air, earth's rarest, most fortunate beings.

Now, in just such a state, he stood as if at the far ends of the earth, leaning against a tree, shifting his weight from one foot to another. There he stood, every so often using his coatsleeve to brush back a legendary reinforced-stiffened-cat eyebrow drooping low over one of the mask's eyeholes.

Not only had this state of blessed immersion in strange visions no timeframe, it also had no correlation in the icy terms of his beloved formal logic. Yet he could sense that this was not just a delirious dream, the surreality of which, however improbable, we take for granted.

Instead, his strange visions seemed to him just what they would have seemed to one of his meticulous opponents in that grossly featureless though uniformly ugly rag in which "Science," represented by all manner of ungodly trash like himself, would loudly and swinishly piss all over essentially unanswered "Religion."

That is, now even to Helium it seemed as if these visions were self-willed games a wakeful soul played with the magical mechanisms of a brain which gets so tired of Reality that overdriven Reason drops off daily (and sometimes even more often) into what might as well be the Next World and conks right out, resting up to further bear the burdens of existence and dealings with that unbearable (unbearable without a cigarette break, at any rate) entity—Reality, that is. And meanwhile the Soul is there romping and playing, whimsically shuffling not just immediate impressions but even those tucked away in memory's privatest of hiding places and cubbyholes: no doubt, as it instantaneously turns round and flies off to the Next World—where there is no Time—to get something you've utterly forgotten, it sometimes happens to grab something that isn't even yours, something that, in waking, you mistakenly think never existed; the Soul takes all this and cobbles it all together, or perhaps itself just follows, beguiled, the self-willed development of improbable and incomparable visions in the nocturnal current of our dreams.

But a dream is a dream, for all the unfathomability of its structure and the fantasticality of its amazing configuration. And amid all the grim action of even the most horrible dream we still somehow contrive to grasp (with just the tip-end of our horror-struck consciousness) one saving straw—the feeling that all this, somehow, is just a dream . . . a dream . . . dream . . . And even inside some pleasant, fairy-tale vision we're never fooled into thinking that the waking state awaiting us beyond its threshold is anything but incomparably more humble, boring, joyless and bleak.

In a word, Helium sensed that these visions of his were not the province of dreams. This was, like it or not, some Unseen Reality which had suddenly and inexplicably condescended to a parley with him—the most insignificant of bipeds—and, by signs understandable even to the blind intellect of a weak man, hinted once again that the Universe was safe in spirit, that not only the Cosmos, not only this puny grain of earthly ground, but also all the stale wasteland of an errant soul were particles in an unfathomable Whole permeated by the living forces of unbroken interactions. . . .

" . . . and besides, the ultimate mysteries of all Existence might possibly remain—until the appointed hour—mysteries vexing to the self-enclosed minds of vampires such as yourself,

Helium Revolverich, because the soulfully live, indestructible wholeness of Creation in everything seen *and* unseen is hyperobvious. That wholeness is, but it's absolutely impossible for the human mind to have any clear notion of its form, its causal forces or the logic of its transmutation from one mode into another. Do you think this kitten has any notion of its own outward appearance, despite the hyperobvious fact that it has one? Is it in a butterfly's or narcissus's nature to react, womanlike, to its outward appearance? Can a mirror-carp really ponder the marvelous chemical formula for water and then issue a bitter opinion on its ubiquitous poisoning?"

These thoughts weren't Helium's own, but his consciousness enjoyed these flashes of long-forgotten arguments, bellicose debates with foes, inexplicable retreats before the pressure of their theses and the faint whiff of an unexpected urge to let himself be taken prisoner—just to get it over with. At that moment a wave of lifesaving mockery splashed over him.

"It must be rather strange for Him," a thought flashed through his mind, "to be looking in from out There, and to watch people playing the sort of dirty tricks on their neighbor that they'd never play on themselves . . .

"It's precisely the clearest and simplest of all hyperobvious things—that I am another You and You are another I—that leads many people (yourself included, Helium Revolverovich) to think that it—the foundation of all moral law—is some ruse dreamed up by the priests. But just imagine for a second that this foundation is real, and that one of the highest senses of the universal order is indeed this feeling of primordial, ultimate, hyperobvious identity and native kinship within the undifferentiated Whole. Just imagine. So of course, the moment when I tragicomically shit on myself by shitting on my neighbor, and my neighbor shits on himself while he supposes he's shitting on me, can't help provoking a Heavenly chuckle or two. So this grand delusion, on the strength of which we treat the *invisibility* of the hyperobvious as *nonexistence*, we may regard as the leaven not only of humans' incomprehensible hostility to one another, but also of the depressingly large admixture of the absurd in the makeup of human history."

Helium's consciousness seemed to be swept up in a wild hurricane-wind of utterly contradictory, mortally-opposed thoughts.

His old thoughts, now forgotten but tested on more than one occasion in the state's victorious battles against "priestianity," were clearly surrendering their positions and starting—in some mysteriously gushing source of real light—to look like the papier-mâché of his mask. And the thrice-branded "reactionary opinions" of his opponents—their "pseudo-scientific theories," their "ultra-antimaterialist hypotheses," their "sacred dogmas of global bourgeois obscurantism," as well as the remnants of so-called theodicies personally routed by Helium himself, were overrunning, occupying, fortifying these once impregnable positions.

Of course Helium couldn't help but remember his "editorial" laughter which was later, in the revised stenographic record of organized debates with Orthodox churchmen, described as "widespread laughter in the audience."

As a political and polemical gesture, so to speak, he had started laughing after words spoken " . . . I guess by that same Zelenkov who just pissed on me, knowing not what he did. . . . *Evil is primordially inept, and therefore excruciatingly envious of Good, and the vicious circle of this existential logic merely brings Evil, with each of its major and minor victories, closer and closer to its*

ultimate, suicidal triumph—not over Good, but over itself. Evil, if
you will, is like Time, in that it possibly, unbeknownst to itself, in-
evitably, works itself out for the best. . . . "

34

HELIUM CONTINUED standing there, leaning one shoulder against the tree, seeming to observe the action of
this lightning-fast skirmish from the sidelines. He was
suddenly amazed that he wasn't cheering for "our side," that is,
for his own routinely stamped-out theses, for the exceedingly
sophisticated rationalism of the logic in certain of his stupid
arguments, for his heaps of articles and reviews, his stacks of
pamphlets, et cetera et cetera.

And in general, the skirmish itself was beginning to look
rather comic to him, since he, who knows how, again felt rather
than thought a certain hyper-obvious thing striking him, something like the way a blind person who briefly regains sight after
a botched operation is struck by the clarity, obviousness and
openness of all those things which were once just abstract concepts in his unfortunate consciousness.

This brief instant suffices for a lifelong memory of sight, in
sight. The world of concepts, despised by a different sort of
blind person precisely because it never becomes a world of
visible essences and phenomena, remains as infinitely closed as
before, but a fond yearning for it and a reconciliation with the
terrible wound (which now seems merely temporary to the
unfortunate cripple) settle into the heart.

Amazed by the strange state of his emotions and even fearing some painful split in his personality, Helium intuited—that
is, thought and felt with his soul—something absolutely incred-

ble to him, but also, having intuited it, thought: "So it turns out that if you were to set up a contest on this little planet for the most ridiculous phenomenon, opinion, theory, situation, anecdote—in a word, the most ridiculous thing that ever was, is, et cetera et cetera—then without a doubt, there are no contenders for the title of universal champion of curious comedy that could even come close to the phenomenon of blind human unbelief in a Maker, Creator. . . . well I'll be damned . . . ha . . . ha . . . ha!"

This thought, appearing out of what seemed to be nowhere, changed Helium's mood so abruptly and sharply that he was suddenly almost convulsed with the naive, childish laughter that no doubt bears witness to a benign, gleeful triumph either of some one person's soul or else the soul of a World that has long and patiently observed all of human reason's laughably confused movements through the labyrinth of its own delusions.

"While the way out, the way to Truth, is as plain as the stupidly pointing (who knows where) noses on our stupid faces . . . and that's, forgive me, the fundamental, Universal joke and, in a certain sense, an unthinkable, pitiless mockery of all our organs of perception, not to speak of our regal brain . . . ha . . . ha . . . no matter how you look at it—the Human tragicomedy . . . ."

Helium's state of inner gaiety was fueled even more by the thought of how touchingly absurd was the tendency of what would seem at first glance the most conscientious and grandly vainglorious of all human minds to invent theodicies—those magnanimous would-be vindications of the Lord of the Universe, the Maker and Creator, of God.

"Oh Lord how perfect are Thy works, but again, begging

your pardon, why is Divine simplicity so complicated that humans have been tormented by their own blindness for millennia now, denying all that's truly most important, while it's right under their collective nose? . . . it's so impossibly hard to push man to the point of seeing through the seeming invisibility of one or two of the most crucial, hyperobvious things. . . . Is it that our likeness to You is so hyperobvious and hypersimple to You Yourself that even if I don't believe in You, You steadfastly believe in me? We'd be less the first-rate bastards we are if timely insight were within our earthly powers. . . . this little planet—even given our temporary difficulties, as they say, and our fascination with the thesis that everything happens 'for the best,' would be a virtual paradise. . . . But then we lived in Heaven once, and our stupid tongue froze to the famous fruit of the famous Tree as if that fruit were a piece of cold iron . . . and we just can't peel it away . . . somehow, more and more . . . *feel the warmth of Your hands.* . . . that little poem of hers says it all . . . I bet neither Eve nor Adam even had time to take a real bite out of that apple, or else they would have recognized the taste of what I'm tasting now . . . it's their own damn fault . . . and besides they ought to have savored that apple with a little more consideration and a lot more pleasure—that is, with torment and suffering . . . but then that's what history is—the savoring and gradual recognition of the taste of sin-ridden existence . . . that's something no history department could ever have taught me . . . 'ah, little apple' . . . and isn't it strange that that rowdy sailor's song was the devilish refrain of our hellbent Russian fall from grace. . . . Of course croaking from spiritual inadequacy is worst of all . . . but freezing to death is at least more aesthetic than rotting alive . . . so every thing, right down to the dissolution of our papier-mâché Empire, is for the best . . . it's dissolving now, and it'll converge droplet by droplet into something not necessarily bigger, but necessarily better . . . can it really be that someday the enigmatic process of our instructive history will come to an end? Can it be that only There, in 'the best,' the transmutation of our stupidly self-generated causes into the ugly rot of inevitable effects will freeze up once and for all? Can it be that someday, oh Lord, all our unthinking mistakes, all our evasive squirming and all our tragicomic qualities will turn into some sum-total, so to speak, serenity, into the indistinguishability of bad and good . . . for the best? but then who can figure it, who can peer beyond Time, into the 'best' . . . then again, old Helium will be peering soon enough . . . it's funny, and very odd that it's funny . . . not frightening . . . ."

35 ANOTHER CONCLUSION, resolution, occurred to Helium, appeared to him. In those minutes he was alive in thought and thought alone, his brain dangerously shut off from the pain of his terribly frozen flesh.

Gradually, without realizing it, he had somehow sat himself down in a snowbank near his tree. And there he continued to gaze into the profound disorder of the life he'd lived, which he had persuaded himself was, if not the ideal life, then at least a finely tuned network of self-justifications, a sort of tricky little relay system hooked up to his subconscious.

Now it seemed as if the phonograph needle had suddenly jumped back out of its pit, and his beloved *Eine kleine* had moved on in all its resonating charm. "This is it . . . the end of my life," he though as he listened agitatedly to what had now ceased to be a mystery. " . . . the grand finale, Hal."

At that instant he might well have drifted off and frozen stiff there in the snow, under the sleeping tree, had he not curled up in a ball and hugged his knees, thereby squeezing the kitten so hard that it let out an involuntary yowl and like a child frightened by the closeness of this strange, incomprehensible darkness, got hysterically overwrought.

But at first Helium didn't quite realize that this pain stabbing his breast in several places at once and seeming to rip right through his skin was not his heart, but rather the kitten digging its claws in. And when he finally did realize that he might be dragging this homeless little furball down with him, he got so upset and distraught himself that some force yanked him out of his blessed numbness back into some understanding of what was happening. "The needle, the needle hasn't quite skipped back out yet, it hasn't climbed out of the rut . . . ."

And indeed his whole body was enveloped in a dangerous, sinister glow. It was hard to breathe. The Brezhnev mask was sopping wet, and beginning to reek of low-grade glue and (belatedly) the rascally gloom of the satirical craft that had made it. He threw it aside, and parted with it once and for all.

He could feel that he had no strength left in his legs, and besides he hadn't the slightest urge to roust himself out of this quiet, tranquil and—strangest of all—fearless state of gradual descent into a profoundly familiar, native abyss (if indeed that was what lay ahead).

He might have stayed where he was, might have just left the kitten to the whims of chance and fate. And in the end he would have felt either an indifferent, infinite detachment from all things living, or maybe just helpless sympathy and forced agreement that there was not a damn thing he could have done. He might soon have been a stiff himself, and then who knows what would have become of the kitten in the frigid air of the free market era fast bearing down on the capital of the former Empire.

But at that moment that same thought—that novel thought—of one of those newly-revealed hyperobvious things stabbed him right through the heart: "I-You-I."

That is, he wasn't thinking at all; his powers of reason had gone numb, but the clarity of this novel feeling shot through him and seemed, with cheerful ease, to sweep aside any barriers between species so distant from one another, and so, as they say, this wasn't the time for debating the question—why, in the name of what, should he hustle, take quick action—or for calculating which of these two perishing creatures should be saving the other.

So in fact it was the kitten who cried out for salvation first, and Helium who instantly responded, shoving his hand inside his coat, poking his nose in as well (where it inhaled the sour despair of growing chill, the remnants of already scarce body heat and the stale bitterness of feline indigence) and, until the kitten finally calmed down, forcing his wooden lips to mumble something loving and ridiculous, in apology for the icy touch of his hand, and also in gratitude for the rustle of life.

Later he couldn't remember getting up or heading off without a clue to what direction he was heading—but propelled by an inner force that acts independently at the very moment a person would seem to be hopelessly done for.

Probably it's that force alone, with only itself to rely on, that undertakes those desperate attempts to hold our bodies back from the border between the Seen and the Unseen, that virtually drags them back from the abyss, and that being done, continues to watch over them.

It sets up some emergency system inside a person, this wise and (in some cases) wonderworking, omnipotent force; it shuts, loads, locks, unlocks, pulls in reserves, and maybe even makes some illicit (from a medical point of view) and unthinkably shady transactions with those kidneys and spleens regarding metabolism and blood supply to a faltering heart. Even in a person who is losing consciousness from sheer weakness, who has suddenly collapsed, the soul does everything in her power to keep that little flame of individual life burning in the helpless body that (in fact) belongs to her.

And now, suddenly looming up before him was the frost-coated figure of one of global anarchism's most fiendishly honorable leaders, caught in a collective squall of darkness, cold and blowing snow. It looked as if by some titanic effort he had bent his cast bronze waist and was dejectedly trudging away against the whirling wind.

Helium skirted mutinous Kropotkin, and felt an involuntary sympathy for this figure whose lonely, soulless bronze was also somehow suffering cruelly in the wind and cold.

At that point he realized that he hadn't lost his way, and felt a joy and sudden respect for himself such as he hadn't felt since his brilliant (silver medal and all) liberation from his hated high school. "And what came then, and what came then . . . a big fat hen . . . "

He tried taking a deep breath to help out his heart, which had suddenly clenched from yet another wave of despair and pain, but he couldn't—he just sucked in a lot of terrible fear and cold, and felt drops of sticky sweat break out on his forehead.

And at that moment he noticed, off to his left, a cloud of dingy steam hanging over some chasm; it was trying to shake off the streetlights' yellow glare and the greenish underglow of floodlights holding onto it and for some reason refusing to let go.

Helium might have walked—or rather dragged himself— right on past this cloud of swirling steam (because by this time he had no more strength to take in each and every little external impression or to correlate this with that) if it hadn't been that his nose—his totally congested and ice-bound nose—suddenly caught a whiff of that same old revolting, hellish chlorine . . . his ears suddenly caught the splash and slap of sprats in a crowded net, the sound the dirty-green vermin had made all round him as they swarmed in the waters of that damned swimming pool . . . a furious hatred, intensified a hundredfold by the pitiless clarity of memory, convulsed him. He stopped in his tracks, gasping from hatred, powerless to cast off—by some reckless, vengeful move—the weight stifling his soul. He was in no condition to do anything—even just bellow until his voice broke, cursing so furiously that dirty strings of foamy, smutty saliva would fly off his lips—let alone go completely berserk, flail his arms, stomp the hell out of something or other, wail, tear his hair, claw his own face or whatever. . . .

Helium's impotent fury was such that it might have suffocated him once and for all if, just one instant before asphyxia set in, something hadn't cleared in his soul and head with unexpectedly marvelous coincidence, the way earth and sky clear when the oppressive storm-laden air is suddenly defused by the playful concord of certain managing elemental forces.

In this sudden descent of mental silence and spiritual clarity, Helium felt utter release, and thought: "Punishment . . . chastisement . . . we praise Thee, Lord (if, of course, this is the work of Thy hands) . . . My return here is my punishment. . . . I accept. . . . But why the demons? Why all the ugliness? . . . But I accept it, Thy punishment, three times over. . . . "

At this instant he had the impression that the tatters of steam from the cloud hovering over the awful chasm had stopped their mad attempts to escape the light, had grown denser, whiter, and begun to acquire the airy contours of an enormous structure sculpting itself with the aid of a snowy, nocturnal wind.

Helium had the feeling he had split in two, and one part of him was getting a matchbox out of his pocket and scraping the matchhead on the box, and nothing in that part of him wavered or trembled as it prepared to touch the evilly hissing, sparking match flame to the black snake slithering from under his heel down to the basement windows of the airy building. . . . But the other part of him, and the eye that belonged to that part, was wincing in expectation of the hellacious rumble and blast, was using its lone weak hand to try and keep the other reckless hand from making this last fateful move, but couldn't . . . it was limp, dangling in weakness and despair . . . the flamelike snakehead, darting from side to side, slithered closer and closer to its aim . . . but for some reason the hellacious rumble didn't come . . . instead a soundless, suddenly descending whirlwind dispersed the innocent rooms of the marvelous airy construction . . . and like snow-white featherdown they rose above the city, as if the explosion of some invisible shell had lifted them up and soundlessly swept them apart, into the untrammeled space of the gloomy skies . . . and on the spot where everything now swept away by that soundless wind had stood, gaped a gurgling abyss, the hellish foundation-pit swimming pool . . .

and the legion of vermin that swarmed in it, emitting a lisping, restive sound like that of the demon small fry caught in the fairy-tale net of the priest's servant Balda. . . . "When you were little, Hal, when you were little, you should have listened to Pushkin instead of your papa . . . the clouds scurry, the clouds whirl, the moon, invisible . . . . "

Then the visions were gone. Instead, he saw five letters on a sign half-written in neon burning soullessly inside its glassy coils: DEMON. . . . The DIVING at the beginning and the STRATIONS at the end flashed and snaked gaudily through the hateful vapors and then flickered out again. . . . "It was right here, right next door on Volkhonka Street that he lived . . . in the headlights' glare. . . . Oh Lord how perfect are . . . not likely I'll live to visit his house . . . but the poet will forgive me . . . ." Helium was horrified by the sudden thought that the demons might hear his senseless muttering and track him down after all, but he did just have time to think that after all it wasn't a hallucination, that sometimes, the truth has to rely on some stupid, frigid neon gas and foolish electricotechnics.

With that he calmed down, and felt a quick, unstoppable rush of weakness through all the main arteries of his body—from leg to heart—from heart to hand—to head . . . from head . . . .

One moment before losing consciousness, he thought he saw someone walking toward him. He never did see whether it was several people approaching, or just one enormously tall passerby suddenly and dizzyingly multiplied into a crowd of smaller people.

36 AT FIRST, he didn't quite realize he'd come to. And that first realization came not so much by realizing any-
thing at all, but from the incredible pain in his hands and feet, which had begun to thaw in the warmth of whatever building he was in. It was neither dark nor bright. One particular lightbulb was peering with apparent curiosity into his eye, prankishly jabbing the pupil with its rays, as if it were trying to arouse and evoke some reciprocal interest in the little light-receiver.

Not too far from him there were some people talking. He couldn't quite hear their voices, but he surmised that they were preoccupied with his situation and therefore were talking about him, this person who had been lying here unconscious for who knows how long.

He was strong enough to stir a little, to let these people know that he'd come to, don't worry yourselves, please. But he didn't, on account of that odd, unconscious feeling of certainty that seems to suggest (especially to someone young) that a mother, say, or a best friend is like another "You" so if everything is OK with you, then they won't worry in the least. It's silly to worry over yourself when you calmly disappear for days on end with-out letting yourself know—making a phone call, leaving a note—where you're off to.

It was precisely this ancient sense of abiding connection, of others being a part of himself, precisely this strange, hyperobvious and therefore unconscious feeling of blood-kin identity with absolutely everyone else—the feeling of common ground typical of an ear of corn lost in a cornfield . . . of a bird in a flock . . . that seemed to intimate to Helium that when he came to these people simply couldn't help knowing, and this is what kept him from wiggling his foot or coughing or groaning.

And he was filled with a quiet, ever-so-light and joyous tranquillity that, imperceptible to the eye of the onlooker, gives the newly-awakened person to understand that one of the trays on the scales of his life and death has outweighed the other yet again, that he's still—as close as those trays might be to a sad equilibrium—breathing.

This quiet state of lifesaving balance over the abyss of the Everlasting is so precious and so infinitely dear at that moment that the person, enthralled, would just as soon die as destroy it with a careless move or foolish talk.

At first the people's voices were just meaningless sounds. He could drive them away without any particular effort, and off they flew, like unimportunate nocturnal butterflies.

Then, directly above him, he heard some barely audible singing, which suddenly changed into speech, or else it was speech changing back into strange song. He couldn't tell the source of these sound effects . . . was it the remains of his semi-delirium, or "Brigadier-General Graves," as his aunt, whose son had been killed near Kabul, always used to call death.

"Well, Helium, you've played yourself out and here's a modest echo from the Higher Spheres," he thought quietly, without fear or trembling, though not without a certain irony—after all, why deny Angels the state of real existence if demons are obviously in possession of that privilege . . . .

"It must be simply that once somebody walks out on the Angels, then all kinds of fiends fall right in step. But now it's the other way around . . . As a matter of delirious protocol, let those angelic voices sing and keen if they're so grieved over my worthless life . . . to each his own . . . the reality of those demons was revealed to me in my lifetime, but that reality might not be revealed to some other person until he's at death's door . . . so who's better off, I wonder . . . excuse me up there, of course, but couldn't you just tack a little sign on Faith that says Knowledge, and another one on Knowledge that says Faith—as a kind of heartrendingly pitiful (that is, humanitarian) aid from the omniscient Heavens? Then again, don't bother. Leave things the way they are. Since you trust us, so to speak, we'll suffer through without any auxiliary knowledge. And who knows who's got it harder—the person who suffers without responsibility, believing in you, or you, who take upon yourselves the responsibility of entrusting the human race with a multitude of ways to suffer . . . but to suffer without believing—now that takes a hell of a hero, don't you know. . . . Now if only we knew history's grand finale ahead of time . . . no . . . better no . . . why skip from life's genesis to any latter-day revelations. . . ."

Helium hadn't quite realized that he'd been carried into the church and laid out on a wide bench in the refectory, a clean and roomy half-basement. Blissful, occasionally delirious, free of pain, Helium suddenly remembered the kitten, and decided that it too must have plunged with him into "so-called nirvana close to the Spheres," since it was so silent and motionless under his coat. He reached for it with one hand, and couldn't keep from crying out as unbearable pain racked his whole body. But the kitten was gone.

37

SEVERAL PEOPLE came over to him immediately, and he overheard the following discussion:

"Father, I'm telling you, he's not sick, he's some drunken old wino. You should call the plague wagon, not the ambulance. He stinks of booze and something else besides. Are we a mausoleum or a collective-farm cowbarn or what?"

"And that scraggly feline's got no business being here either. See that little scarecrow heading right for our humanitarian aid? It's those democrats let them all breed . . . and then *they* run for the joint-venture underbrush. Really, we'll be a regular animal farm by morning mass."

"And where do you think He blessed us with his Birth? Some deodorized-sanitized King Herod Memorial Maternity Wing?"

"Here's the main thing, Maria Ivanovna."

"I swear you're as evil-tempered as a nurse in a district clinic."

"I just wanted to say, reverend father, render unto the drunkards their drink, the sick man his ambulance, but let the beasts of the fields find their own roof. . . . oh, fine, we'll put up all the cats and dogs, herd in plenty of crows along with the refugees and the pigeons, give all the sparrows shelter . . . and just who is it going to clean up after them, do you think? Your hoity-toity intellectuals?"

"We shall! If it's necessary, we shall! These hands have also known the feel of sleaze and grime, I mean grease and slime!"

Helium decided to open one eye just a little.

This latter declaration had been made by a woman of powerful build, whose inspired-commander's face bore an expression of stoic readiness to take on any and all sanitation duties, however disgusting or complex.

"Maria Ivanovna, could you really bring yourself to toss that kitten out onto the street?"

"You're not in the sisterhood, no you're not, you've got no . . . you just stir up trouble, tithing a few kopecks and then blathering a thousand rubles-worth and distracting the father here . . . just go on down to Manezh Square and yap into some microphone why don't you . . . !"

"Do you know what?" said the mighty, nearly ceiling-high lady, artistically restraining her fury so as to let the spiteful old churchwoman know that in another place, another time, she might have squashed her like a bug, without a second thought.

"Here, kitty, kitty, kitty!" said yet another lady who only came up to the first one's belt and so looked like she might be her elder daughter, "here, kitty kitty . . . " she said with challenge and support for the kitten in her voice. "Your faith, Maria Ivanovna, is dead without works. We need to help even our lesser brothers live through this winter."

"I've got no problem with the brief span of beasts' lives, and I'm not bidden to shelter puke-covered drunks on church property—we're not the drunk tank here, but the House of God."

"Father Vladimir, I'll try and rouse Sliptsov . . . Slipslimov . . . whatever . . . believe me, he's a very conscientious pathologist, even though he did once work in the Kremlin emergency room. You could wait until kingdom come for a regular ambulance . . . haven't you read the *Literary Gazette* lately?"

"Greta, dear, the doctor has a hyphenated name—Sliptz-Slimov," the shortish lady corrected her. "Is that really so hard to remember?"

"This is all I have to say: if the fellow didn't puke on himself, well who did? And for that matter, why didn't you just haul him on home to your place? It's not that far. A clean house for you while you're fouling our nest?"

"Really, Marya Ivanovna, don't you see that the man's near death, after all? And besides leftovers on him are clearly of external—not eruptively immanent—origin."

"Greta, more validol, quick!"

The shortish lady who could have been Greta's grown daughter suddenly threw herself on top of Helium and pressed her lips to his.

This was so unexpected that he choked for an instant from the pressure of her breathing, from embarrassment, emotion and a fit of laughter brought on by his rescuer's spiky, tickling mustache which, apparently, she never plucked. So, of their own accord, his lips somehow parted in an involuntary, smiling grimace. The sympathic woman, thinking that these were death pangs, searched his wrist for a pulse. Then she again swooped down to listen for a heartbeat.

Greta immediately came to her aid. With both know-how and self-assurance, she pumped on Helium's breastbone with her huge, manlike hands two or three times—so hard that he let out not a groan, but something more like the wheezing whistle usually emitted by old, worthless bicycle pumps.

Under Greta's hands he for an instant felt himself a bedridden little boy, passionately—almost heart-stoppingly—wishing he could turn into a grown-up man so that he could marry the pretty doctor who always spent a long time rubbing his ailing little body with some kind of disquieting salve. . . . This friend of his mother's smelled of cigarette smoke and mysterious work carried on in the uncharted reaches of adult life; she smelled sometimes of snow from the street outside, sometimes of violets from her dacha, and no one ever understood why Heelie had suddenly and soundlessly begun to cry that one time.

But what he'd been sobbing from was a sharp pain that resembled unbearable happiness, when the doctor had accidentally sunk her long raspberry-red fingernails into his flu-ridden little body. . . . He whispered to the women, "Everything's great . . . thanks . . . . ," and remembered his mother's doctor friend who once, long ago, when he was cranky, feverish and kept home from his damned, despised school, had helped him dispense with his virginity.

"It's beating! Beating! . . . Faint, but beating! He's already thanking us!" joyfully cried the shortish lady, and her whole body gave a shudder as she wiped her lips on one sleeve. Helium couldn't help sensing this was a gesture of instinctive disgust, nobly overcome by the passion to help someone in distress. All this touched him even more deeply.

"I suspect he got roughed up at some fancy banquet and then got thrown out of the restaurant. Or else he was simply hit by a car and then lay somewhere for a long time, got frozen stiff. By the look of him he's cultured enough, all designer clothes—although he does give the impression he's just crawled out of a platter of assorted meat, fish and vegetable hors d'oeuvres from the good old days."

"In Stalin's time you could get anything, not like now, with your tubby Mayor Popov . . . looks like a roast pig stuffed with buckwheat kasha, he does . . ."

"Suckling pigs are 1500 a head at the market, and what have I got for a pension? Birdseed and chickenfeed . . . "

"Odd that he's still got his overcoat and, I think, his wallet."

"Slipov. Slime-Sipsov should show up any minute now!"

"Greta, it's Sliptz-Slimov. . . . Why is it you've got Slimy on the tip of your tongue all the time? Is he one of your grad students, or what? Just try not to mangle a perfectly good aristocratic name. Please."

38 SOMETHING HAD jogged Helium's memory. He'd seen both of these gentlewomen somewhere before—if, of course, this wasn't just one of memory's little tricks; he seemed to remember one of them, at some meeting, categorically attempting to establish a terribly thickheaded, tasteless, and quite precise correlation between one's patriotic love for Russia and one's love and reverence for the genius Solzhenitsyn.

Helium, for all his years of government service, hadn't quite managed to destroy either his mind or his taste, and this unseemly, purely Soviet-style foisting of expressions of love and reverence onto one's fellows grated on him terribly.

And after all he felt a certain—not exactly sneaking, but somehow involuntary—sympathy both with his homeland, gracelessly ossified into a pompous-pegleg Empire, and with the legendary exile. True, he revered him in private, and more as a genuine hero of our time than as a literary genius and magician of the classical word.

"Marina Ivanovna, please, get on the phone and don't get off until you reach the rescue squad. Thanks to all of you," said the priest. "Nastasya, towel off the kitten and mix up some dried milk from that torn German package." It was evident that the person saying this was sick and tired of all the chatter.

"Father Vladimir, if I might tear you away for literally just one minute?"

"Yes, yes, of course, but just for a minute. I should be up there . . . with her."

"Oh, she was literally a saint . . . we're absolutely prostrate with grief. . . . What happiness that you didn't treat the funeral mass of such a pure angel on a holiday night in clerical-bureaucratic, excuse the expression, fashion. . . . In a word, well, your preliminary agreement is absolutely necessary here. . . . This won't take long. . . . in a word, the fact of the matter is that in our native Russian literature profanity is . . . does that word annoy you?"

"The word itself doesn't annoy me. But when people don't . . . well, for example a few days ago I heard this with my own ears; someone was singing . . . 'the unequivocal ring of the harness bells . . . ,' and then, you know, it's upsetting."

"Good. Profanity is, with hyperobvious rapidity, becoming one of the many strains of spiritual AIDS. It is simply essential, now that the Church has been given permission from on high (all praise to Boris Nikolaevich) to participate in the affairs of society and even state, to cry anathema, to excommunicate at least one of our particularly undisciplined scribblers. They have no right to be called Orthodox Christians. A wake-up call is just what we all need. Let the Patriarch or the Synod decide just whom to excommunicate. As for the rest of the slip-slimey foulmouths, we should impose the very strictest of penances;

deny them confession or communion until they swear off their dirty little contextual tricks. We've already begun collecting signatures among outraged believers and even from a number of important representatives of scientific atheism to append to the Patriarch's memorandum. Delay could be fatal. . . . "

And suddenly Helium remembered that this very woman had called him at his department a couple of days before, and had fired the very same salvo into the receiver, adding that among those authorities invoked in Patriarch's Memorandum were the Epistles of the Apostles, as well as both Johns (Chrysostom and Climacus), and that this powerful movement in defense of the ecology of everyday speech and litspeak was assured the active support of Yavkovleltsin and Khasbulevernadze themselves, as well as the tacit sympathy of Shevbulatov and Alksnis and the sponsorshop of Svyatoslav Fydorov, who by day and by night, an eye for an eye, was bringing the nation foreign currency. In fact, the Movement might bring leftists and rightists together and this coitus, that is consensus, might become the cornerstone of re-de-construction, and the signature of Alexander Isaich Solzhenitsyn himself was anticipated in the very near future, which he would affix here, in Moscow, in a suitable auditorium or hall, because otherwise the entire country was heading down the slippery slope to you-know-where . . . .

Helium had been doubled up with laughter, thinking how he would give this restructured inquisitoress and arrant fanatic of fideism a true sailor's send-off to—well, to the very place she was no doubt going anyway. But then she said that calling down anathema "on even one slippery songbird of genitalia, i.e., parts below, would save our culture, not to speak of the long-suffering nation's secondary sign system, from communal-collective collapse. We must think, Helium Revolverich, of the children."

And so, indeed thinking about them, he finally made up his mind to promptly father a child and hung up without answering her.

"Can it really be that this whole thing started with a phone call from this gigantic garter, I mean guardian of morals, and now it's ending with her too?" he thought, not without a certain exalted horror at the mysterious, so to speak, architecture of everything that had happened and continued to happen to him. . . .

"Moreover, we all think that the reinstitution of anathema, a rite destroyed by the October Catastrophe, would serve as a timely conciliatory gesture toward our law-enforcement agencies," the stubby woman chimed in. "With jointly forged iron, Father Vladimir, let us burn the pollution from the poetry and prose of our culturo-religious space!"

"Forgive me, but what about ballet, painting, cinema? Who should we expel for that episode in Muratova's film—the director or that authentically foul-mouthed actress?"

"Muratova and the writer, provided they're card-carrying churchmembers, of course. The others involved deserve perhaps a few small doses of penance.

"After all, if the Church excommunicated Tolstoy in spite of his enormous international reputation and almost impeccable moral purity, then it would be a sin to just wink at the slut and smeaze, I mean smut and sleaze that some of these literary hoodlums are dissolving into their streams of muck. And then the rest of them—" and with one enormous iron hand Greta made several chops to the backbone of Russian profanity, "won't dare to . . . "

"Forgive me, but let's discuss this another time," politely but firmly said the priest, interrupting her. "Don't leave our patient alone. Thanks to you all."

"Don't forget, Vladimir Alexandrovich, that we have invoked the Epistles and both Johns in our Memorandum campaign."

"Oh, no, how could I forget something like that?"

"Greta, I'm going up to Veta too . . . then I'll come spell you."

39

WHEN HE HEARD the name, Helium didn't connect it with her—he'd blocked this name out of his mind so completely that in all these years he'd literally never once uttered it, even to himself.

The pronouns she, her, hers had always echoed inside him with such a tone of deadly hurt and bitter reproach for the casualness, the heartless cruelty of his instantaneous reaction to something which could hardly be held against him, even on their Judgment Day.

It was as if these simple little urns, these pronouns, were the final resting place of the depersonalized name of his one true love and that lost love itself, while Helium's unbearable yearning had gradually been transformed into an eternal, stony, heartfelt weight—into true, lifelong sorrow.

And so when he heard the name he didn't connect it with her. True, he quickly thought to himself: "Back then every other little girl was named Veta, even more often than Marfa, or . . . " And he never could picture her face or her form or her personality. Nor, say, when down in the subway's underworld he encountered some gray, fluffy mustache beneath a crimson, al-coholic nose, or any other features strikingly like his father's, did his heart—which organ usually indulges itself in such illusions more readily than does the sceptical mind—skip a beat. Let the dead bury the dead. Even if they're only dead in memory.

He squinted off to the left, at the floor, under the table, and could just barely make out some kind of awful beastie bearing no resemblance whatever to a feline. Helium's spirit sank in despair at seeing how much the kitten had shrunk. Under Helium's wing, under his coat, the icy weals and the snow caked on its chilled hide had melted, but it hadn't been warm enough there for its fur to dry out completely. Now the fur was pathet-ically stuck together, shrunk back to normal, and the outsize, bony frame of this living creature looked more like a run-down hostel for a dozen tiny kittens than a proper place for just this one. The eyes in the kitten's sharp, almost ratlike face seemed unnaturally large, and they bulged madly from its greedy, fran-tic efforts to lap up the last of whatever was in its bowl. Its skeleton swayed from side to side, rose and fell like a pump.

"He's OK," thought Helium, "he'll dry off, warm up, perk up, come out of this a fluffy little furball and scratch my leather couch to shreds . . . might scratch up my nose, too . . . couch . . . nose . . . what am I talking about . . . I won't be around to see it. . . . "

"Your pulse is weak . . . I just took it . . . almost down to thirty, but for the time being that's high enough. . . . Pardon me, can you hear what I'm saying? . . . "

He realized that Greta was holding his hand, and he nodded. He might even have been able to answer, to talk or to whisper, but at the moment he wasn't up to speeches.

In his brain, in the same spot on that overplayed record, the skipping needle again started chewing into that same musical bit. But it wasn't the music that was frustrating him, insistently chiseling away at his memory—there was something hiding behind it, something else insisting, insinuating, unwilling to back off, something arousing mindless fear and strange alarm. "Fate is always dark, impenetrable . . . you can never see what's ahead. . . . " he thought.

But if he had listened better he might have sensed that the needle stuck in the rough pit wasn't trying to foist anything at all on him, but was in fact saving his disturbed consciousness— which had shut tight all its doors and windows to the outside— from having to face the awful specter of unimaginable inevitability that any event sets loose.

In order to shake off something—just what, he didn't know—he began listening to the everyday chitchat of the women who were sitting in the refectory and, as far as he could tell, drinking tea.

His attention to what they were saying, what they were telling one another, indeed helped distract him from a premonition which was threatening to become a thought, or perhaps from the thought drumming on all the doors and windows of his conscious mind, wanting in . . . let me in . . . let me in . . . I have to turn into some feeling! . . .

40

AND WHAT DIDN'T Helium hear, as he gave himself up to those conversations!

They made up an unpretentious but quite head-strong commentary to practically all the events of recent Russian history. And he regretted that in general that history's pyramidal apotheoses had been built of the tragicomic—if not downright idiotic—skulls of those great Russian politicians who had done nothing but push the world closer to the brink of the abyss, and out of the dead stones of events, rather than the noise of small-scale wars of words, or the restlessly sounding cries and murmurs of existence, or the intimate whisper of Time itself, through which all these events had flowed and would continue to flow.

As he listened to these conversations, he felt a passionate nostalgia for a calling he'd long ago betrayed—that of a psycho-historian, specializing in "the phenomenological analysis of time-distribution preferences in the lives of individuals and de-funct human groups" . . .

He was about to drift off into contemplation . . . "it's comical that we call everything that's happening 'news,' because it's all happened a million times before, just with a different face. . . . All news is old news. . . . Crime . . . the debauched orgies of the nouveaux riches right in front of half-starved old women like these . . . red pythons, choking as they simultaneously gulp down the remains of the Empire's gross national product and shed skins split right up the belly by that voracious gulp . . . awe before the mysteries of life turning into a dull hatred of reality and then into the deadly dangerous illusion that it's possible to radically restructure the labyrinths of that life . . . while those labyrinths are standing on a foundation of shit cooled to the temperature of liquid—like it or not—helium . . . trusting, herdlike adoration of leaders and the beastly humiliation of their pitiful corpses and dummies . . . the eternally unfathomable spirit and passion of human hostility . . . it's high time we acknowledged that as obvious, as chief among the forces of history, so that somehow before the end of the world we can sensibly regulate those bizarre flashes of a passion for mutual destruction seen even among the most civilized of nations . . . or else channel that hostile energy into collecting Perrier empties in the Sahara, or pave all the roads in Vologda province with the good intentions and cobblestones of the proletariat . . . you can regulate your appetite to fend off, say, a stroke . . . after a third heart attack sex can still mercifully be allowed . . . so what else is new, ladies and gentlemen . . . . "

As the women chatted, Helium gave himself over to all sorts of reflections, amid which there were thoughts that were in themselves quite new to him, as well as old ones he had himself once dismissed.

Suddenly distracted both from the conversations and from his own thoughts, he gratefully squinted his good eye in the direction of the anathemist-Greta's grenadier bulk, as she fussed with something over by the kitten. He even, out of old, lewd habit, looked her up and down with a lecherous eye. He sighed in nostalgia at having to part with one particularly wonderful verb, forever persecuted by "decent folk" . . . past tense . . . adieu, adieu . . . The thought struck him that next to this Mistress Gulliver even such a fearless man (but bantam-weight writer) as Yuri Vlasov would feel like a Lilliputian. . . .

And again he passionately took in all the "news" of the tea-drinkers, as they brewed up their shared bulletins of miraculous occurences, disastrous omens, signs of change for the better, outlandish prices, the greed of the entrepreneurs and the worthlessness of the politicians who had multiplied faster than rats, crows, mosquitoes and cockroaches put together . . . and of all the other strictly-urban phenomena of recent Russian life.

It never occurred to Helium, by the way, to wonder just where the ambulance was, or just how long he'd been lying there . . . or what would happen to him . . . or how this would all end . . . . What was his general condition and his proximity to . . . to what, actually? Why should the pain sometimes vanish entirely and sometimes slip from one spot to another—from fingers to ears, from feet to bruised ribs, straight to the heart and then fuckin' bitch (sorry Greta) clap the suckers of its foul, slimy tentacles right over his temples and throat?

Nor did he think of NN, although he was about to blurt a question to the "anathemist" . . . "would you, my dear lady, be so kind as to find out if there's a woman with unusually expressive features somewhere upstairs . . . with a temper like a neutron bomb . . . that is, she tends to incinerate all the roast pigs and sauerkraut-with-sprats in her vicinity . . . green, yes, she wears a green sheepskin coat with blue, fairly worn fleece . . . general impression: spirited, unspoiled, a certain repressed aristocracy of manner . . . but headstrong, recklessly headstrong . . . you know, Greta, you and I run in the same circles . . . " he almost blurted out his question—and immediately recoiled from the grim shadow bearing down out of depths of the unknown.

In sum, if in those minutes when the needle was skipping in the same spot inside his head, tormenting the totally innocent *Eine kleine Nachtmusik* and sadistically hinting at something-or-other, someone had asked him "Do you have any one single wish at this moment?" he would have answered without a second thought, "Let it all stop, as long as it's now, now, let it all stop *now!*"

Because no matter how he tried to distract himself from whatever it was bearing down on him, no matter how he waved away the grave premonition of some unthinkable and inevitable thing, it still bore down on him, shrouding its unimaginable face.

Helium's conscious mind resisted even guessing at its features, with the kind of horror that even in unimaginably awful nightmares has little to do with whatever it is that has terrified us to madness. You let out such a bloodcurdling yell, break out in such a cold sweat precisely because of the obvious incongruity between the chase, the violence done you, or your own bloody deed, the irreversible loss of a precious possession or some such thing, and whatever it is that hovers menacingly behind those hellishly awful forms of dreams, waiting to breathe a blast of otherwordly chill straight into your soul, and in comparison with that blast the all-devouring element of fire seems like nothing more than a parlor trick of the naive Dieties dying of mundane boredom in their Olympic Village, trying to keep themselves amused with a little kitchen chemistry.

But however that horror (which by the way seemed to Helium a genuine novelty in his life) might distress him, however he might try to resist it by using all manner of mental and spiritual tricks, he kept getting tangled up in his own snares, enmeshed ever more tightly—all the while believing that the catch in his chest would go away, would let go, would let him take a breather . . . that was why it was called a catch, so it could snag you, torment you, hook the very breath of life and reel it out of your miserable, half-dead self. . . .

When it did let up a bit, he wanted to yell his head off, yell the way he had often yelled in dreams, to make it all stop now, now. And then, in one of his attempts to fathom the nature of this looming, absolutely unbearable thing, he suddenly recalled a friend's son, a schoolboy at the time, whom Helium had, at the parents' request, tried to instructively disincline from religion and the priestly calling.

This young pup was informed with some profoundly felt, precocious wisdom, mysteriously acquired (where, from whom, from what?), taken on faith. One could see all too well how deeply infected he'd been by the religious contagion which had suddenly begun creeping out of the national woodwork.

Helium didn't even attempt to divert the young man from his spiritual course. He knew perfectly well from experience that attempts at "dissuading this personality type by actively logical means is a waste of time, an exercise in adding grist to the priestly mill." All such attempts would merely reinforce those born-again fanatics in their frenzied desire to suffer. And indeed it is in the most lucid readiness to suffer persecution that they see the most forceful demonstration of their absolute rightness, which, by the way, they've never been able to prove in words, either to others or even to themselves.

So in their discussion Helium employed an offhanded, sophisticated cynicism, so flattering to the minds of the young, and also a charming, down-to-earth irony. Moreover, this was all applied in homeopathic doses. Believe what you will, young man, he'd say, that's all wonderful, but even within us—permit me to assert this from the vantage point of my experience—the church must be pragmatically, so to speak, separate from the state; that is—from our personal, social, and official affairs. Dear boy, after all, nothing stands between you and an esoteric diplomatic-corps career. . . .

The boy heard out all of Helium's quite civil, commonsensical admonitions, and then spouted a great deal of bizarre nonsense about the terror of falling "v ruki Boga Zhivago" . . . into the hands of the Living God.

41 "OH LORD. . . ." Helium tried to fend off this recollection too, especially the "nothing stands between you . . . " part; he jumped out of the way as it rushed past without knocking him over, though it did just clip him, and seem to blind him for an instant with an insinuating flash of fateful consonances and meanings . . . when suddenly, from all the questions of the nurse who sat shaking her head . . . .

The Mighty Greta had just asked him if he wanted any water. He again shook his head no.

"Hang on, my dear, we just have to hope that the ambulance or else Slipov . . . why *does* that name make my tongue just go dead somehow . . . you are doing better, believe me . . . at first we thought you were just stewed . . . then that you were really scr—, oops, what a foul linguistic atmosphere we and our children live in, really . . . you're much better now . . . you just hang on . . . your kitten stuffed itself and fell asleep . . . you don't have a bad heart, do you? . . . is there anything I can do for you? . . . "

He lay silent, his teeth clenched to keep them from chattering, and Greta went away. And once again he was gratefully convinced that it was magically but truly possible to turn one's entire self into hearing alone. Several people were still talking.

"Marya Ivanovna, let's not quarrel, especially on a day like today, " said Greta. "After all, you're not really such a shrew as you pretend to be."

"How can I help but rail at the likes of you democrats when you and your partner-lady here keep telling me that Judgment Day has already come and gone and all our daily life is one long term at hard labor? Don't you wish! Oh no, Madame, you're just hoping to get off easy. But you won't. The judgment's not come yet. But it's gathering. . . . The day lies ahead when certain folks' gold crowns will melt right off their teeth and other folks' lead fillings will pop right out just like their eyes, and the raven-bird will wind our guts round its claws. And there's no hope of anything different, mark my words, and besides how can you call this eternal bondage if here I am treating you to humanitarian tea? There won't be none of us sipping tea with American crackers or Japanese fruit drops on Judgment Day. It's written: and all thy bodily sustenance shall be essentially transformed, in accordance with the Heavenly food program."

"You've misunderstood Greta Klimentievna. She wasn't at all intending to imply that history—by which I mean the preliminary investigation prior to the Judgment itself—is an expanded form of punishment following a Last Judgment, but instead was attempting . . . . "

"There you go again with your smarty this-way-that-way-on-the-other-hand business, you keep on jawing and I swear it's quicker buying a horse off a gypsy than settling anything with you. Look at you . . . fine punishment that you've set up for yourselves—excommunicating cussers and blasphemers? Fine judges you are."

"Somebody else here one time was harping on the idea that there never would be any Last Judgment, and how we shouldn't be sitting around twiddling our thumbs waiting to bury each other. It was high time to have a real Russian Orthodox shock-work revival, she said, wake the dead and reassemble them into solid citizens, bone by bone, instead of sitting around swilling vodka."

"I wish morning would hurry up and come—back to work, no smoke breaks. . . . "

"Here's the main thing . . . ."

"And besides, what kind of common punishment is it after the Last Judgment when there's people can't scrape two kopecks together . . . and there's others stuffing thousand-ruble bills down some half-naked floozy's bra in nightclubs? Are we, what, back in the camps . . . you're breaking your back and there's all kinds of scum brewing up their jailhouse chifir and polishing the bunks with their you-know-whats . . . . "

"Here's what I say: if it's a punishment we're to bear, then we should all bear it together, so it's fair to everybody. If I'm sorry for you and you're sorry for me, then before you know it we've already forgiven each other. But we need to try and sin old-fashioned-like, separate, because there's no justice in this life. It won't come till everyone's bearing that long-awaited punishment together."

"And besides, who ever heard of such goings-on, the Mafia racing around in old Brezhnev 'Chaikas' and getting the runs from eating those French snails and here we're sucking lousy lemon drops and teawater with no tea . . . "

Helium sang a doleful little song to himself, putting this last phrase to the tune of a heartrending folk melody that had suddenly popped into his head, and he suddenly felt such a pang of pure kinship with these bickering people that their squabbles temporarily tuned his snarling heart to a cheerful key, the native, indulgent key that in some purely biological fashion reconciles adults to the psychopathic hyperactivity of children at play. . . .

"So my granddaughter strolls in in the wee hours of the morning and shamelessly announces that from this historic moment on she's going to be giving me a little allowance for candy and other treats in foreign money, the slut, and that from now on her name isn't Nadezhda Zvyagina but some fancy Sonya Marmeladova. . . . Granny, she says, we'll start all over again, because you look for justice and what do you get . . . and why should Nadezhda, I mean Sonya, have to suffer in this life?"

"If people don't suffer, if they aren't tormented, then that's the ultimate penalty . . . that shows up their infinite, total soullessness. The chosen suffer, the damned suffer, and soullessness is what struts its smutty stuff in this perestroika show. The nightclub hustlers and the smutpeddlers and the racketbrokers are all bonafide walking corpses, according to the ingenital . . . I swear, the very devil's got my tongue . . . *ingenious* Law of Pentadomov, Marya Ivanovna."

"So what new bigheaded law have you come up with now? La-a-w. What's it ban, what's it mean?"

"Pentadomov has formulated it with absolutely unheard-of simplicity: the essence of life's absurdity is that we have too many bodies per capita."

"If he's got five heads you'd think he could come up with something a little smarter than that."

"Here's the main thing: they've all gotten very smart, but of course it's not just heads but souls that are lacking, and not just in the body politic either—it's even in the government and Popov's city council."

"Now don't you get all relieved and easy in your mind supposing that you're already bearing your punishment just because somebody cusses right in your face or some mugger snatches that fur hat right off your head and prices are shooting up again and there's nothing to buy anyway. And it's not for you to judge whose soul grieves or whose has been knocked out for good and all by roast pig or leg of lamb. We're a lot closer to Judgment Day than to that communism of yours. Dying early won't save you either. The archangels can find sinners on the sea floor and six feet under; they'll yank them right out of their nightclub where they're showering money on those shameless Marmeladova hussies. . . . They'll pry your Berias and your Trotskys and your Bukharins right out of their mausoleums, the archangels will. . . . they'll raise them up and wave those bras like warrants right in their shameless faces, see, and proclaim— hands behind your heads, assholes, latrine break . . . !"

42 THE PAIN HAD EASED a little. Maria Ivanovna's exceedingly grim and naive prognostications seemed to postpone the onset of that hyperunimaginable thing— which had been about, he thought, to set on him personally any minute now—for some yet-to-be-determined time.

This immediately put Helium in a more optimistic frame of

mind. Like the myriads of people who had lived before him, there in that fatal atmosphere he caught the tempting whiff of the shady deal available to each and every mortal mind.

This was the sweet smoke of possibility, the possibility of cutting a deal for oneself with the Higher Powers. The main thing was to do it right now, and then later—well, time would tell. Later some other chance for salvation might just turn up.

In a word, Helium had sensed that if at this instant someone were to offer an exchange—deliverance from the specter of this strange horror or from the hands of the Living God Himself (if he really had stumbled into them) for a readiness to, at some yet-to-be-determined future point, undergo the eternal torments of hell, then he would have unequivocally accepted those conditions—granted, with a certain embarrassment at his own sleaziness.

He gratefully drifted off again, thinking that the obvious underhandedness of such a deal was perfectly excusable, given his weakness. . . . "Given this dreadful story, Lord, the unfathomable trials of my existence, the unthinkable, unbearable pain, suffering and fear and to top it all off, the depressing inequity of my existential, so to speak, position in bio- and noospheres in comparison with the enviable situation of a flower, a bug, a fish, a bird, or a cat . . . why not use a little guile? On the other hand, you can't exactly envy a cat . . . and who knows what a geranium feels when it's left unwatered, or when a butterfly is pinned to a naturalist's board live, so its death-throes won't shake the pollen off its wings . . . rats driven through Nobel labyrinths . . . a head transplant on a chimpanzee, with an eye to the Lenin Prize. . . ."

43

A NEWCOMER suddenly interrupted these distracting thoughts. This woman simply started wailing right off: "Lord, what's the world coming to! They say Brezhnev —people have seen him with their own eyes—has been roaming the streets reciting poetry, asking for Gorbachev's address. And complaining that Yeltsin is a foulmouth alcholic and an enemy of the Party, saying he's boundlessly hurt and surprised. . . . Some crack reporter from the *Independent* managed to get his voice on tape. . . . But who really cares about that anyway. . . . In my daughter-in-law's building some famous lady got murdered. She was rich, this lady, mafia-connected, with a Polish name like Zamoskvaretsky or something. . . . Furs, diamonds, two cars, five lovers at least and all of them Politburo hotshots. I know for a fact that hound Yanaev spent the morning after there more than once. She had a whole warehouse of deficit goodies for . . . I can't bring myself to speak the obscene names of those fat Party cats in a church . . . and anyway she kept her hounds and her cats pretty well fed . . . practically tossed them sprats and tongue-in-aspic out her window. Well, it would have been one thing if somebody'd just robbed and raped that Polish slut. . . . It's not like us women aren't used to that. . . . But the Mafia tortured her, stuck her fingers in the sockets and then literally grilled her over a hot stove . . . the neighbors heard her admit to something or open up some safe . . . you so-and-so, the hoods were saying, you Polack hag, bloodsucker Beria's hired skag, where did you stash whatever it was. . . . I don't know what, but anyway she was yelling and screaming . . . they cut her up and then finished her off with a pistol, bless her soul, nobody should get killed like that . . . and there was blood running over the threshold and all the way out onto the staircase . . . and they tacked a note to her door saying that aliens from the planet Kildim had arrived to put the Kremlin mattresses in order . . . and then they took off . . . well, what else . . . not too far from here some gangster got his leg run over by a car and froze to death before the ambulance could even get warmed up . . . and some other co-op hustler got his head split like a melon on a lamppost but got up and walked away like it was nothing . . . and some Party type, used to be a hotshot, embezzled a whole pile of money and tried to run off to America but they chased him down in an OMON armored car on the Smolensk highway and he started shooting at them but they nailed him right there on the spot . . . turned out he'd slipped that Polish woman his share too . . . so there you are, girls, tonight's news final . . . Merry Christmas everyone . . . I fried up some feast-day cakes in French olive oil. . . . Lord have mercy Lord have mercy Lord have mercy. . . . Personally, I carry cayenne pepper for those shameless Mafia eyes. . . . I can't afford cottage cheese, let alone those Mace cartridges . . . "

"What would you need Mace for? Who would want you, Annushka, or have you got some trinkets stashed away somewhere too?"

Helium's shock, as he instantly correlated what he'd heard with what had just happened to him, was so great that he managed to tear himself out of the claws of that looming horror, sit up sharply and, groaning in pain, slip one hand into the inner pocket of his overcoat. The little package with the artifact K had given him, the package he'd utterly forgotten in his mortal anguish over what had happened, was safe and sound.

"Horrible, it's horrible . . . news . . . final. . . . Can the mind really take this all in? . . . And if it can't, where does it all get taken? . . . Thank God I'm in no wise to blame here, not for this death anyway . . . that poor bitch . . . how could she not have cracked under torture and told them who had the thing? . . . she must have. . . . I'll put up a statue to her on the very spot where Krupskaya's was, if . . . Now there's something nobody gives a damn about anymore, not a damn . . . who needs any of it . . . Cuba . . . sweet deals . . . fencing leftover Tsarist trinkets to petroleum princes . . . my generous cut . . . Madison Avenue . . . then again I could have bought a whole new wardrobe in Italy . . . red lobster, white wine, black-haired girl . . . then espresso and Benedictine . . . funny how that demon crew always backed away from that marvelous liqueur . . . the little stinkers knew who made it . . . she, on the other hand, preferred Chartreuse . . . and so did they, it was green . . . but who cares now . . . if she cracked, then the jackals were obviously on my trail . . . unbelievable . . . that means that those little devil-mites did look out for me one last time . . . or maybe they didn't, and if they didn't . . . then *He* did? But what did I ever do to You, that I'm the one You turn inside out like You were frisking somebody's dirty shorts? . . . Am I any worse than some Feuerbach or Voltaire or even Suslov or Yemilyan Yaroslavsky*? Have I really outdone all the outright Judases, icon-mongers, whoring-drunk bishop snitches, all the other scuzz of Scientific Atheism? . . . After all, I never did prove You didn't

*Author of a 1937 propaganda pamphlet entitled "Pushkin's Atheism."—TRANS.

exist, and certainly couldn't prove the unprovable . . . so why is it me You're after and why the hell didn't You protect me from that gaggle of demons?!!!! . . . I might right this minute have been sweetly entering Danilov Monastery or swinging the censer for a certain former baron of mathematical logic, lately a priest . . . and right now, this very minute, I sincerely wish to make my donation to the restoration, that is, the transformation, that is—die . . . take it, take it . . . just let me go . . . I'll bow down at Your feet, hide me in a coffin and then in a grave . . . I'm a thing made by Your hands too. . . . "

But no matter how feverishly Helium grasped at any opportunity to draw a breath, to fight off, fend off any images of this unheard, unseen thing tripping at his heels, this thing so full of grim meaning that he'd sooner have gone blind than come face to face with it—those images just kept getting closer and closer.

He sensed that despite his readiness to distract himself, detach himself from everything on earth—that is to simply croak—he now had neither the time nor the strength to engage in this beloved pastime.

Now he understood that he wasn't fated to comprehend the gaming configurations, the odds ratios of improbable chance, or all the indescribable peculiarities of his no-doubt-starring role in this lethal, fateful story. He would never plunge headfirst into the quest to unravel the tangle of mysterious causes inspiring someone's omnipotent, providential fantasy to . . . "just think of it—to go ahead and foreordain that reality be the coincidence of the merest of details and brushstrokes in some scheme decades in the making . . . demons . . . a holiday evening . . . my delighted anticipation of something singular, something lovely . . . NN's furious rage . . . some treacherous scum leaking K's plans to those three jackals . . . that driver . . .

theoretical physicists pissing on me personally in my gomer mask . . . but then why even wonder about that driver, or that vain and venal bushy-browed bursar of the Empire, or those physicists newly come to believe that the Universe was *created*, when each and every one of them had long been brought up, coupled to this train of events, drawn up tight . . . when even the pitiful scrap of chow thrown in my face, that attracted the poor kitten . . . if it hadn't been for a bite of ham I wouldn't be here at all . . . not to speak of this frigid Christmas (what else could it be?) Eve . . . or in the elements, wind, snow . . . or in that tiny pit on the record, or in my *Eine kleine Nachtmusik* serenade or, in the end, in the final hideous stunt by those lowlife devils corkscrewing down into the belly and nostrils of the beast. . . . I swear it's like some celestial Rezo Gabridze Puppet Theater—He's sitting there in state, behind an impenetrable curtain, sitting there pulling the strings of each and every one of us, despite humankind's harangues on the free will supposedly bestowed on each of us from on high . . . and suddenly He takes a few thousand strings and twines them round and round His fingers and He won't let go for anything, because at that point He knows that your will never has, as it turns out, been free, but has been terminally corrupted (not without, of course, your own slavering help) by the demons of fatal delusion? *Your* free will, Hal, was what you and Papa Revolver chugged down with those two bottles of Martell at the Prague; and then again, if it was your will, then it had always been free, and if it was your papa's, well then it was never yours to begin with. Now do you get it, you idiot wrapped around that scum-green demon little finger . . . ? And what if that's really is how things are, with fate and fortune's little tricks? . . . Oh Lord! . . . "

44 HELIUM SUDDENLY FELT how extremely, hopelessly close that inevitability was, felt it with such clarity that, strangely enough, something inside him relaxed, let go. And not so much from the clarity itself as from a sudden all-embracing agreement with everything that was now bearing down on him.

And even his teeth started aching in his sweet longing to touch any, every, even the smallest—like a doorknob—part of the space of visible life from which he'd been whisked by Time's draft as it whistled endlessly back and forth out of Nonbeing into Being; the roof of his mouth felt prickly, then so did his throat, as if he were swallowing the honey of his flu-ridden childhood, of country vacations . . . and then his half-delirious brain as accidentally (was it accidentally?) as the primordial sense of that word, Nonbeing, suddenly yawned before him like an abyss—a word that embraced Being itself: No, Begin . . . in the Beginning. . . .

And then he was visited by an agonizing envy toward everything his eye could take in—and everything it couldn't: envy of the grannies and aunties drinking their tealess teawater as if they were in some friendly little whistlestop halfway to nowhere; of the dim lightbulb hanging above him; envy of the incessant gurgling of water in the church toilet's tank; of the kitten, blissfully stretching over there by the radiator; of Greta's bustling figure, hectoring the grannies and aunties, preaching the restoration of the rite of anathema—even of the very texture of his clothes, which had their own lives to live and weren't planning on rotting away with him; he envied them all passionately, and would have given anything for the chance to turn into one of those humble little fruit-drops . . . or, if it came to that, not even into the candy itself, just its brief crunch . . . even just the water in the toilet tank . . . or the chairleg . . . or the bulb's light—not one photon of which, it seems, goes to waste; it hooks up with some sweet little molecule on the margins of the Unseen, and they cook up something, take part, dammit, in the business of the universe, help make, well, if not the pie, then the starry flour, the resplendent stuff of Matter.

Had a sly whisper sounded in his ears and, right then and there, made a businesslike offer to turn him into a rank-and-file imp, to let him raise a little hell, he would have signed up for the nastiest of nasty jobs without a second thought and spent his time off reflecting on the essence of all ugliness (that of the unholy vermin included) as remarkable proof of the principle— eternal, shining throughout the entire Universe—that each and every thing, even those things that at first glance would seem to be a brazen challenge to life itself, has its life's work. . . . "I'd prove myself, however nasty the job . . . on my word as a gentleman . . . I would . . . I keep my word and you know that perfectly well, by the way. . . . I'd probably even get promoted . . . become a strain of HIV, say . . . that's not so bad . . . I'd do in all the addicts and queers . . . but I'd sabotage all the syringes aimed at the flesh of children and Marmeladovas of easy virtue . . . and maybe in the meantime I'd crank out a dissertation on the historical inevitability of the metamorphosis of global Evil into viruses and microbes . . . 'A

Metaphysics of the Nature of Origins, Genetic Transmission and Rapid Proliferation of Human Disease: Toward the Current Question of the Ontological Status of Agents of AIDS . . . ' or something on that order. . . . Then a lavish banquet at the Seventh Heaven, another promotion . . . another interesting research project, maybe even as a simple janitor at the EVOLUT Institute for Scientic Research . . . you can't just sit around doing nothing, after all . . . there's no empty places under Jesus' wing . . . or if they do exist, then it's only as some true hell of excommunication from spiritual participation in those perfect works. . . . I feel the warmth of Your hands, You hold me like a handmade thing and hide me. . . ."

Suddenly he heard someone sobbing. Opening his eye with some difficulty, he saw Greta comforting her friend as if she were a weeping child. "There, there, Mina . . . it'll be all right, look after this gentleman and his kitten and I'll go see her . . . all right now . . . " "All right, all right . . . nothing will be right, she's gone . . . !" cried the woman called Mina, through tears and convulsive sobs.

In Helium's brain a voice suddenly uttered a strange phrase he'd once heard at some fiery rally, one of those civilian wakes for the Empire. . . . The voice had uttered this phrase over a microphone with such unnaturally quiet but intense (thanks to the absence of oratorically r-r-rolling consonants) thunder, that its meaning seemed to be absolutely firmly and clearly expressed by the tone alone. . . .

"Even the Deity cannot undo what has already been done. . . . "

In the gust of air carrying this flock of words beyond the horizons of hearing and the borders of consciousness, Helium sensed such humanly understandable, frank and genuinely

tragic regret on the part of Heaven itself—a regret in comparison with which the historical necessity so revered by the slaves
of history (executioners and victims alike) seemed nothing
more than a dirty scam which soulless (alas) human reason
had tried to pass off as the most powerful of all philosophical
categories and Forces, the prime mover of events and
worlds. . . . "Yes, yes, namely *tragic* regret . . . in connection
with . . . and then I'm in total agreement . . . thank you for
your candor . . . withal with all in agreement . . . Meet the
grandedame Kategoria Istneobkhodimka Historical Necessity,
mother of intervention? . . . grandedame my ass . . . You're
just some dim Katka, Kategoria indeed . . . not even a sweet-
cream-lady-marmelade-whore (excuse the expression, Greta
and Mina), not even a simple boob or a two-bit tart. . . . You're
nothing but the puling rat offspring of practically dumb and
factually blind human reason, a prodigal byblow of divine
Logos. I acknowledge It, at this dreadful moment! . . . That's all
you are, you bitch, not some grand high-and-mighty Kategoria!
In foresight and hindsight both and those lifelong communo-
cretins are the only ones who think you're the justification for
all the evil deeds grandly committed throughout history by
misanthropic ghouls like . . . . What, was it historically necessary for me personally to become a piece of shit? No. I could
have stepped in it the way other people do—with just the
we-e-e-e tip of the big-toenail on my left foot. Yes, left! . . .
stepped in it and then wiped it off with a page out of *The
Communist* or *The Atheist's Companion*."

Even the Deity cannot undo what has once been done. . . . It
was fading away within him, that echo of frank regret which the
Voice, that Golos, had shared, not so much with Helium personally as with all Humankind . . . and just for a moment, in the

mirror-clear, soundlessly freezing current of his mind it seemed
to be reflected . . . Golos . . . Logos . . .

 45 MUSTERING WHAT WAS LEFT of his strength, Helium was
nonetheless again distracted from the sense of these
sounds and visions.

He realized that a feeling of acute sorrow—which may suddenly release people who have lost someone close, only to (as if
fearing to dull and disappear altogether) begin gnawing at
them all over again—the feeling was shared by Greta as well.
And at that moment it seems that it's not sorrow, but the dead
themselves, pitifully clinging to those from whom they cannot
imagine themselves forever parted . . . impossible . . . not possible . . .

Greta, however, had taken herself in hand and headed reso-
lutely upstairs, but . . .

In these moments the inevitability of everything looming
ahead weighed so heavily on Helium, bore down on him so
painfully that if he'd had the strength for it he'd have screamed
bloody murder.

Someone had begun skinning him. Obviously his skin was
ripe for it—it was blistered, heavy, but, like the stucco on the
city's derelict buildings, not quite ready to fall off on its own.

He flailed inwardly, shrinking from anything that touched
that burning layer of skin; he felt like a piece of meat shoved
body and soul into some hellish oven to roast there in an air-
tight crock. His scorching skin hissed, crackled, and mockingly,
teasingly smelled of the Hotel Astoria kitchen and the smoke of
that never-to-be Havana banquet with a bronzed yearling piggy

on an enormous platter . . . his skin was shriveling up, separating into layers; then someone began stripping it off in big pieces whose edges thinned and curled into ashy white twists; they were stripping it carefully, agonizingly slowly, like white birchbark from a denuded treetrunk, so that the bark twist was as long and thin as possible, so that it glowed pink in this dim light, like a baby's hand in the sun, or the fingers of an old woman considerately shielding her candle from the small quirks of the atmostphere.

He let out a groan—not to ease the torment, since he had already figured out that in operations such as this there is no such thing as anesthetic—but just to attract attention to himself.

Both women leapt to his side. Moreover Greta instinctively drew air into the bellows of her broad ribcage—for lifesaving pneumatics—and rolled up her sleeves to thump on his heart, pump on his ribs.

Then he sat up slightly, and both women realized the obstinate meaning in his unstoppable impulse to get up, go upstairs . . . "Upstairs . . . I have to keep in step with my punishment . . . I should have done this a long time ago, I should have done it, gone to meet it . . . not lay here on the bench with my hands folded on my chest. . . . "

This had become his goal—to act in concert with his torment "to get it over with . . . it can't last forever, after all . . . it's still, thank God, only *life*long . . . but what if . . . "

A horrible, indescribable and infinitely grim conjecture suddenly flashed through his mind. It outsped the psyche's capacity for resolution (which is more or less accustomed to coping not only with the most surreal and fantastic efforts of everything painfully anticipated by imagination, but also with the lunatic surprises of an "off-the-wall" reality) by such a degree that it wrenched Helium out of the women's arms as if it had been a whirlwind's blast, and carried him up the steps into the sanctuary, the House of God.

The women were stunned by the inexplicable strength with which he pulled them along.

It was the same force of movement, fueled by who knows what sources, as can sometimes be observed in absolutely decrepit, half-dead old women who nonetheless shove their way to bus exits, elbowing aside crudely complaining bruisers twice their size, or charge unstoppably up to the humiliating shop counters where the System, barely alive but still kicking, has suddenly put out (at excruciating prices) cottage cheese or egg noodles or darning thread to mend their rags and tatters.

46

HELIUM DIDN'T seem to notice that anyone else was in the sanctuary. Or rather, the few people present seemed fleshless phantoms to him. It also seemed to Helium that the candles' flame fell hungrily on him and him alone, as if it had been waiting for this very moment.

At first he saw nothing save these tonguelets of fire, which for some reason did not recoil as the door's movement sent a ripple through the peaceful air of the room, but were instead drawn from all sides toward the entering man; which painfully stabbed him in the eye, tried to interrupt with his already uneven breathing; even at a distance these tongues of flame seemed not cold but terribly hot, penetrating his clothing, reaching deep inside him. And his chilled-through body broke into a seemingly impossible sweat.

If it hadn't been for the sweat he might have collapsed—from weakness, from the torment of stinging pain and the old horror that refused to leave him.

And so he was embarrassed, like some of us at, say, a concert, are embarrassed by that provocatively causeless, self-igniting internal combustion which flouts all of nature's thermodynamic guarantees. You practically black out, disgusting sweat trickles down the channel of your poor spine to who knows where and then from there brazenly heads for the elastic in your socks, and you make your way—rear end in the faces of the other concertgoers who with forced civility suppress their indignation and annoyance—to the toilet, or the snack bar, there to suffer those unusually sharp pangs of loneliness which are the precise equivalent of, again, our solitary "I" . . .

He was embarrassed, and by sheer force of will, rolled his eyeball up and back underneath the lid, to get those intangible specks of searing light off his pupil. Now, he could make out all the orange, cherry-red, dark-lilac, crimson, blue, green votive lights burning unwaveringly in their circular filigreed holders, moving his soul to an infinite envy of their quiet purpose and image of everyday peace.

The tapers' light, multipled a hundredfold in the gold and silver icon settings, did not reach out at his pupil, his skin or his clothing, did not frighten him but instead seemed, there in its housing of silver and gold, to live a life of its own which, though reflected, was even more mysterious than the freely flickering life of the little votive tongues of real flame.

The tapers drew his gaze, held it, beguiled it, seductively luring him into those reflected depths which give your image of self an ideal peace—without, however, depriving it of the opportunity to contemplate the external vanities of existence to which (perhaps in some final sorrowful yearning) all things made manifest but hopelessly mortal do cling.

And having felt something of the sort, Helium came to his senses, and realized that he could call what was hyperapparent *non*apparent as much as he liked, but that, alas, would not make it nonexistent.

And then he was drawn irresistibly back to that inevitability, which he had fought so stubbornly, only to make its assaults of hellish pain and terror more frequent and fierce by his very passion to distract himself from them.

This surge—or rather, wave—of understanding of what had happened covered him from head to toe, whisked him out from the women's supporting grasp like woodchips or featherdown and carried him off toward the unbearability of the known.

One of his saviors—the one so much shorter than her friend and comrade-in-anathema—glanced at her companion with unconcealed fear, and with one finger made a circling motion at her temple.

The wave that had swept up Helium might have crushed him with its weight, taken his breath away and tossed him to the floor face down had he not grabbed, with his last remaining strength, either the bow or one side of a coffin sailing, as it turned out, toward him but heretofore hidden from view by the candles' blaze.

He steadied himself and leaned over the side, seeing at first only hands, obviously abandoned by the spirit of movement and hence folded—by someone else—across a dead body, yet by their own final, posthumous effort shielding the place of birth and rift from both the womb and all those thresholds of other worlds.

Then somehow he made out a small icon of the Mother of God, held in the fingers of one hand, and at that moment the pain and horror began to leave his heart, and it was once again filled with the feeling which had been an inseparable part of him ever since the moment the demons had seemed to pry open his lips in that utterly unexpected and grossly indecent howl.

It was that feeling of infinite heaviness, that is, of the instantaneous death of love and life's happiness, the feeling that had arisen in that accursed swimming pool when she, Veta, had swum away from him in horror, away from a grimacing face twisted in mockery of her poet's fine and tragic revelation, away from a voice whose very tone breathed the stench of truly demonic death.

He wasn't aware of the priest breaking off his quiet reading of prayers and taking his arm so he wouldn't fall, nor of yet another person, alarmed by his demeanor and his state, approaching.

Without taking his hands from the coffin he again prayed in a voice unabashed by its spiritual nakedness for God to strike his one good eye blind, to fill that eye with soothing sand, wind, salt, darkness, anything because he couldn't stand it any longer, couldn't bear to look . . . couldn't bear it . . . oh Lord strike me blind. . . .

But before the pure desperation of such a plea could rise to Heaven, he, at the very limits of his mortal strength, turned his gaze to the face now detached from all earthly cares.

Her face was turned toward that very thing which had opened before him beyond that last threshold, and which cast an all-consoling, bright, quiet calm onto the clear brow from which it had wiped every single line, onto the eyelids which like two small curved palms caressingly and lovingly shielded her eyes from the world seen by the living. . . . Below the eye-lids, over the deep shadows and the waxiness of her cheeks, her lashes swept like two final signatures in her quick, elegant, decisive hand, signing for something remarkable, inescap-able . . . it almost seemed that the Angel of breath hadn't yet flown from her lips, and yet its sad, slight leavetaking had made them go cold, and they were about to quiver one last time before its final good-byes. . . . Her whole body was awash in imported flowers. If it hadn't been for the old-fashioned cut of her severe, dark suit and the gray in her hair—which looked as if some sudden natural disaster had streaked one lock on her forehead pure white—the face of Helium's dead love, lost to him so many years before, might have seemed no more than a girl's.

His heart was suddenly bursting with a surfeit of words meant for her alone in all the universe, but his already wooden tongue had now gone completely numb and a mad fear crept over him—that he wouldn't be able to tell Veta even a small part of what he himself never knew had been accumulating all these endless, melancholy hours and days and years . . . and now all these drops and droplets had converged into something pounding against his heart muscle, straining to get out, to have time enough to . . . to . . . before the exit, before the departure, before the blizzard's final windblown whistle could bear her body and its coffin away from this platform, this dock, and only the flame of a white carnation would flicker and flash blind-ingly for one instant before vanishing in the murk and rumble which themselves would fade away as the flame disappeared round the last curve between mortal darkness and the blessed Silence of the Unknown.

He understood that there wasn't much station-time left, so to speak, but that there was some roadblock in the way of the heart-felt words and sincere explanations now rushing toward speech.

And then, on the verge of utter discouragement, it mournfully occurred to him that perhaps the heart's memory was truer than sad reason's, that the key to all its secret caches lay hidden at such depths that the frivolous person could never retrieve it, couldn't dive so deep or so far in a million years.

He wanted to share this observation with the dead woman, and with pained attention searched her face for any signal of quick agreement, any trace of puzzlement, or frank sign of the good-natured laughter with which she had always greeted certain of his theories. His lips quivered.

At that moment it seemed to him that she had somehow perceived his unspoken thought, and that her lips had pinkened with barely discernible movement, with the light of an answering smile, ever so slightly baring both rows of strong, straight, snow-white, smart, merry teeth—now dulled by a dead-matte finish.

Then he shot a grateful look and bent even lower over the dead woman, smiling his same rather strange, dazed smile. It was the smile of a man who has lost the only key to the box containing his precious personal papers, who has already reconciled himself to the loss—and then has accidentally found the key, and is dazed by this absolutely inexplicable miracle of unexpected luck.

His swollen, chapped lips began moving by themselves, whispering to the dead woman what the demons had prevented him from saying back then, what he should have caught up and repeated with her in the Moscow pool, and what he *had* been ready to recite from heart along with her—just the way two people recite, read, sing or just mindlessly chatter in tandem, drawn together by some loving mutual spell and heart's accord.

He whispered her fateful poem from start to finish. And although the truth it held was already revealed to him in part, this time he drank it down like a mug of water after days and days of deadly thirst, as if sharing it with this woman, swallow for swallow, word for word that constricted the palate and the heart with lifesaving, heavenly coolness.

Toward the end it seemed to him that she was soundlessly repeating everything he said and when the words and lines of this wondrous revelation had run out, Helium sensed that the words of the last line were still with him . . . and You hide me like a ring in a case. . . .

He repeated them over and over, as if under a spell, never noticing that those present and those standing beside him were quite disturbed by what they observed happening at the casket.

It's quite possible he might have simply slipped into quiet madness, the first grim blast of which had already swept through his brain; he might have dug his nails into the casket rim and no power could have torn those hands away as long as there was life left in him . . . had it not been for the fear of setting off some fiendishly ugly outburst or other, had it not been for the will to hold it in . . . hold . . . hold . . . .

He looked around in fury, suspecting that the devils might have cooked up some final ugly farewell ball-bacchanal, that everything leading up to this moment was simply their fiendish *nachtmusik*, but the gleaming tapers and votive lights went calmly about their thoughtful business of illuminating the sanctuary, and convinced him that nothing of that ilk could disturb them here.

And all this quiet burning, shining, this gleam and radiance and magnificence suddenly brought back an utterly forgotten feeling—that he had a refuge, or rather, a hiding place, under a trustworthy, friendly, protective roof, just as he'd felt as a toddler hiding in his mother's full skirt, or under his blanket, or in a homemade branch hut . . . where he could curl up in a ball, under Jesus' wing. . . .

And You hide me like a ring in a case. . . .

The line was still with him, refused to leave, until his hand crept unbidden into his pocket and brought out the packet that had safely outlived its unfortunate mistress, outlived her killers, outlived all the night's dangers laying in wait for any poor woman's handbag—let alone such a rare, precious thing as this.

Without understanding why he was doing it, Helium quickly untied the string on the flannel-wrapped packet with his teeth. The rag fell to the floor at his feet, and instead of the nagging word "case" there was immediate silence.

The little case, the black-market parcel that he was supposed to deliver over the ocean-sea and so make a frogskin fortune to last him the rest of his life, was held shut by a tiny, elegant bolt.

It was reminiscent of a miniature casket covered in buttersoft, patrician burgundy leather, bearing initals stamped in gilt. The leather had long since outlived all possible discussions of the object's age. It looked aristocratic, as do all those things whose appearance and manner retain the nobility of their owners' origins. It's precisely because of this gift at making such an impression that little cases like these have long accompanied rare artifacts through museum life, private collections or cacophonous auctions. Or have dozed quietly in warm chests and bureau drawers while the precious things themselves sparkle on the living hands of fabulously wealthy women and royalty.

Helium's fingers had no intention of cooperating. He again

had to use his teeth. He pulled the little bolt out by its chain, tapping on its little pin with his fingernail, without understanding what was directing these strange actions, seemingly knowing something was hidden inside but tormented by his inability to remember what it was exactly. Tormented, too, in the very same way, trying to remember the source of that strange vision of the demons standing in embarkation line at the pig. . . .

He was struck by understanding at the very moment he'd despaired of remembering: "That's it! The epigraph! . . . to *The Possessed*. That's it then—that's the end of them! They're done for! Oh Lord . . . and You hold . . . You hide me like a ring in a case. . . . "

The little case's spring suddenly popped open by itself . . . and there in a comfortable little hollow in the black velvet lay a marvelous antique platinum ring, and its enormous emerald eye, set in large diamonds, gazed directly up into Helium's only remaining one.

In those green depths a face was reflected . . . or perhaps two faces . . . or several faces with features impossible to make out because flames of the the burning candles, the gold of the settings and the bright paints of the icons had all merged in this bottomless stone gaze.

Somehow, everything surrounding Helium at that minute had somehow fit into it. And so the gem's omnipotent gaze assured the man gazing into it that the copy—more perfect than two identical drops of water—the copy of this instant and everything contained in it was absolutely guaranteed safekeeping in Eternity. "So this is it, Goethe's wait, oh minute, you are fair—that's what it meant . . . a cry of love for the unfathomable mystery of death . . . "

Tearing his gaze away from the ring, Helium again bent over

the dead woman, and everything went dark . . . this death-night, this night-city . . . he was trying to hold on the casket's rim and couldn't, his hands were full and so he began to sink, forgetting where he was and even who he was, and at the last minute he had the impression that he wasn't bending over the dead woman but that she was bending over him as he sank serenely and gratefully into a profoundly native abyss—she was bending over him and her face suddenly came alive but it wasn't her face at all, it was NN's, begging him not to slip away, to try and stay a while yet . . . I'm here, Hal, I'm here with you . . . Oh Lord. . . .

47 THIS WAS A GIFT from the Heavens—that is, a blessing he in no way deserved, to be buoyed up on the floats, the little rafts of her agitated, entreating words instead of flying downward into the beckoning abyss as the priest and the women carried him back into the refectory.

Rocked as sweetly as if in a cradle, he hardly even noticed NN hastily putting something on the eye which had now swollen into a rainbow-hued shiner, wiping his cheek and neck with her scarf, hastily brushing off the scraps of hors d'oeuvres still stuck to his coat, rubbing his fingers, unlacing his shoes, feeling for a pulse . . . hardly even heard her exchanging remarks with Greta and Mina.

Nor did he notice that they laid him in the same spot downstairs, that a sleepy newcomer in a sport coat hurriedly tossed over wrinkled, rumpled pajamas was assessing him in one quick glance, calculating just how to go about resuscitating this strange, obviously beaten-up and frostbitten figure wearing an old-fashioned black overcoat with a beaver collar on which frosty silver no longer gleamed either because it had long since melted or else the beaver himself had just finished climbing out of his pond.

"Air, give him air . . . back away please . . . Greta, a syringe. . . . Mina, some alcohol. . . . You should both be serving on the rescue squad instead of working to deprive the Russian people of the spontaneous, free lunacy of its street language. . . . Thank you . . . if only you knew how I hate the Russian intelligentsia—as a phenomenon . . . although there are certain intellectual individuals of either sex whom I adore . . . I'm not talking about the practical professions— engineers, doctors, our scientific brethren et al. . . . mean that revoltingly persistent, worthless (worthless to everyone but demons anyway) ideological activity . . . careful . . . don't scrape the skin off his fingers! . . . here we all stupidly pride ourselves on the historic novelty of these gophers between God and the Devil and forget that the Russian intelligentsia—literary critics mostly—were the chief architects and clerks-of-the-works in the hell of Soviet history. . . . It's wonderful to be able to say this openly! . . . Who here knows how to take blood pressure? . . . It's rather strange, and this fact remains to be interpreted, ladies and gentlemen, that doctors, philologists, lawyers, teachers, engineers et al. have existed and continue to exist in all countries of the world. They even exist in Uganda, despite Idi Amin's efforts to boil them all down or fry them on a spit à la bokassa. But there literally is not a single other country where the ideological pastimes of the professionals keep them from practicing their own useful callings. They don't leave their microscopes, books or blueprints to go buzzing around in the faces of workers or traders or farmers with their spiritual advice. . . .

That's precisely why . . . his blood pressure is god-awful, his pulse is just barely ticking . . . that's why neither France, nor England nor the States have never gotten around to 'all power to the Council of Workers et cetera' . . . Counciled to death, we are . . . oh no, you say, we're the Paladins of Intellect, the Spiritual Elite! . . . In a pig's eye. . . . We're the paladins of the grandly inept ruin of a country, a people, a culture. . . . That's who we are. . . . Lack of sleep makes me grumpy. . . first let's prop him up . . . here we go . . . excuse me, you're the wife? . . . be very careful unclenching that right hand . . . I think we'll get by without having to amputate . . . if he can pull himself out of this of course . . . Greta, the kitten's already dead so I need your help here, don't go dashing back and forth between our patient and the wee corpse of that poor creature . . . we can do without fits of temporary insanity while this man is in mortal danger . . . you can't imagine, reverend father . . . excuse me, Vladimir Alexandrovich . . . just how much I hate the self-absorbed, perverted narcissism of the Russian intelligentsia . . . do you know what the intelligentsia sees mirrored in puddles where its face should be? . . . Thank you . . . higher . . . a little higher . . . they see an *idea* . . . can you feature it? Again THE IDEA—after seventy years of the most disgusting third-rate hell (not, if you please, Dante's inferno, but some boondocks hell, a Tambov, Kuntsevo, Sumgaiti hell) . . . where did this gentleman manage to get himself so plastered and half frozen to death? . . . It's all some sort of narco-boozy lunacy, and the intellectual-ideological-leeches don't want to treat the hangover with the water of pure work, oh no, they want a shot of that 'special Russian idea' . . . Mina, there in my bag, off to the left, there's a little jar of goose fat . . . and just imagine, there's no historical abstinence to be observed in certain exalted personages of this Knightly Order. . . . They just steer their course and its our banged-up heads that ram full speed ahead against their hypernovel id-e-a . . . it's not life these guardians of the people need, it's our irrepressible desire for new absolutes . . . they assign us hyper-historical-tasks, don't you see, then toss a few 'regulatory ideas of practical reason' into our empty troughs . . . and then they cluck and cluck, those shameless intellectual fowl, that the idea they hatched was great and wonderful, it was just the omelette that stunk to high heaven . . . sorry, folks, the over-easy came out a little hard . . . sir, where the hell are your veins? . . . now he should feel a little better . . . take a lesson from the Swedes, damn it . . . it's vodka that should be named 'Absolut,' not the latest crackbrained theory . . . cafeterias for hungry old people, well-fed nursery schools, pharmacies piled high with lifesaving drugs—those are what you should call 'Idea' . . . christen a little all-purpose farm tractor—not some heap of 'national ideas' 'Ideal,' and produce as many of those 'Ideals' as you want. . . . There, I gave him the same dose I used to give (bound by the Hippocratic oath, mind you, which is not your Stalin's-oath-at-Lenin's-graveside) Brezhnev, Suslov and Chernenko . . . he's got the pulse of a corpse, but in our business that doesn't count . . . Oh Lord, smite the Russian intelligentsia for . . . a swab, please, with some alcohol . . . for its squeamish horror at the tragedy of natural existence and its whorish adoration of that pair of pimps Idea and Principle . . . now Mina, our dark-age medicine is powerless here, I'm sorry. I hate to say it, but the poor thing is absolutely and ideally dead, and I assure you, judging from the expression on its sweet face, it died perfectly happy . . . you want cat resuscitation when our former pets can't even find anything in

Russia's garbage heaps to eat? . . . he's better off this way . . . all that's left is to give him a decent burial, and that's the end of it."

48 AFTER THE INJECTION, the doctor's last words suddenly penetrated Helium's consciousness. They provoked a sharp, instinctive objection in every cell of his body, an itch for a nice little physiological "scene."

He opened his good eye, rolled it round in search of NN, who at the moment was rubbing his bare feet with something. He found her, and moved his lips. She noticed the movement and asked him in a voice that would have instantly melted the ice of loneliness in the abominable snowman, "Do you feel any pain in your feet? No?" He shook his head no and tried for a jaunty smile, as NN continued massaging his feet, then his hands, then his feet again.

The only way to attract her attention was to blink his good eye desperately. She understood and quickly moved closer.

The fear of death suddenly shot through him when, awaiting the touch of that lovely ear against his lips, he could feel neither the warmth of her earlobe nor even the shell-like ear itself which had always seemed to breathe purely on its own, with the intoxicating, inaudible rush of the body's free element.

"Where is it?" Helium thought he had whispered these words about the kitten quite distinctly. At first NN didn't quite understand, and thinking he was talking about the ring, she answered:

"Don't worry, I have it. Just don't worry. Don't think about anything right now."

"You take it . . . this fix . . . not likely I'll get out alive . . . please just honor my last . . . "

"What are you talking about! Just trust yourself to fate . . . just stay quiet . . . hold on . . . "

"Can you believe . . . " Again NN didn't quite make out the meaning of the words straining to be understood . . . "Can . . . you . . . believe . . . me . . . believe . . ." She nodded quickly. ". . . it wasn't me being so crude to you . . . it was them . . . the demons . . . I'm not crazy . . . believe me . . . I beg . . . then I'll croak a hap . . . " He started wheezing in agitation.

"I believe you, I believe you. . . . I came to my senses after a while and knew it was something . . . really, really . . . I could see it in your face . . . but . . . "

"My dear, darling . . . I'm . . . I'm . . . a total shit, be-lieve . . . but I could be a good father . . . I wanted . . . re-ally . . . "

"Just stay quiet . . . just be quiet . . . " She had been massag-ing his hand, and gave it such a squeeze that he yelped in newly awakened, unbearable pain. . . .

He passionately wanted to explain that he loved her and had always loved her, but that some sort of hellish disease had afflicted his consciousness or maybe even his whole exis-tence . . . "Yes . . . an existential disease, a plague of infinite miscalculation . . . which also killed off any possibility of recog-nizing fate, acting in concert with fate . . . that's what you're all about, *Nachtmusik*, that's what you're all about . . . about love for the unforeseeable . . . no, no, it's not fat Sophia Union the slutty regime, not environment, it's no one's fault, this private, terrible disease, I spawned those demons myself . . . my-self . . . now I know how it's done . . . but exterminating them apparently takes outside, so to speak, help . . . a person can't pull themselves out of quicksand, my dear . . . it's not croaking I'm afraid of it's . . . I want our love more than I want life . . . I'd trade twenty eternities for it . . . " But he knew he was in no shape to tell her all this right now. Besides, he needed a voice for that, and his was gone.

Helium thought that if he got out of this fix alive . . . his thought embarrassed him and he broke it off, sensing how outrageously nervy it would be, making promises to certain Powers that he'd spent a lifetime shitting on. . . . "an enormous donation to Church coffers, for the poor and hungry, for a few repairs here and there . . . and in foreign currency too . . . in thanks for the recovery, the continuation of a life . . . but I wouldn't turn down just plain goodness and mercy, if that was all . . . "

This latest mood struck him as comical, and he felt even more embarrassed, but nonetheless ventured another desperate prayer, a meek, almost wordless prayer for deliverance, as trusting and unselfish as those prayers addressed to Heaven by people gifted with a pure, inborn faith that assures them their prayers will be heard. . . . "But if it's not, for some reason . . . there must having been something lacking in it . . . a proper deference for fate's decrees. . . . "

NN had stopped listening to his whispers and was massaging his other hand, while Greta and Mina sat at his feet, massaging them, rubbing them down with something.

The doctor assured them that in such cases it was better not to get involved with hospitals, that the gentleman's ribs were apparently whole and that the contusion, though unusually extensive, would heal on its own. The man was clearly not dystrophic. The old women gave advice on how to make salves. Father Vladimir bent over Helium and said soberly, more in doctorly than priestly fashion:

"Please, just keep saying your prayers, and do your part to help your guardian angels, so to speak. Are you a believer?"

This somehow struck Helium as funny. He smiled, and again yelped in pain.

"Father, I'm an atheist by God's grace . . . and now chief prosecutor in my own case . . . and grateful . . . theodicy's . . . " he whispered confidentially, fighting the sting in his cracked lips, to the closely-listening priest.

"All the more reason to pray gratefully, and with hope. If you yourself don't believe, that means the Almighty is personally sure of you, because otherwise you'd be someone else—God knows who or what—and somewhere else (although you *are* here in awfully sad condition, good sir)—May the Lord bless and keep you. Try not to drink so much in the future. . . . " He made the sign of the cross over the sick man, then couldn't help but complain, "Last fall I was at some rally, and there were two orators waxing eloquent over the rebirth of Russian nationhood et cetera. I was quite caught up in it at the time. It was all true, if a little too superficial. . . . So there I was on my way home, and there they were, the pair of them, wallowing in some puddle, hugging each other and burbling, burbling something or other about rebirth. . . . "

Helium swallowed back tears and prayed frantically under his breath, this time not for salvation, but simply, "Don't let this peace leave me, this peace I haven't felt since I was a babe in diapers . . . just as long as she's with me . . . and the father . . . he's my father . . . everything hurts right down to the quick . . . I don't care, let it . . . better quick than dead . . . ."

"Hang on . . . hold on . . . you're my drugas . . . ich bin friend . . . spice and sugar . . . happy-end . . . my half-English, quarter-Lithuanian and quarter-German grandpapa used to sing me that little song . . . can you feel my hand?"

He couldn't keep his lips from stretching into another smile.

"Of course . . . I'm a piece of shit . . . but I do love you . . . the kitten saved me . . . and you did . . . and I guess Heaven must have had something to do with it . . . call the father over . . . for a minute . . . "

When Father Vladimir came over and bent down once more, Helium asked passionately, "I have to . . . I'm sorry . . . my last confession . . . do you believe in demons . . . devils . . . all that . . . do you?"

"I don't *believe* in them at all, because I simply *know* them: the Evil One is an unseen but absolutely obvious part of our demonridden reality."

"Thank you, thank you . . . but now why is there evil . . . why does it . . . I have to find out . . . I can't . . . ."

"The true nature of evil . . . now don't get so agitated . . . is known only to the Creator. But of all the possible explanations, this is the one that seems clearest to me: 'Evil is resistance to the free will bestowed upon us by Divine Grace.' Gregory the Theologian said that. He said it many centuries ago, but we began resisting long before that, and who knows when we'll stop. When you get back on your feet, stop in—we'll chat."

"Colossal!" exclaimed the doctor. "That formulation of evil covers all my years of torturous doubt! Colossal! I'm ready to swim a marathon in the baptismal font this very instant!"

Helium resisted the sly hint at the swimming pool contained in this last too-fanciful remark, and felt a little embarrassed for the good doctor. Despite the pain which was creeping ever more stubbornly from his hands and feet toward the tip of his nose, his lips, his cheeks, he suddenly and blissfully drifted off, lulled what he'd heard and by the presence of NN, who was still trying to tidy him up.

In an effort to distract herself from her own fears and worries, she was hurriedly recounting how she'd just missed him . . . "It was because of that damn, busted windshield wiper, but thank God everything's come out all right . . . we'll go home . . . you'll sleep it off . . . I'll steam the room with cypress, make an infusion. . . . Zelenkov brought me some Buryat herbs from Siberia. . . . I'll make some compresses . . . the doctor says you can have just a swallow of cognac . . . you absolutely should have just one swallow to thaw out your insides, they're all chilled. . . . Hal, it really is all for the best, though I couldn't bear to go through all this ugliness again . . . I'll straighten up the apartment, straighten myself up . . . I'm so sorry . . . I'm a crazy woman sometimes, I can't control all those technicolor genes . . . . I should have knocked the stuffing out of you, just annihilated you, ripped you up one side and down the other, dunked your head in the toilet and whipped your ass, anything but put you out on the street . . . anything . . . I'm sorry . . . and then everything would have come clear . . . ."

"But you know it wouldn't have come clear," thought Helium, "if she hadn't put me out . . . nothing would have come clear, not until the time for clarity had come of itself . . . and there was something I had to get through first . . . it's right what the old ladies said, that I died happy . . . it's right . . . it's only the lucky ones strike happiness right off . . . and here I've struck a nugget or two of it in maybe my last hours and it's enough, enough for me, anyway . . . any more and there'd be enough for everybody . . . I need to make some arrangements. . . . Let them sing a mass for me along with Veta and that poor murdered woman . . . and say a prayer for those three jackals while they're at it . . . who's counting now, after all . . . on the third day after, a month after, forty days . . . and once a year from then on, and Veta and I will be somewhere out there talking things over in our own sweet time . . . that's not such a bad thing . . . Lord, just let me live till they can get a notary . . . Greta and Mina . . . witnesses . . . I'll leave everything to her . . . everything . . . but then there's no one else anyway . . . but I won't leave out the aunties and grannies . . . never . . . what kind of self-respecting Empire would lead all these aunties and grannies and cats and dogs to such downright hunger and degradation? . . . Madame Sophia Union, you were nothing but a miserable sewer rat and a stinking whore, jangling your nuclear jewelry at international fêtes and gouging old ladies for their calico, fruit drops and soft bread-and-butter . . . just look at all the toadies you spawned . . . and the bloodsucking bureaucrats that grew all over that thickskinned spine of yours . . . at the generals you ignored while they were turning army bases into filthy labor camps where the sergeants were busy reaming out the sorry-ass recruits . . . and what you've got now isn't cultural space or economic space or imperial space but just shamelessly empty space and the only thing there's no shortage of, you lead-eyed bitch, are those ridiculous officers' hats everyone's selling to tourists . . . I'll make sure I leave some money for repairs, for candles and lamp oil . . . no one expects anything out of the Empire anymore . . . the only glimmer of hope is that there may be enough individuals to put together a decent community of responsible citizens . . . but what are you thinking, Hal, you boob and champion dickhead, here in the final moments of your life . . . maybe you're hoping to be revived and live happily every after in civically-aware Mother Russia?"

Just before drifting off again, he understood from their conversations that they wanted to move him to NN's car. The doctor had final say, but they couldn't tear him away from the priest. The doctor was pleading:

"Greta and Mina, please, just give me one minute's peace . . . Stop pestering me . . . Vladimir Alexandrovich, you decide—and that's how it will be. What am I to do if I'm, as it were, a leftist-progressive-agnostic, but my right leg seems to be dangling over the abyss of genuine doubt? I'm using up all my inner resources on this balancing act."

"It's hard to say . . . I'm no guru, you know . . . but no doubt you need to find your support in a certain clarity of thought and deed, in order to . . . "

"But how, if you'll permit me to interrupt your very important thought, am I to find it if I'm literally like Esenin tiptoeing on one foot and slip-sliding with the other? How do you resolve the rending contradictions between the two poles of sceptical and optimistic agnosticism and establish, once and for all, in short, a sentimental balance between faith and knowledge?"

"Well, for pity's sake, if you've got nothing else to lean on . . . just rejoice and be glad . . . "

"That is—well what do you mean 'rejoice'?" The doctor was taken aback.

"Just that, rejoice."

"At what?"

"At rejoicing, if nothing else."

"That's it?"

"Yes. That's it. God grant each and every one of us the same. The rest will come in its own time."

"Are you sure this isn't just the exceedingly sophisticated sophistry of applied theology aimed at an overly risky simplification of existence and a formulaic amelioration of the tragedy of being?"

Helium was suddenly shaken by both convulsive laughter and a surfeit of life's experience. In his chest and throat something cracked and gurgled. It was obvious he was suffocating. Everyone in the refectory went still. The doctor rushed over to him and squeezed his wrist. He asked Greta and Mina to hurry and get his stethoscope out of his bag. He started poking it into Helium's sides and chest, which made Helium feel like laughing even harder, but he couldn't inhale or exhale either one.

Only after the doctor gave Helium a painful pinch on the soft part of his thigh and, asking NN to prop up Helium's head, poured some wondrously warm water into his mouth. . . . "For God's sake don't choke on this . . . these spasms are hysterical, not physical . . . at least you can crow, thank God, though you may have a nice case of pneumonia . . . cling to life . . . rejoice . . . you've got a lovely wife, after all . . . I envy you . . . in the most moral and ethical sense, of course . . . I mean I'm genuinely happy for you . . . girls, hold his coat the way Muscovites spread out that long-suffering Russian flag back in August . . . we'll make a quick run . . . and to bed with him . . . I'll help you into bed and then run see my wife for a minute . . . I'll leave something just in case . . . keep a syringe, an ampule and some smelling salts on hand . . . ah my dear, put that away, we'll split a bottle of champagne if . . . no, no, he doesn't need any hospital . . . as Louis the 13th's attending physician said, l'hôpital, c'est moi . . . from five o'clock on the whole hospital, dying atheists and agnostics included, will be drunk as skunks, it's a holiday, ladies and gentlemen, and this is Russia . . . who needs a hospital! Merry Christmas to you!"

Helium tried getting up, ashamed of his helplessness and not wanting to be any trouble, but he realized his body didn't have the strength even to sit up, and his soul . . . well his soul . . .

"Just relax, Hal, don't worry, you're as safe as in a cradle . . . everything will be fine . . . you just sleep . . . try not to think about what happened . . . " NN was saying as she answered someone's holiday greetings. Suddenly she gave a cry, thinking that . . . and Helium quickly opened his eye to let her know he wasn't . . . we're still . . . the agitation made it hard to breathe . . . .

49 HE AGAIN SURRENDERED to that random but now familiar, sweet plunge into the spiritual depths of a word, the ultimate meaning of which was at first glance ordinary and superficial, seemingly self-evident—this time it was the word Nativity.

This happy entry into the *word*, we might note, inspires not only poets, but leaves any person so remarkably detached from reality for an instant, face-to-face with the Mystery of Time, the darkest, most essential side of its unseen nature.

Sometimes this sudden comprehension of the Mystery of Mysteries disappears from memory just as instantaneously as a swoon during lovemaking. But that brief moment of comprehension remains forever joined, in the person's shaken and surprised soul, with a certain awe at the possibility of continuing the improbably simple process of discovering the secret meanings of once seemingly incomprehensible things.

This instantaneous disappearance of states of orgasmic ecstasy—Reason coupling with the Cosmic Mysteries—isn't *this* the mysterious fuse that sparks our stubborn ardor in acts of scientific inquiry? This passionate impulse to relive the swoonlike state that so shook the person in that joining—isn't *this* the very reason for man's inexplicably fantastic lust which has, in 99% of all cases, little to do with its biological purpose? . . .

Helium brushed away such thoughts with the sudden feeling that he was already—without any effort at reason, or strain of will, or attempt to concentrate on the topic of his musings—beginning to fathom the unfathomable.

It was just like back in the foyer, when his half-delirious reflections on the properties of memory had revealed to him the reality that any one of a myriad of instants was forever captured in the Other World—be it one fleeting instant from one individual life or from the sum total life on Earth (or maybe in the whole Universe) from the moment of creation on.

He felt that what was being celebrated today was not just the latest anniversary of the Nativity of the One about whose "sublime but mythical shamanism" he had produced a dozen or so "scholarly-scientific" articles . . . . "If," thought Helium delightedly, again involuntarily returning to consideration of "the main thing," "if I'm not completely crazy, then how can believers not understand—for all their prayerful intent and pure-hearted adoration of the Mother and Newborn Son, that this isn't just his Nativity they're celebrating. How can they not see that the communion they celebrate today—in its manifest simplicity—is communion with the Mystery of Time? How can they not fall still in exultation and transport—like Helium on his portable bier, not just in some symbolic attendance on that midnight crèche among the magi and the oxen and a few lucky onlookers, under those same skies that lit one single star among all the stars in the wintry chasm over Bethlehem, the star of the Nativity, but in the knowledge that we are *all* there, even I'm there, as the Virgin is delivered of her miraculous burden? . . . The fire is forever alight there . . . and it's forever warm enough for everyone . . . the milky breath of life and salvation forever rises cloudy-white from the nostrils of the oxen . . . deliverance from the horror of Time . . . breathe-in, breathe-out, it all happens at the same time, just as Christmas and every single twist and turn and miracle of the earthly life of the Child and all His stations of the cross, His crucifixion and death, the inaudible rumble of the stone rolled from his grave by the Angels of the Resurrection . . . it all happens at the same time there . . . here *and* after . . . in the Hereafter Time lacks any universal—not to mention earthly—properties like span or length which are intrinsic to it only in lifetime Motion—not in Divine Rest . . . how can my pygmy reason grasp the essence of the Trinity and also agree to that highly improbable circumstance—that its three Persons are forever separate and indivisible? But *There,* that's exactly how things are, and it's clear even to me, it's as clear as two-times-two . . . it's even clear just what Judgment Day is . . . always prepared, that's my motto . . . I'm in total accord that everything past is now in Eternity's keeping, . . . everything superfluous—that is, all the individual sins and dirty rotten tricks of human history that have disfigured the beauty of a World transfigured by the Creator—everything

superfluous will be burnt to ash in in the pit of nonbeing . . . And that, quite simply, is how Beauty will save this
sorry bastard of a World which in any case has (with my help)
never done anything but gracelessly destroy that Beauty . . . . "

Helium drifted off again. In these minutes, nothing save
death could have torn him from this strange, captivating feeling which resolved all the absurdities of existence, this feeling
of deliverance from the forces of omnipotent Time's length
and span . . . . "Moses is forever leading the Israelites out of
Egypt, Buddha is forever feeding himself to the starving ti-
gress . . . today is Christmas now and forever . . . his Nativity . . . " he whispered through amost immobile lips.

Helium moved one hand, and when NN noticed, and took it
in hers, he gave her hand a squeeze, hoping she would understand the impulse of a spirit with almost no strength left to
inspire coherent speech.

"Hal, just stay alive . . . not that I forgive your thickheaded,
stupid . . . I don't . . . just stay alive, I mean . . . forgive
me . . . will you?"

He drew her hand to his cold, swollen lips. Then weakly let
go.

50 SEVERAL OF THE women, the priest, and the doctor,
holding the supine Helium's coat by the collar, tails,
and lapels, awkwardly carried him out. It really was as
if he were being rocked in cradle, rolling left, then right, head
lolling backward, then forward, as they descended the church
steps down to the car. . . .

Lulled by the motion and by the concern of the living, he

was already sinking softly into some deep place when he suddenly remembered his nocturnal companion and was upset at not finding it there beside him. NN again put her ear to his lips, and managing to understand his question this time, tried to distract him from his worries over the kitten.

The little creature dying so happily in its sleep must not have been able to survive some internal shock. And it was clear to NN, and to Greta and to Mina and to all the old ladies and their priest, that this shock had been brought on by the happiness of having a human quite unexpectedly share its fate, of being kept warm and close to a living body, of being given shelter from the elements, of, for once, filling its belly—a yearning for which had managed to develop this mite's natural-born instinct for self-preservation into sheer desperation and lunatic bravery.

Although it was certainly possible that this happiness, coming as it did right out of the stormy, gloomy blue, might have seemed just a wondrous dream to the weary kitten, and so, to keep from ever waking up again, it went back to this deepest of sleeps.

Helium calmed down, trusting in NN's word, and was again struck by the loathsome fashion with which his reason (trained long ago by himself and that green scum too) had always stubbornly converted something like, say, his love for NN (suddenly revealed to him with such indisputable clarity that this "life-sentence" was both a tender passion, and a joy of liberation from the vain despair of senselessly filling up time) into a question of infinite calculation. " . . . and you kept tallying, second-guessing—love her, love her not . . . get married or, putting it politely, keep up the courtship with careless mimosa bouquets and some trinkets from Paris or wherever. . . . I was thinking, well what if it all falls through and then there's the dreary business of divvying up the property . . . who needs it? . . . oh my heart-and-soul, forgive me for all the mockery and humiliation, forgive me and then . . . actually, when all is said and done, you're all I've got. . . ."

Then he realized he was in NN's car and felt a stab of hurt—that not once in all the years he'd known her had NN confided in him about her affairs or the minor torments of their everyday hell, or about her latest purchase—of this very car, for example—or about her apartment exchange (with a charming eye to motherhood, as it turned out) with that damn Zelenkov ("why a scientist and theoretician, by the way?"); could you believe it, not once did she ever hint—with a word, a gesture, a capricious cock-eyed scowl or a frontal attack of mood or hysterical mood swings that he ought to bring some clarity to their relationship . . . and rejoice . . . rejoice . . . it's clear we love each other . . . not once did she . . . there's your mongrel ancestral pride . . . there's a temperament . . . there's the villainously secret song of human nature . . . I love you . . . I love you . . . love . . . I respect and adore you madly . . . but I'm . . . well of course I am . . . just an incredible shit. . . .

Every so often she turned from driving or talking with the doctor to look around at him and ask him how he was doing. In her voice, which seemed to be coming from far far away, he couldn't help sensing something which would give even the most pitiful person on earth a feeling that he wasn't alone, wasn't abandoned, whatever the wilderness.

He somehow managed to stretch one hand to the back of the driver's seat, and she quickly touched it, stroked it and squeezed it, and he again sank deep into . . . the paramedic swayed back and forth with her vial of smelling salts . . . passersby, streets, faces flashed by in the headlights' glare . . .

it's sweet in the dim light . . . Oh Lord how perfect are Thy works. . . . You hold me like a handwrought thing. . . . and You hide me like a ring in a case. . . .

Suddenly, though not for the first time tonight, an absolutely wordless thought (or maybe it was a feeling) filled with some mysteriously undisclosed meaning, flashed through his mind (or maybe it was his heart).

This feeling confused and dismayed his quickened conscience—that is, his mind and his soul, which had survived the horror together and seemed to be zealously reproaching each other for the ease with which they had suddenly made their peace with the obvious hopelessness and inevitability of all that had happened . . . all for the best. . . . "Oh fine, for the best . . . when it couldn't get any worse . . . "

Nonetheless, when we damn all beginnings and ends, when we grow deathly cold in the mystery of ever-flowing Time, when we puke up—blood, scraps of lung and all—the plebeian poison of cruelly instructive Soviet history, when we grow twisted in hurt and hatred for the ridiculous order of things which, by all accounts, tends toward the misrule of chaos, soul-less, heartless vulgarity and the triumph of crude force rather than the organic and honorable norm of justice, when life seems more than we can stand, as the blows of fate strike at the very roots of our inner strength or destroy us through the misfor-tunes of our loved ones, this wise feeling nonetheless guaran-tees those of us who do not shut it out—even in the darkest hours of our lives—that everything works for the best . . . somehow . . . for the best. . . .

Just what is for the best, how it's for the best—is unclear. All the clarifying detail, all the details intelligible to human reason remain hidden in the mist that swirls over the rift between our individual lives, our common Times—and Eternity.

But if in some fashion it has penetrated our being—this mysterious, unfathomable Heavenly wisdom, and the Heavens' own belief not only in the structure of historical Being, but also in our own insignificant but not incoherent presence within, then we are indeed at that very instant making our communion with the Miracle of sharing in Divine Hope, and also in Him Whose love hazarded the Universal Creation, and risked bestowing upon Humanity—in its very becoming—the gift of tragically free, unforeseeable selfhood.

" . . . all for the best . . . all for the best . . . " Helium exulted as they carried him, draped over NN's and the doctor's shoulders, through the courtyard, and up the foyer stairs to the elevator . . . NN's keys jangled . . . she couldn't find the right one . . . the needle was still stuck, digging out that same pit in the record, scraping away at the pitiful remnants of the lovely beginning cadences, a melody gone hoarse, its voice cracking but by some miracle still sounding—until it jumped at the jarring footsteps of the returning people, until it revived and moved on to its long-awaited continuation of itself, just one moment before suddenly ceasing to sound, both in the apartment and in the ears of a perfectly happy Helium.